PURL UP AND DIE

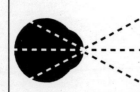

This Large Print Book carries the
Seal of Approval of N.A.V.H.

PURL UP AND DIE

MAGGIE SEFTON

THORNDIKE PRESS
A part of Gale, Cengage Learning

GALE
CENGAGE Learning®

Farmington Hills, Mich • San Francisco • New York • Waterville, Maine
Meriden, Conn • Mason, Ohio • Chicago

Thorndike Press® Large Print Mystery.
The text of this Large Print edition is unabridged.
Other aspects of the book may vary from the original edition.
Set in 16 pt. Plantin.

LIBRARY OF CONGRESS CATALOGING-IN-PUBLICATION DATA

Sefton, Maggie.
    Purl up and die / by Maggie Sefton. — Large print edition.
        pages cm. — (Thorndike Press large print mystery) (A knitting mystery)
    ISBN 978-1-4104-8261-7 (hardcover) — ISBN 1-4104-8261-8 (hardcover)
    1. Large type books. I. Title.
PS3619.E37P87 2015b
813'.6—dc23   2015020682

Published in 2015 by arrangement with The Berkley Publishing Group, an imprint of Penguin Publishing Group, a division of Penguin Random House LLC

Printed in Mexico
1 2 3 4 5 6 7 19 18 17 16 15

CAST OF CHARACTERS

Kelly Flynn — financial accountant and part-time sleuth, refugee from East Coast corporate CPA firm

Steve Townsend — architect and builder in Fort Connor, Colorado, and Kelly's boyfriend

Kelly's Friends:

Jennifer Stroud — real estate agent, part-time waitress

Lisa Gerrard — physical therapist

Megan Smith — IT consultant, another corporate refugee

Marty Harrington — lawyer, Megan's husband

Greg Carruthers — university instructor, Lisa's boyfriend

Pete Wainwright — owner of Pete's Porch Café in the back of Kelly's favorite knitting shop, House of Lambspun

Lambspun Family and Regulars:

Mimi Shafer — Lambspun shop owner and knitting expert, known to Kelly and her friends as "Mother Mimi"

Burt Parker — retired Fort Connor police detective, Lambspun spinner-in-residence

Hilda and Lizzie von Steuben — spinster sisters, retired schoolteachers, and exquisite knitters

Curt Stackhouse — Colorado rancher, Kelly's mentor and advisor

Jayleen Swinson — Alpaca rancher and Colorado cowgirl

Connie and Rosa — Lambspun shop personnel

ONE

A Monday in early July, one year after the High Park Wildfire

Kelly Flynn pushed open the heavy wooden entry door of the Lambspun knitting shop and stepped inside the foyer. Shop owner Mimi Shafer Parker was draping a rainbow-hued knitted shawl across the doors of an antique dry sink in the corner.

"Good morning, Mimi. I thought I'd get a coffee refill and hear how your camping trip went this past weekend."

Mimi gave Kelly a big smile. "It was great. Weather was perfect. Cassie had a ball learning how to cook over the camp stove."

"I tried scrambling eggs over a campfire once, and they got pretty hard. Almost inedible," Kelly said as she walked through the central yarn room to the main knitting room and dumped her shoulder bag onto the long library table there. "Hopefully Cassie did better than I did."

7

"Well, a camp stove is easier to cook on, Kelly. You can control the gas heat. So don't throw in the towel on campfire cooking just yet," Mimi said as she followed Kelly into the large room where fiber workers regularly gathered.

"Ohhhhh, I threw in that towel years ago, Mimi," Kelly said, grinning at the maternal shop owner. "When there are so many good cooks around, there's no reason I should get in the kitchen except to make coffee. That I can do well. Did you three go up into Cache La Poudre Canyon? There are some great campsites right on the river."

"Oh, yes. We went to one of our favorites, where we reserved a site right there on the river. Cassie just loved it. She'd never gone camping before we took her last year." Mimi stared off into the wonderland of yarns she and her staff regularly created. Yarns and fiber creations filled the rooms, spilling out of bins and spread across tables. Color, color, everywhere. "There's nothing like the sound of a river nearby to lull you to sleep at night."

"That's for sure. I sleep like a log whenever Steve and I go camping up in the canyon," Kelly said as she took her oversize mug and walked toward the back hallway, which led to the café in the rear of the shop.

"That is, until I hear the early-morning birds singing. Or the telltale sounds of a raccoon trying to get into the locked cooler outside."

"Oh, yes. Raccoons and other critters that roam around looking for food." Mimi followed her down the hallway.

"One time we took Carl, and I swear, we barely got any sleep. Carl heard every animal sound for miles around. Kept growling or barking or making little growly sounds all night."

"Carl was being protective. That's his job."

"I don't know how he managed to hear those critters with the sound of the river so close. Tiny scratching sounds would be drowned out," Kelly said as she walked into Pete's Porch Café and spotted good friend Jennifer loading plates of tempting breakfast dishes onto her tray.

Mimi laughed her little musical laugh. "You forget about Carl's keen nose. That's how he knew critters were afoot. He smelled them."

Jennifer balanced the tray on her shoulder and walked over to them. "Good morning, you two. Can I get you anything?"

"Just a coffee refill when your hands are free," Kelly said with a grin. "Mimi was telling me how much fun Cassie had on the camping trip this weekend."

"I'll say. She regaled Pete and me with every detail. Seems she really liked cooking on that camp stove. So she must have inherited some of Pete's cooking genes."

"She did a good job with those cheese scrambled eggs," Mimi said. "They were better than mine."

Jennifer grinned. "That's because she's been watching Eduardo. He's the master." She glanced toward the familiar grill cook, who was busy turning pancakes and strips of bacon and sausage on the large grill.

"Well, tell Cassie she can come over to our place and make some cheesy eggs for Steve and me anytime." Kelly pulled out a chair at the closest café table. "If this is Monday, then she's out at tennis with Megan this morning."

"Yep. She's actually playing in a tournament this weekend. In between softball games, of course. This is getting heavy, so I'll catch up later." Jennifer turned toward the main part of the café.

Mimi pulled up a chair across from Kelly. "It's hard to believe Cassie's been here over a year. It's gone so fast. Last year in July, we were still helping Jayleen and other folks repair fire damage to the canyons." Mimi shook her head. "Time really flies faster nowadays. I guess that's a sign I'm getting old."

Kelly leaned back in the chair and smiled at her friend: Mother Mimi, who always took a motherly interest in everything Kelly and friends were doing. "Well, if it makes you feel any better, Mimi, I think time is passing faster, too. And if I think it's my imagination, all I have to do is look at Cassie and see how much she's grown in a year."

"Hasn't she ever? I declare, that girl must have shot up three or more inches. Why, she's as tall as I am!"

"I remember Burt saying last year that Cassie would be going into a growth spurt judging by how much her appetite increased. She was eating more. Looks like Burt was right."

Julie walked up then and placed Kelly's refilled coffee mug on the table in front of her. "Here you go, Kelly."

"Thanks, Julie. By the way, how did your church group's canyon repair go this past weekend? When Steve and I went up to help with canyon repairs, we really had great weather."

"Ohhhh, we got a *lot* done." Julie gave a satisfied nod. "We shored up several hillsides that had rain damage and lost soil. We made more waddles with straw and put them up. And we reforested several areas with tiny tree plantings. We were exhausted by the time we finished. But, boy oh boy, were we proud of the work we did. Those people on that property had most of their house burned, so it felt really good to help them. The wife started crying, watching us at work."

"I'll bet. You and your church group did a huge good deed for those folks," Kelly said. "How far down the road from Jayleen's ranch was that place?"

"A couple of miles. When we drove out of the canyon we went up and over the hill toward Masonville, so we passed by Jayleen's ranch. It's looking a lot better, too. Jennifer told me how much you guys did this past year with replanting and shoring up those hillsides. Looks like we've got a ton of new growth all over Bellevue Canyon now. I saw a lot of green on Jayleen's hillsides."

"All of you should be proud of yourselves," Mother Mimi said. "So many of our friends needed help after that awful High Park wildfire last summer, and lots of people showed up to help. Now Burt and I drive through the canyons and we see green plantings and new growth all over. Restoring the land."

Julie grinned. "Thanks, Mimi. It felt good to make a difference. Talk to you later. I've got to check on my other customers now." She scurried back into the main café.

Seated in the back alcove, it was still surprisingly quiet for a summer morning, Kelly noticed. The breakfast rush must have come and gone. After all, golfers and tennis players like to be out early so they can avoid the heat of the midsummer sun. She'd seen several foursomes out on the greens already when she and her boyfriend, Steve Townsend, took their early-morning run by the river.

"I'd better check to see if Rosa needs any help up front," Mimi said as she rose.

"Oh, yes. Work beckons," Kelly said, joining her.

"How's that new building project Steve's working on in Denver going?" Mimi asked as she and Kelly walked toward the hallway. "You said he was working some late nights."

"It's going well. Construction has moved into the next phase. Framing is all done, so they'll get the roof on and then start on the interior." Kelly took a deep drink of the hot black coffee that was Eduardo's specialty.

Mimi's cell phone sounded, and she dug it out of her pocket. "Oh, it's Barb. She's teaching an intermediate advanced knitting class early this afternoon. I hope nothing's come up. Talk to you later, Kelly." Mimi scurried down the hallway, phone to her ear.

Kelly didn't feel like scurrying this July morning. She was looking forward to sitting inside the knitting shop's comfy air-conditioned surroundings and working on her client accounts. Tonight was a Little League softball game with Cassie's team on one field at Rolland Moore Park, and Curt's grandson Eric playing baseball on another field. Back-to-back ball games. Luckily, Kelly, Megan, and Lisa didn't have a game tonight, so they could relax and cheer the kids instead. Steve's team played tomorrow night.

Walking back to the main knitting room, which was still empty of customers, Kelly pulled out a chair at the long library table, popped open her laptop computer, and settled in for a morning filled with accounting and numbers. Lots of numbers. Thank goodness for strong coffee.

A familiar voice sounded in the adjoining yarn room. An authoritative woman's voice. Kelly looked up from her laptop screen and the accounting spreadsheet pictured there and saw former nurse and part-time knitting instructor Barb Macenroe stride into the main room.

"Hey, Barb, good to see you. Mimi said you were teaching an intermediate advanced knitting class today."

Tall and big-boned, Barb dropped her huge fabric bag on the table with a big thump. "Good to see you, Kelly. You should sign up for the class, too. There are a couple of spots open."

"Ohhhh, I don't think I'm advanced enough for your courses, Barb. I've heard that you really get into some tricky knitting techniques. It's all I can do to keep to the basics so my stitches are even."

Barb's face took on an expression Kelly recognized as the "schoolmarm" look. Kelly made sure she kept a straight face. Barb was stern but had a good heart and could always be counted on to help out Mimi when there was a time crunch.

"Don't underestimate yourself, Kelly," Barb said in that schoolmarm voice. "You can easily master those techniques."

Kelly chuckled. "Just the word 'master' and my name in the same sentence is a contradiction, Barb. But I'll promise to peek in today and see what you're up to. When are you teaching?"

Barb glanced at her watch. "In less than

an hour. So let me go and set up the workroom right now. We have five signed up, so with me, we'll have six around that table." Barb smiled at Kelly. "Plenty of time to reconsider, Kelly. I've never seen you back away from a challenge."

Kelly refused to take the bait and laughed softly. "You're right, Barb. But all things knitting related have the power to confuse me no end. So I don't push my luck." Remembering something, Kelly switched subjects. "By the way, how's son Tommy doing? It's hard to believe he's finished his medical studies. I believe you said he was an intern the last time we spoke."

Barb immediately turned from the doorway, her face alight. "Ohhhhh, Tommy's doing *wonderfully*! Because he'd taken so many extra anatomy and physiology courses for his EMT training, even advanced ones, he was way ahead in the classes he needed. In fact, he's finished his fourth-year requirements." Her chin went up in obvious motherly pride. "Now, he's a *resident* in family medicine."

"Oh, Barb, that's wonderful!" Kelly exclaimed. "You deserve to be proud. And Tommy does, too. Why, he's taken courses throughout the summer every year. That's to be commended. You tell him I said that, okay?"

Barb beamed. "Thank you, Kelly. I'll tell him. And you're right. He has been taking courses nonstop ever since he was awarded that scholarship a couple of years ago. Thank goodness for that philanthropic organization. Because of that, Tommy was able to cut back on his EMT hours to once a week so he could take classes full-time."

"Is he actually working at the hospital now?"

"Well, he's doing his residency there with several doctors in different specialties. And he's on the staff of one of the emergency care clinics located around the city. Focusing on general practice. Everything walks in the door of those clinics, from bee stings to burst appendixes." Barb chuckled. "So, he's getting an education, that's for sure."

"Did you ever work in one of those emergency care clinics?" Kelly asked.

"Ohhhh, yes. We nurses go wherever they need us." Barb suddenly checked her watch. "Well, enough of my maternal bragging. I'd better set up for class. These are very good students and they deserve my full attention." She headed toward the doorway to the workroom once more.

"I may check in on that class, Barb. Just

17

to see what you're up to," Kelly called after her. Draining her coffee mug, Kelly decided it was time for a refill.

"Now, watch how I wrap the yarn and then slip it off the needle," Barb instructed the class, holding up both knitting needles. A soft pink yarn spilled into a pile in her lap.

Kelly leaned forward exactly like the five class members and stared at Barb's needles as she went through the movements. One needle double wrapped the yarn and then slipped it off onto the other needle. Kelly blinked. What was that again? She wasn't sure she'd seen what Barb was demonstrating. It looked like the yarn over stitch, but a little different.

"Ohhhhhh, now I get it," one middle-aged woman said, nodding her head.

"Can I see that again?" another woman asked, peering at Barb's needles.

"Yeah, do that again," a couple of younger women said, nodding, holding their needles and yarn in front of them.

Kelly watched Barb's needles work through the motions again. She thought she saw the yarn being wrapped twice, but she wasn't sure about the rest of the motions. Clearly, she would need Mimi to walk her through it, step by step.

She watched the rest of the class try to imitate Barb's movements. The two middle-aged women and the three younger women all looked like they understood what Barb was trying to show them. Obviously, knitters were not created equally, Kelly concluded.

"How's your son Tommy doing?" one woman asked, her needles moving smoothly through the motions. "Didn't you say he was an intern?"

Barb's big smile returned. "Actually he's moved on and is a resident in family medicine now," she said, face glowing with motherly pride. "He's even working in one of the emergency care clinics."

"Really?" another woman asked. "Which one?"

"The one near Drake and Timberline. It's open twenty-four hours. Tommy gets the middle of the night since he's the resident."

"Lowest on the totem pole," a younger woman commented.

"He won't stay there long," another said. "He sounds like a rising star from what you've said."

Barb's face glowed, clearly basking in the praise for her son. "I think so, too. The other doctors seem impressed with him. So he should move up fast."

"Well, you know what they say," a middle-aged woman said. "Cream rises to the top."

A couple of the women chuckled as others concentrated on their stitches. Kelly was about to add her affirmations to the others when her cell phone rang.

"Excuse me, folks, sorry to interrupt," she said, jumping out of her chair and heading toward the doorway. She quickly dug into her pocket for the phone, which was playing loud Latin music. Steve's name flashed on the screen as she clicked on. "Hey, there. Will you be able to make the kids' ball games tonight or will you be stuck at the building site?"

"Actually I'll be home earlier. You and I are going to dinner. I've already made reservations at the Jazz Bistro for six o'clock tonight," Steve said, the sound of a smile in his voice.

"Sounds great. Any special reason or do you simply want something other than fast food or pizza tonight?" she teased.

"Matter of fact, there is. Sam Kaufman officially made me a partner today and wants me to expand our construction business into Northern Colorado."

Kelly could feel Steve's pride coming over the phone just as she could hear it in his voice. "Oh, Steve! That's *fantastic*! I know you and Sam were talking about it, and we were hoping. It's official?"

"Yep. We signed the papers at the lawyer's office this afternoon. I was going to head back to the work site, but Sam told me to go home and celebrate." He laughed softly.

"I love Sam. Great advice. So, where are you now?" Kelly asked, walking over to the knitting table.

"Actually, I'm halfway home. I should be there in forty-five minutes at most. Do you have any appointments scheduled?"

Kelly slid the laptop into her over-the-shoulder bag, then checked her watch. "Nope. No appointments until tomorrow. I've finished my accounts, and I'm free as a bird. You want me to meet you at the Bistro? We can have drinks before dinner."

"Actually I was thinking we could have our own celebration before we head to the Bistro," Steve suggested, a teasing tone in his voice now.

Kelly caught his meaning immediately and smiled. "Sounds like a plan. I'll see you at home."

"Count on it."

Kelly grinned and clicked off, then headed out of the shop.

Kelly took a sip of the crisp clean sauvignon blanc wine and savored. Fruity pear flavors hinting. She leaned back into the cushioned booth in the Jazz Bistro's cocktail lounge and watched the jazz pianist, Mark, take a familiar melody and riff through it with a jazzy twist. The bass player closed his eyes and took the lead, alternating with the piano. Good food, good wine, and good jazz. Hard to ask for more.

She looked over at Steve, who was leaning into the cushions beside her, and placed her hand over his on the table. "I'm so proud of you, Steve. You worked wretched hours, driving back and forth to Denver, helping Sam build up his business. You deserve this partnership."

Steve turned to Kelly and smiled into her eyes. "That means a lot, hearing you say that." He lifted her hand to his mouth and kissed it.

"When do you think you can open an office up here?"

"Not for a while yet. I'll keep commuting to Denver until I've gotten a couple of projects started up here. I'll be talking to some builders I know who used to be in the business a few years ago. A lot have survived by switching to remodeling. They've had to transform themselves. Hell, we've all had to transform ourselves." He sipped his Scotch.

"Well, you're in the top of that group," Kelly said. "I know a whole lot of folks who went belly-up but didn't transform. They just went to ground and got into other work. Some had enough savings to survive with remodeling. But most didn't. They've never come back. And you're the only one I know who did the hard job of leaving town and learning how to be successful in a bigger city like Denver. That takes guts. And brains." She winked at him and raised her glass before taking a sip.

Steve grinned. "My biggest fan." Then he leaned over and kissed her, lingering. "What do you say we go home and have dessert there."

Kelly grinned back. "I say ask for the check."

Steve laughed softly and raised his hand to signal the waiter.

Two

Tuesday morning

"You tell Steve 'Congratulations' for me, okay?" Arthur Housemann said, smiling across his polished mahogany desk at Kelly. "He deserves to be a partner in that business. Steve worked harder than most to recover from the building bust a few years ago. Most builders I knew then have gone out of business and haven't returned. They've either moved on or moved into remodeling full-time. It's not as risky as building new homes. Steve not only survived, but he came back stronger."

Her words exactly, Kelly thought and returned her client's smile. "I couldn't have said it better. And coming from you, Arthur, that's high praise indeed. You've seen many a building boom and real estate bust, and you've survived as well." She lifted her coffee mug in a salute.

"Oh, that I have, Kelly," Arthur said, lean-

24

ing back farther in his upholstered desk chair. "Only the strong survive. And the strong and smart will prosper." He winked.

"I'll tell Steve that, too. He'll be meeting with some of his old builder contacts here in town as well as the new ones on the scene."

"You tell Steve I'd be glad to meet with him, too. I've been listening to my tenants and landlords and getting ideas. I wouldn't mind tossing them around with the new partner of Kaufman Construction."

"Actually, it's now Kaufman and Townsend Construction," Kelly said, not bothering to conceal the pride in her voice.

Arthur beamed. "I stand corrected. Kaufman and *Townsend* Construction."

"I'm sure Steve would love to meet with you, Arthur," Kelly said, delighted at Arthur's suggestion. That would be a great opportunity for Steve. "Changing the subject, have you done any more wildfire restoration work in the Cache La Poudre Canyon? The last time I drove by there, I noticed that your place and Dennis Holt's place next door are both looking good. The wildfire didn't touch either of them. But down the road that left side of the upper ridge is still blackened."

"Yes, it is. And a whole bunch of us in the

canyon are going to volunteer to plant some more seedling pines this September. Like last year, we'll get past the August heat and let them take root before the winter snows come. We ought to be able to plant more, too. Last year the soil was freshly charred and not in good shape."

Kelly took another sip of Arthur's office coffee. Not as strong as Eduardo's but passable. "That's a great idea, Arthur. Will Dennis be helping with that?"

"Absolutely. Dennis has been clearing out dead brush on his land and also on his neighbors' properties since spring." The buzzer on Arthur's phone system sounded. "Oops, that's my secretary. Reminding me that my next appointment is here."

Kelly drained the last of the coffee and gathered her portfolio into her briefcase bag. "I'd best get back, anyway. You're in good shape, Arthur. So now I need to see what Don Warner and company have waiting for me."

Arthur Housemann rose from his chair. "Well, knowing Don Warner, I'd vouch to say he's got projects of his own on the table and up his sleeve."

Kelly slipped her briefcase bag over her shoulder. "Oh, you're right as always, Arthur. Warner is constantly coming up with plans. And it's my job to find the money for them."

Housemann laughed as he accompanied Kelly to the door of his office. "I don't envy you that task. Take care, Kelly. Are you and your friends playing softball tonight?"

"We are, and wish us luck. We're playing our archrival, Greeley."

"Well, hit one out of the park for me, okay?" Arthur teased, opening the door.

"I'll do my best. Talk to you next week," Kelly said as she walked past the waiting client. Once outside in the hallway, Kelly heard her cell phone's music. She clicked on, seeing Lisa's name. "Hey, there. Ready for Greeley tonight?"

"I hope so. They're tough. Say, I just saw Jennifer and she told me about Steve's big news. Partner in the construction firm. Cool! We'll have to celebrate tonight after the game. Have you told Megan yet?"

"I left a message on her voice mail. She's in an all-day conference with one of her clients. The demanding one. So I expect to hear from her —" The beeping sound of another call coming in sounded in Kelly's ear as she pushed out the office building door. "That's probably her now."

"Okay, I'll hang up. See you at the ball field," Lisa said, then clicked off.

Kelly spotted Megan's name and clicked on to the new call as she walked through the parking lot. "Hey, there. You got my message?"

"You betcha. It made my day. *Way to go, Steve!*" Megan yelled into Kelly's ear. So loud, Kelly had to hold the phone away as she laughed.

That afternoon Kelly watched as Jennifer poured a black stream of coffee into her oversize mug. The rich aroma wafted toward her nostrils. *Ummmmmm.* Caffeine. She took a sip of the hot brew without blowing on it. The brain cells that hadn't reported for duty yet snapped to attention.

Jennifer laughed softly. "I still don't know how you do that. Doesn't it burn your mouth?"

"It's supposed to," Kelly teased. "That's part of the enjoyment. You'll be at the ballpark tonight, right? Cassie said you guys were bringing her."

"We'll be there. Cassie's team is playing before you guys. So we'll make it a doubleheader."

"Well, she and several of the girls I coached last summer have improved so much they made their middle school teams last fall. And now, they're even better."

"I love to see Cassie run around the bases. I swear, those long legs just sprint across the ground."

"I know. Didn't you tell me she'd grown at least three inches this past year?"

"At least. And that gangly phase has started." Jennifer started to laugh. "I swear, she's bumping into walls, knocking mugs off the counter. It's hilarious."

"Ohhhhh, yeah. I remember that phase in junior high. Stuff used to jump off the table as I passed by. And if you think that's hilarious, you should have seen me play basketball. Arms and legs everywhere."

Jennifer laughed out loud this time. "It sounds like you were a female version of Marty." She glanced about the beginning of the early lunch crowd filling the café tables. "Well, that's enough for memories right now. Gotta get back to my customers. See you tonight."

"See you then." Kelly raised her mug and headed toward the corridor leading back into the Lambspun shop. Numbers were calling her name.

Kelly tabbed through the accounting spreadsheets, entering revenues in column after column. Warner Construction had a very profitable month. Now, if only expenses were in line, all would be well.

Mimi walked into the main knitting room, a stack of magazines in her arm, and pulled out a chair at the knitting table. "I thought I'd do a pattern search in here. Connie can handle whatever happens up front."

"Good to have the company. It's really quiet this afternoon for some reason."

"It could be the hot weather. People forget about yarns and fibers on hot July days. Your team is playing tonight, right, Kelly? Make sure you all have enough water," Mimi said, glancing up at Kelly.

Kelly had to smile. Mother Mimi. Always worrying about her people. "Don't worry. We always bring a couple of huge water containers. That way we can keep refilling our water bottles. We decided last year we needed to cut back on those plastic bottles, so we're going back to the way we handled it years ago. Save the planet."

Mimi smiled as she paged through a magazine. "I think that's a wonderful idea, Kelly. You and your team deserve to be commended for their efforts."

Just then Barb strode into the main room. Her face was red as if she'd been hurrying. "I'm so glad I found you two alone," she said, sinking into a chair beside Mimi.

"Barb, what's the matter? You look so . . .

frazzled," Mimi asked. "Your class isn't until an hour or so."

"It's not that," Barb said, glancing about the room and then over her shoulder. "I heard some *awful* news from Tommy a little while ago . . . and I have to tell someone. Someone sensible."

Kelly noticed Big Barb was sweating, water had ringed the sleeveless shirt she wore, and it trickled down her neck. "Well, Mimi and I are nothing if not sensible. A business owner and an accountant. So what's up? Has Tommy's scholarship run out or something?"

"Oh, Lord, I don't know. But if these awful accusations become police record, Tommy may lose his scholarship entirely!"

"Good heavens!" Mimi said with a shocked expression. "What accusations?"

Barb frowned and her lips tightened as she leaned over. Kelly leaned closer so as not to miss anything Barb was about to say. "Tommy told me last night he was covering the emergency clinic during the nighttime hours like he does every week, and this young woman came in the middle of the night. No other patients were there, just the nurse on duty and him. This woman complained of stomach pains, so the nurse took her into the examining room and had her remove her slacks and then get on the examining table and cover herself with a drape." Barb took a deep breath.

"Tommy said he came in then, asked her several questions on the medical information form she filled out, and started to examine her. The nurse was out front answering a phone call. The young woman said she had these recurring stomach pains that started yesterday and were getting stronger. Tommy said he started pressing on her stomach in various places, trying to eliminate obvious things like appendicitis, when all of a sudden the woman sat up on the table and yelled 'Stop that!' Then she jumped off the table, grabbed her clothes, and ran out of the room, crying. She stopped at the nurse's desk and accused Tommy of groping her during the exam! Can you *believe* that!"

Kelly stared at Barb, trying to digest what she'd heard, shocked. She'd met Tommy. He was a good guy.

"What!" Mimi cried, sinking back in her chair. "That's *ridiculous*! Whatever is wrong with that young woman?"

"I don't know! Tommy swore to me he did nothing wrong. He was pressing on her stomach and never put his hand between her legs . . . or anything like that. There has to be something wrong with the girl. A mental problem or something . . . to accuse him like that."

"What did Tommy do after she jumped off the table and ran out of the room?" Kelly asked. "Did he tell the nurse what happened?"

Barb nodded vigorously. "Of course. He told her right away. She was stunned and told Tommy that the girl said he groped her." Barb closed her eyes as if she didn't want to picture the awful images she was describing. "The nurse said the girl yanked on her slacks outside the glass front door, dropped the drape on the floor, then ran outside."

"Do you think the girl will go to the police?"

Barb's face contorted and reddened even more. Kelly thought she might start to cry. "She already *has*! Tommy said police showed up at the clinic as he was getting off duty this morning. The two officers told him that the young woman had reported an assault at the clinic last night when she was being examined for stomach pains. The officers told Tommy that they had to question him since he was the only physician on duty last night. They called it *sexual assault*! He's just beginning his medical career. That . . .

that can hurt him!"

This time, Kelly did spot tears brimming in Barb's eyes. She reached over and placed her hand on Barb's sweaty arm. It felt clammy in the air-conditioned shop. "I'm so sorry, Barb. That is terrible."

"Oh, Barb, that can't happen! Tommy is innocent. Surely the police will find out," Mimi said, her face revealing her concern. "Tommy told them everything, right? Told them how the girl jumped off the table and ran off in the middle of the exam?"

Barb nodded, swiping the tears from her cheeks with one hand. "Yes, yes, he did. But he told me the officers just wrote everything down in their notebooks but didn't give him any feedback. They did tell him that the girl had filed a complaint, and that was official. Tommy told me he got a bad feeling after that."

"Wha . . . what did he mean?" Mimi asked, her voice lowering because customers had entered the adjoining yarn room.

"Tommy told me one of the other doctors who'd come in early was close by and advised Tommy to get a lawyer. An official police report goes on file and has to be investigated. And there will be a record of it in the police department." Barb shook her head. "And that could mean Tommy might lose his scholarship! And if that happened, he could lose his intern spot at the emergency clinic!"

"Oh, no!" Mimi said, hand to her breast in her familiar gesture of concern.

"We need to ask Burt exactly what all of that means. When's Burt coming in, Mimi?" Kelly asked, checking her watch.

"Oh, dear. Maybe not until this evening. He's in Denver doing errands."

Kelly leaned toward Barb. "I think it would be a good idea for Tommy to speak with an attorney. I can highly recommend Marty Harrington. He's Megan's husband and an excellent lawyer. Several people we know have used Marty's services."

"Oh, yes!" Mimi enthused. "Marty is excellent! I could call Megan if you want his number."

Barb shook her head again. "No, no, we have a family attorney who has known Tommy since he was a baby. I used him last year. You know . . . when that malicious crook caused all of us such grief." A different expression crossed Barb's features this time.

Kelly recalled that Barb had been a suspect in Jared Rizzoli's murder a little over a year ago. "Well, if he knows Tommy, that's an even better choice."

Cassie suddenly appeared around the corner, can of soda in her hand. "Hey, Kelly! Are you ready for that big Greeley game?"

Kelly quickly focused on the slender young girl, her dark hair pulled back in a ponytail. She could really see the jump in height. Cassie was much taller now. "I'm as ready as I'll ever be, I guess." Kelly smiled back at Cassie. "Are you ready for your game? You're playing a Loveland middle school, I think."

Cassie took a sip of soda. "Yep, we're playing Loveland Central. Then my friends and I will come over to your game and watch you guys." She straddled a chair backward in the way Jayleen Swinson did. Kelly figured Cassie had picked that up from one of her adopted grandmothers.

Barb swiped her face again and rose from the table. "Well, I'd better get ready for my class. I'll talk to you later."

Mimi rose as well. "I'll help you set up, Barb." She glanced back at Cassie. "Did you have fun at Greg's lab, dear?"

"Oh, yes! The geeks had a new project they're working on so they were explaining it to me. Greg also showed me some of the newest computer chips." Her big blue eyes grew even larger with delight. "It was *awesome*!"

"Take care, Barb," Kelly said, watching Barb head for the doorway.

Barb nodded but didn't say anything as she followed Mimi into the workroom. Kelly noticed Cassie staring after them.

"Is she okay? It looked like Barb was crying," Cassie asked, smile gone from her youthful face.

Kelly sought for an answer a young teenager would understand. "Barb's had kind of a rough day. A really rough day."

Cassie pondered that then nodded. "Kind of like when we lost that close game to Lafayette."

"Yeah, like that," Kelly nodded. "But worse. Now, tell me, are you and the team ready for that Loveland batting lineup? As I recall, they were really good last fall when your middle school played them."

Cassie took a sip of her soda and smiled at Kelly. "Oh, yeah. We're gonna take 'em. You watch."

Kelly chuckled. The sound of Youthful Confidence. You had to love it.

"Wow, that is serious stuff," Steve said, reaching for another piece of barbecued chicken.

"It is, indeed," Marty said, following suit and stretching toward the metal café table and the platter stacked with chicken.

Kelly tipped back her bottle of Fat Tire ale and relaxed in the wrought iron chair at their favorite café in Fort Connor's Old Town plaza. After all the congratulations to Steve and the accompanying lifting of beer mugs, bottles, and soda cans in salute, Kelly ventured into a more serious subject. The normal postgame conversation became considerably subdued when she described the situation Barb had related earlier in the afternoon.

"It sounds like a 'she said, he said' situation," Greg offered as he snagged a larger piece of chicken.

Megan dipped her chicken morsel in the spicy sauce sitting open on the table. "I've never met Tommy but all I've heard are good things. You know . . . worked as a paramedic, got accepted for med school, worked hard, and is now a doctor. Sounds like a homegrown success story."

"I have met him and Tommy comes across exactly the way you described him. Workaholic and high achiever. I just don't see him as someone who'd make a move like that." Kelly reached for one of the fast-disappearing BBQ chicken pieces.

"Well, I've been on the other side of that situation," Lisa said. "No one has ever tried it with me —"

"Because you'd give him a fist in the ribs, right?" Greg probed.

Lisa gave him a patient look. "No . . ."

"Knee to the groin?"

"No, I —"

"Well, put those on your to-do list," Greg decreed, then tipped back his bottle of craft brew.

Lisa rolled her eyes. "I was about to make a different point. I've been around girls and women who have been in the situation of being groped. And there's no 'type' of guy who does it. And they're not drunk at a bar, either. It can happen in offices, all kinds of places. So, I'll reserve judgment on Tommy." Lisa gave a nod of experience and sipped her beer.

Kelly pondered what Lisa said. With her position as a physical therapist, Lisa was exposed to all sorts of patients and people. And with her graduate studies at the university, she was in contact with scores of female students. Lisa had a breadth and depth of experience that the rest of them lacked. Consequently Kelly had to admit Lisa's observation was valid, disconcerting as it was.

"I see your point, Lisa. You're right. None of us knows Tommy that well. So, naturally the police are looking at him exactly the same way. Tommy's story may indeed be true, but there's no way to prove it."

"Listen, I didn't mean it to come out sounding like a joke, but I was serious," Greg said, leaning forward and looking at his girlfriend of several years. "One of the grad students who worked in our lab a couple of years ago was complaining about being groped at a party. And she was really mad that she didn't say anything at the time, like 'Watch it, dude!' or 'Back off!' The guys and I told her to call 'em on it if a guy tries that."

"Yeah, but that's kind of hard if you're in a place where you don't expect it. Like a doctor's office," Megan added.

"Excellent point," Steve said, leaning back in his chair, ignoring the last pieces of chicken.

"Whether Tommy is innocent as a lamb or a guilty troll, tell me what happens next, Marty?" Kelly asked, turning her empty Fat Tire bottle on the chair arm.

"It sounds like the woman filed an official complaint, and the police followed up on it. They questioned the man who was accused of assault, as well as the alleged assault victim. Now, the police will make a report of their investigation and file that. The next move will be up to the woman. If she presses charges, then Tommy will definitely need a lawyer because he may be headed for a trial. The court will decide how to handle it. So, it all depends on what the woman decides to do."

"Wow. Being charged with sexual assault with a patient could really jeopardize Tommy's medical career." Megan toyed with the chicken tidbit.

"Even if Tommy's not officially charged with assault, there would still be a police record on file. And you're right. That could definitely damage his medical career. This is a patient that accused him. Not good," Kelly said.

"Okay, we agree that is one bad situation. But there's nothing any of us can do. So, personally, I'd like to change the subject back to Steve's good news. So we can finish off the evening feeling a whole lot better than we do now."

Kelly grinned at Greg. "Wow, sleeping with a psych major really has rubbed off on you. That was positively therapeutic advice."

Greg extended his hands, palms up, in a "but of course" gesture.

"The doctor is in," Steve joked before

draining his favorite ale. Laughter floated into the summer night air.

THREE

Wednesday morning

"He's just pretending to fall, Carl," Kelly called to her Rottweiler in the backyard of her cottage. "He'll take off once you get close."

As usual, Carl ignored her as he raced toward the chain fence, barking furiously. He'd paused for a head and ear rub and stopped paying attention to Patrol Duty. Brazen Squirrel, the ever-observant, ever-ready little creature that he was, had taken advantage of Carl's lapse in attention. Now, Brazen was racing along the top rail of the chain-link fence, nut in his mouth, almost at the low-hanging branch of the huge cottonwood tree. Only a few feet outside the fence, the cottonwood shaded most of Kelly's backyard. It also offered refuge for weary golfers who were searching the edge of the golf course for their stray balls.

The very second Carl charged the fence

where Brazen was running, the little rodent leaped for the cottonwood branch. Piece of cake. Kelly observed the familiar drama. Yet another easy squirrel escape, eluding Big Dog once again. Carl, for his part, was barking his angry accusations and venting his frustration. *Curses! Foiled again!* Kelly laughed softly. No matter how many times she watched this familiar backyard drama, it still amused her. It was like one of those daytime television dramas, minus the romance.

Glancing over the golf course expanse of green, Kelly spotted a few sun-resistant golfers. Playing their rounds, no matter the hot July sun. Compared to last June and the Wildfire Summer, these July temps were normal. High nineties and creeping into a one hundred reading once or twice. Normal for a Northern Colorado July summer. Still, Kelly had to wonder at the golfers who were out on the links. Most wore small hats with brims in the front. Or those cloth hats that had droopy brims all around.

She didn't think either of those hats would pass muster with her dermatologist. She'd advised Kelly to wear a bigger sun hat with a wide-drooping brim whenever she was outside in sunny, mile-high Fort Connor. A mile closer to the sun, Dr. Hayes always reminded. And her constant mantra: "Never leave the house without sunscreen." Kelly had vowed to try. So far, she had a fifty-fifty track record, but it was a beginning.

"Keep those squirrels in line, Carl," she called to her dog as she slid the patio screen door shut. Carl lifted his head briefly then returned to sniffing all traces of squirrel feet on the morning grass along the fence. Wait . . . was that a raccoon?

Lifting her briefcase bag with laptop over her shoulder, Kelly drained the last of her morning batch of coffee into her mug and headed out the cozy cottage front door. She spotted Burt Parker across the driveway separating her cottage and the Lambspun knitting shop. Kelly called to him and waved. "Hey, Burt!"

Retired Fort Connor police detective Burt turned at the sound of his name and waved back. "Hey, Kelly. Got time for coffee?"

"With you, Burt, always," Kelly said as she sped around the wrought iron fence to the gate.

Burt had already chosen a table in the shady part of the garden, so Kelly headed straight for it. She noticed most of the outside tables were full this gorgeous July morning. Without even going inside, Kelly knew the inside café was packed at this midmorning breakfast hour.

She plopped her bag onto the ground and settled into a chair across from Burt. "I see you've already got a start on the coffee break. Man after my own heart." Kelly took a big sip from her oversize mug.

Burt's weathered face crinkled with his familiar smile. A fatherly smile. "Right about that, Kelly. How'd that game go last night? I was still in Denver. Mimi's looking at two different suppliers of looms and wanted me to go take photos and ask questions of the craftsmen."

"We lost, but just barely. Only two points. So I think we're inching up on them." She gave a shrug.

"Next time, right?" Burt said in his encouraging way.

Julie hastened up to them then, notepad in one hand, coffeepot in the other. "Morning, guys," she said, swiftly refilling both Burt's and Kelly's mugs. "Isn't it beautiful today? The heat won't rise for a couple hours, so it's positively balmy." Julie glanced toward the golf course.

"It's gorgeous, all right," Kelly agreed, watching Julie's attention. "Are you a golfer, Julie? Have you ever golfed?"

Julie returned her attention. "Lord, no. I could hit the ball, but then I'd spend hours trying to find it. Just like those poor folks over there." She pointed toward the greens.

Kelly looked and saw yet another couple of golfers walking about the edges of the course, staring at the ground. Meanwhile she could hear Carl barking in the backyard. "I agree, Julie. My balls would be all over the place. Plus, I'm not sure I'd be able to hit anything that small. I'm used to softballs and tennis balls. And both those sports are confined to certain playing areas. Golf courses, on the other hand, are big. You could spend hours covering all that ground. I don't have that kind of time."

"Me, either," Julie decreed. "Now, what would you two like?"

"I'll have one scrambled egg, one strip of bacon, and one small pancake. And coffee," Burt replied.

"Sounds kind of meager, Burt," Julie observed.

Burt released a long sigh. "Mimi's got me on another diet. She's on it, too. We've both been eating too much over vacation and, I confess, we didn't work out at all."

"Horrors," Julie said in pretend shock.

"I know, I know. *Wea culpa,* instead of *mea culpa.* We both are guilty. So now that we're home, we have to get back to our regular routines. Meanwhile, we're cutting

47

back on food for a while."

"It'll come off once you two start walking again every morning," Kelly said encouragingly. Burt looked mournful.

"How about you, Kelly?"

Kelly debated. She'd already had a fruit and yogurt that morning. Now she was going to dive into her spreadsheets for the morning. Surely she would need more sustenance than that. Surely.

"I'll have one of Pete's cinnamon rolls, warmed up, please. And coffee, of course."

"Of course," Julie said. "Okay, I'll get these orders to Eduardo right away. Might take a few minutes longer than usual. We're pretty full as you can see."

"Oh, yes, and I love it," Kelly said. "Small businesses that have become successful make an accountant's heart go pitter-patter."

Julie laughed then hurried off. Burt sipped from his refilled mug and looked over at Kelly. "Mimi filled me in on the bad news that Barb shared yesterday about Tommy. It's a damn shame. I hate to see something like that damage Tommy's reputation. He's worked so hard to become a doctor. And from people who've been to see him, they've had nothing but praise. Saying he's meticulous and conscientious." He wagged his head in a manner Kelly had watched for years.

"Marty was walking all of us through the legal details last night. It looks like now that the official police report is filed, then the next move is up to the girl who accused Tommy."

"Marty's right. If the girl decides to press charges, then the police will have no choice but to officially charge Tommy with sexual assault."

"Maybe she'll decide not to press charges?" Kelly offered.

Burt shrugged. "Who knows, Kelly? Maybe she won't. We'll all simply have to wait and see."

Kelly stared out at the golf course again. Fewer golfers there now. Heat was slowly beginning to rise. "Wait and see," Burt had said. That was going to be hard, especially for Tommy. Wondering what was going to happen to him.

Neither she nor Burt spoke. They simply sat quietly together, gazing out into the beautiful July morning until Julie arrived with their breakfasts.

Kelly walked into the main knitting room of Lambspun and set up her laptop. She'd worked outside in the shade for an hour until the July heat drove her inside to the shop's air-conditioned surroundings. Thank goodness Colorado had low humidity, so the heat was dry. That was a whole lot more comfortable. Kelly had lived in both the East and the Midwest, and summer heat there was hot, humid, and sticky. Oppressive.

Earlier, Kelly had grabbed a small table in the back of the café until the lunch crush arrived. She'd ordered one of Eduardo's yummy salads for lunch and left the cozy spot as soon as she finished. There was no way an accountant would deprive a small business owner of customer revenue by occupying a table longer than necessary.

Removing file folders from her briefcase bag, Kelly was all set to dive back into her spreadsheets when she heard women's voices coming from the workroom. Several voices, talking at once. Loud voices, too, as if they were arguing.

Is that a class? Whatever in the world is going on? Checking her watch, Kelly realized that it had to be Barb's class. Curiosity got the better of her, and she left her open laptop and walked toward the workroom. As soon as she entered the room, Kelly could feel the electricity in the air.

Barb's normally quiet intermediate

advanced knitting class was no more. Knitting needles and yarns sat on laps and lay forgotten on the nearby worktable. Instead, the students were either sitting and talking animatedly or standing and gesturing and talking. Barb sat quietly at the end of the table, her face flushed, as the women peppered her with questions.

"How can she make a charge like that without . . ." An older woman gestured, obviously searching for a word.

A younger woman sitting next to her filled in the gap. "You mean 'proof'? There is no proof in a case like that."

"It's a case of 'he said, she said,' " a middle-aged woman added.

"That's awful! A wonderful young man . . . a doctor . . . is accused of something like that," the older woman said, frowning.

"I know," the younger woman replied. "But the police still have to follow up on the complaint. In other cases the young women are telling the truth. It *does* happen."

"It happens more than you think," one of the college-aged girls added.

"Oh, yeah," the other concurred with a nod. "A couple of years ago I heard about a student accusing one of her professors of sexual assault in his office."

"Good Lord!" The older woman rolled her eyes.

"What happened?" the middle-aged woman asked.

"There was a lot of gossip around campus. Some students who had the professor in class didn't think he did it. They said he was a good guy."

"That doesn't count for squat with the police," the older woman said.

"The professor denied it, if I remember correctly," the college student continued.

"Was he fired?" the younger woman asked.

"If he had tenure, the university wouldn't be able to fire him," the middle-aged woman replied.

"What happened? Did the college student ever press charges?" the older woman asked.

"I don't think so, but I'm not sure," the college student replied. "One of my friends actually had a class with the professor. And I remember her saying he was innocent."

"How would she know?" the younger woman said.

The college student shrugged. "I don't know. I remember her being upset about it. Apparently she knew the professor and his family."

Kelly glimpsed Mimi leaning on the door-frame that led to the back-room office and storage area. Clearly Mimi was doing exactly what Kelly was doing — silently watching and listening to the reactions and comments bubbling up from the class. Big Barb sat quietly at the end of the table, not saying a word. Her expression said it all. It was a mixture of sadness and apprehension. The variety of comments surely were a jolt for Barb to listen to. The class spoke bluntly about the situation and their reactions to similar incidents.

Mimi beckoned to Kelly as she stepped farther back into the office storage area. Kelly quickly edged around the class, which was still animatedly commenting on Tommy's situation, and joined Mimi in the box-filled area. "Well, that was interesting," Kelly said quietly.

"Oh, my, yes," Mimi said. "Just listening to those women, all ages, and their comments. They think it's awful what's happened to Tommy, but they talk about other incidents when the young women were telling the truth. It was an education listening to them." Mimi's worried expression claimed her features now.

"I know. Burt and I had the exact same conversation outside on the patio this morning. Both of us are worried what the young woman will decide to do next. Will she press charges or not?"

"That's what worries me, too. And you can see how poor Barb is holding up." Mimi pointed toward the workroom outside the office. "Good Lord! I've never seen Barb look so awful. Even last summer when she was a suspect in that awful man's murder."

Kelly smiled to herself. Mimi had never been able to say the name of the man who had caused so much turmoil and loss in Fort Connor before his death. "I agree. Barb looks like she's been kicked in the stomach. Poor thing. It must be hard for her to hear all the comments from the class. They're speaking the truth. No one will ever know whether Tommy is innocent or guilty. For a devoted mom like Barb, that must be devastating."

"Burt said almost the same thing."

An idea came to Kelly then and she pondered it. "You know, I think I'll talk to that student in the class outside and ask her for her friend's name and e-mail. Maybe I can contact that student and ask her what she remembers. Then maybe Lisa can ask around at the university about that incident with the professor. We can learn what happens in a situation like that."

"I think that's a good idea, Kelly. Please keep Burt and me informed," Mimi said, then turned toward a large open box on the floor behind her, one of many. She withdrew three skeins of turquoise yarns.

Kelly thought the twist looked smaller than many wools and reached out to touch them. "Is this wool mixed with . . . mixed with what?"

"It's mixed with baby alpaca, believe it or not. See how soft it feels." Mimi handed Kelly a fat skein.

Kelly stroked the soft yarn. Wool mixed with baby alpaca. So soft. "Wow, that is soft. These are for the fall season, right?"

"Absolutely. It's July already, so we'll start putting out fall yarns at the end of August."

Kelly drew back with a pretend look of horror. "Don't even mention fall, Mimi. You know how much I love summer. I want it to go on forever."

Mimi smiled. "No, you don't. You'd get bored if it did. Fall is a great change of pace that prepares us for winter."

"You're right, of course. But I still don't want to lose summer." She heard the sound of chairs scraping against a wooden floor and returned to the doorway that opened into the workroom. All the women were standing now. "Looks like the class is finished. I'll see if I can grab a moment with that college student."

Kelly walked over to the yarn bins on the side wall of the workroom. Baby- and toddler-size sweaters and dresses hung along the shelves. Mimi put all of the yarns for baby and infant garments in these bins. Most of them were smaller twist, soft cotton yarns. Washable and easy care, plus nothing that could bother a baby's delicate skin. Wool was beautiful but could be scratchy and itchy.

Kelly touched and stroked several small skeins of baby blue and white yarns, then found some pink and white as well. All the time, Kelly kept watching the class members talk to each other and move toward the doorway leading to the main room. The college student was talking with the younger woman in class as they both headed toward the main room.

Walking behind them, Kelly waited until they finished talking and the college student walked into the adjoining central yarn room next to the foyer. Not knowing the girl's name, Kelly walked close enough to tap the girl on the shoulder. "Excuse me. Were you in that class?" she asked.

The college student turned quickly, a felted knitting bag over her shoulder. "Yeah. It's a good class. I've learned a lot. Did you want to join?"

Kelly grinned. "I'd better not. My knitting skills are mediocre at best, so you guys would leave me in the yarn dust. Or, lint. Whatever."

The girl smiled. "I've seen you around here a lot. You're that accountant, aren't you?"

Kelly held up her hand. "Guilty as charged. I'm Kelly, and I'm a lot better with numbers than with yarn. Hey, I wanted to ask you a question. I was listening to what the class was saying and I heard you mention that a professor at the university had been accused of sexual assault on a student a few years ago. You said you had a friend who was familiar with the incident."

The girl nodded. "Yeah. I've had some classes with her, so we've studied together a few times. We're both premed majors. My name's Elizabeth."

"Well, congratulations, Elizabeth. That's a hard major from what I've heard. I wondered if you would mind giving me your friend's e-mail. I'd like to contact her and ask about that incident. I'm trying to learn what's involved in this kind of situation. What do the police expect, and what does the person who's accused do once they've been questioned by police? Stuff like that. Mimi and I are trying to educate ourselves so we can help poor Barb through all this." Kelly held up the notepad and pen.

"Sure," Elizabeth said as she took the pad and pen. "I felt so sorry for Barb. She looks traumatized, I swear. And I've never seen her be that quiet. Normally, she's nonstop talking as she teaches."

"I know what you mean. Barb looks like she was punched in the stomach. Everyone here at the shop feels so sorry for her. We'd like to help Barb any way we can."

"Sure. My friend's name is Cathy. Cathy Craig." She tore off a page from the notepad and handed it to Kelly. "You can tell her you talked to me first. And I said it was okay for you to e-mail."

"Oh, that's great. I can't tell you how much I appreciate this." Kelly folded the little sheet of paper and shoved it in the back pocket of her cropped jeans.

"I have to get to class. Let me know what my friend says," Elizabeth called as she headed for the foyer.

Kelly dug into her front jeans pocket and pulled out her cell phone. She flipped through the directory as she walked through the foyer and outside onto the front entrance porch. The July heat had increased significantly since this morning, so Kelly chose the closest shaded outside table to find a chair.

Lisa picked up on the second ring. "Hey, what's up? Don't forget we have softball practice tonight."

"Got it on the schedule. Steve's working late in Denver finishing up that commercial project. Listen, I've got a favor to ask of you."

"Shoot. What do you need?"

"Barb's knitting class was today and she told the students about Tommy's situation."

"You're kidding. What did they say?"

"Well, they were all shocked, and some were mad that it happened to Tommy, stuff like that. But a college student in the class mentioned that one of the university professors was accused of sexual assault by a student three years ago. Apparently the professor denied it. Elizabeth is the girl in Barb's class, and she said a friend of hers had classes with that professor and knew the professor's family."

"I think I remember that incident. I was buried in exams at the time all the gossip was buzzing around campus."

"I wanted to see if you could ask around your friends at the university and see what you learn. I don't know if the professor was officially charged with assault or not. But I'd like to educate myself about what happens when someone's been accused of assault. The better to help Barb get through all this. You should see her, Lisa. She looks like she was hit by a truck but is somehow still standing. Kind of a glazed expression comes over her eyes, and she just stares."

"Oh, poor thing. I'll see if I can get in there in a couple of days. I'm doing some teaching of one of the elementary psych classes. But I'll make some inquiries. Put it out with my friends and see what they turn up."

"Thanks, Lisa. I figured you'd like to help me 'sleuth around.' "

"Yeah, right. It'll probably take a few days to hear back from them. I'd like to refresh my memories of that incident as well."

"By the way, the girl in Barb's class gave me her friend's name and e-mail. Her name's Cathy Craig, and both she and Elizabeth are premed students. I thought I'd send her an e-mail and see what she says. Elizabeth told me to tell Cathy that she gave me her name and e-mail. Giving permission, kind of."

"Okay, I've made a note of it. Now I'd better get back to my study notes. And I know you have accounting to do."

Kelly laughed. "Now, you're getting psychic in addition to being a psych major."

FOUR

Thursday morning

Kelly closed the cottage front door and walked toward the driveway that separated her cottage from the red-tile roofed, beige stucco Spanish Colonial–style house that held Lambspun knitting shop and Pete's Porch Café. It had been Kelly's aunt and uncle's home for decades. Kelly had fond childhood memories of time spent with her father and Aunt Helen and Uncle Jim on their sheep farm.

Once Uncle Jim died from a heart attack, Aunt Helen sold the farmhouse and moved into her quilting cottage across the driveway. The much smaller cottage bordered the golf course and was a look-alike version of the shop, complete with red tile roof and beige stucco.

Kelly had inherited the cottage from her aunt Helen years ago. Aunt Helen's death and funeral had been the reason that Kelly had returned to her childhood home, Fort Connor, Colorado, six years ago. Her aunt had been murdered. Police found her strangled body lying in the open doorway to the cottage. Kelly stayed on in Fort Connor, determined to find the actual killer of her aunt. And in the process, Kelly was attracted to the warmth and friendliness she felt coming from the people who were regular knitting patrons of Lambspun. After working remotely from her corporate accounting job in Washington, DC, Kelly finally made the decision to stay in Fort Connor permanently and become part of the great group of friends she'd found at Lambspun.

Walking along the sidewalk bordering the inviting greenery which surrounded the backyard garden area of Pete's Porch Café, Kelly admired the brilliant-colored annuals and the softer hued perennials that were scattered here and there among the lush green plants. Bright red salvia and orange marigolds waved in the slight breeze like little flags in their sunny spots. Hardy plants, they were able to withstand, and even thrive in, hot July summer sunshine. Soft lavender and blue pansies moved gently beside the yellow and purple violas. These plants loved the sun, but in less intense doses. Part sun and part shade suited these flowers much better.

Kelly continued through the garden, heading for the café front door, admiring the flowers hiding in the greenery while others boldly proclaimed their presence. Skirting the decorative fish pond, she sped toward the flight of wooden steps leading to the front entry. Kelly walked into the café, glanced about the tables filled with customers, then spotted Jennifer at the grill counter, loading breakfast dishes onto her tray.

"Looks like a busy morning," Kelly said as she set her mug on the counter. "I'll sit at the counter over here. No hurry with the refill."

"No problem, Kelly." Jennifer glanced over her shoulder toward the front windows. "Why don't you grab that smaller table beside the pond outside? I'll bring your coffee out there. I wanted to tell you something."

"Sure thing," Kelly readily agreed. Intrigued, she headed toward the café front door and down the wooden steps, back into the inviting greenery. Spotting the small table for two beside the fish pond, Kelly settled in. The table was too small for her to set up her laptop and work space, so Kelly focused her attention on the fish pond itself. A large orange goldfish swam lazily across the ornamental pond, which was surrounded by colorful rocks. Another fish, gray with orange tail and fins, swam across the pond in the other direction. Then two smaller black fish appeared, swimming quickly, swishing through the water. Kelly had never paid much attention to the pond with the water cascading peacefully down the side of the rocks. Every now and then she'd notice the fish, then almost forget the pond and its inhabitants were there.

Staring at the fish swimming around their kingdom, Kelly suddenly wondered if they were ever threatened with natural predators like raccoons. Night creatures like raccoons were very clever and adept with their agile little hands. Did the fish hide behind the rocks at night, she wondered?

"No, we don't serve fried goldfish," Jennifer's voice teased.

Kelly looked up to see her friend walking over to the table, Kelly's mug in hand. "Thanks, Jen. I appreciate it," she said, accepting the mug. "So, what's on your mind?"

"I wanted to share with you the conversation Pete and I had last night with Cassie," Jennifer said, sitting in the chair on the other side of the table. "We brought home some fried chicken from the café for dinner, and while we were eating, Cassie looks at us and asks if Barb's son was going to be arrested. She'd been hearing several women in the shop talking about Tommy. And of course they mentioned his being accused of sexual assault."

Kelly stared at Jennifer, surprised. "Really? What did you say?"

"Well, I didn't say anything at first. I figured Pete should be the one to answer." Jennifer gave a crooked smile. "I could tell he was surprised at first, so he asked Cassie if she knew what sexual assault was. She said she'd read about it before in the newspapers. It seems Grandpa Ben had always given the newspapers to Cassie to read and answered her questions."

"Good for Grandpa Ben."

"Then Pete looked over at me, and I could tell he wanted me to jump in and give a woman's view. So, believe it or not, I carefully explained what that term referred to . . . in more specific terms." Jennifer met Kelly's gaze.

Kelly smiled at her dear friend. "I have no trouble believing that. Cassie and Pete are lucky to have you with them. Did Cassie ask any questions?"

Jennifer's eyes went wide. "Did she ever. Apparently Grandpa Ben's explanations had been short on specifics, which we can totally understand. So, Cassie asked some *very* specific questions. Pete and I did our best to answer completely, in detail, and . . . how shall I say it . . . matter-of-factly."

Kelly laughed softly, watching Jennifer wag her head. "That brings back memories of my dad explaining to me about men and women and babies. I sat and listened politely, even though my friends and I had learned all the explicit details from a girl at summer camp. Her mother was a nurse and explained everything early on. This girl set out to educate everybody." Kelly grinned. "I didn't let on to my dad, but I did ask some specific questions, just to see how he'd respond. He blushed a little but, bless his heart, he gave me a good answer. Not as many details as the summer camp girl, but good enough."

Jennifer smiled. "That brings back memories. Sister Catherine, back in my old parochial elementary school days. She was a jewel. Believed in full disclosure. No details left untold. Boy, was she thorough." Jennifer chuckled.

"It looks like you and Pete did a great job. You two are great parents. Cassie is really lucky to have you both." Kelly smiled into her friend's eyes.

Jennifer smiled back. "Thanks for saying that, Kelly. It's nice to hear." Glancing over her shoulder, Jennifer pushed back her chair. "Well, I better get back to the customers. I just wanted to share that with you. Feel free to share with the others."

"I'll be happy to. Talk to you later," Kelly said, then reached for her briefcase bag and rose from the chair. She had places to go and people to see.

Kelly stepped into the Lambspun foyer and stood for a moment, drinking in the wonderful cool air that washed over her. *Ahhhhh.* Blessed air-conditioning. Having spent the entire morning on errands and a short appointment with client Arthur Housemann, she was out in the mid-July heat constantly. Kelly could tell it was going to be a one-hundred-degree day. Temperatures were already in the upper nineties, and it was only twelve noon daylight saving time. There was definitely more heat to come.

Deliberately taking her time, Kelly fingered some of the knitted garments Mimi had displayed. A cherry red open-weave triangular shawl dangling from the ceiling enticed her fingers first. "Wool and mohair," the tag said. A tiny baby sweater hung above a stack of the soft cotton yarn skeins in the same bright pink. Bubblegum pink. And a brilliant blue scarf was draped across the antique dry sink. Kelly stroked the scarf. It wasn't knitted like the other garments. This one looked like the scarves Mimi created in her Wet Felting class. The royal blue silk scarf had layers of varying shades of blue overlaid onto the silk. *Gorgeous,* she thought to herself and wondered how hard it would be to learn that technique.

After another minute of indulging in the sensual paradise surrounding her, Kelly walked toward the main knitting room. She saw Lisa and Barb sitting together at the far end of the long library table. They looked deep in conversation to Kelly, so she deliberately didn't interrupt. Instead she settled at the other end of the table and pulled out her laptop, ready to work. Having been out and about all morning, Kelly knew she had lots of spreadsheets demanding her attention.

At the sound of chairs being pushed back, Kelly looked up from her laptop screen. Barb, her face pale rather than flushed like before, gathered her huge tapestry bag and walked through the door leading to the workroom. Kelly could almost see the dark cloud hanging over Big Barb, weighing her down. Normally energetic Barb even walked slower now, like she was tired.

Lisa turned and looked at Kelly. "Hey, there. Do you want to take a coffee break outside? We're going to need privacy so I can tell you what my friends learned."

Even though she'd spent all morning moving about in the hot sun, Kelly readily agreed. "Sure thing. Let's make it iced coffee." She powered down her laptop and grabbed her coffee mug. Time for a refill anyway.

"Good idea," Lisa said, grabbing her bag and following Kelly into the central yarn room.

"Is that what you were talking about with Barb?" Kelly asked as they walked down the hallway which led into the café.

"No, Barb doesn't need to know everything I learned from friends. I simply asked her how she was doing, then listened when she talked. I tried to reassure her the best I could. I said that her friends here at Lambspun would help her through this difficult time. And I told her that the best thing Tommy could do was to continue to be the wonderful young doctor that he is. Tommy's reputation will help to counterbalance these accusations."

Kelly and Lisa entered the back of the café and signaled Julie, who was placing lunch orders on a tray at the counter.

Balancing the tray on her shoulder, Julie walked over to them.

"What do you need, guys? More coffee? Let me guess."

"Right as usual, Julie, but please make mine iced this time. It's hot outside."

"Me, too. We'll leave our mugs on the counter. Go back to your customers, Julie. The sight of that heavy tray makes my shoulders hurt. I hope you do exercises lifting weights."

Julie grinned. "I sure do. Gotta stay strong in this job." She walked into the main café.

Kelly and Lisa settled at the smaller two-person table in the corner. Customers filled practically every table. Waitresses Jennifer and Julie moved about them in a choreographed dance, never bumping into each other.

"Like I said, it would probably take a few days for them to get back to me," Lisa said.

"Barb still looks awful," Kelly said, watching part-time waitress Bridget filling both their mugs from a glass pitcher.

"I know," Lisa said with a sigh. "She's so afraid that this incident will ruin Tommy's medical career. That eats at her inside. All I could do was to sympathize with her."

"Hey, guys. Here're the iced coffees. If you want to head outside now, you can snag that smaller shady table in the corner of the garden patio."

"Thanks, Bridget. We'll go pounce on it now." Kelly took a cold sip of the black iced coffee — sustenance — and headed toward the café front door. Lisa followed behind her. Skipping down the sunny front steps, Kelly hurried toward the still-vacant table in the shady back corner of the garden patio.

The adobe stucco walls that edged the entire front of the patio yard and garden behind the knitting shop created a fair amount of shade on their own. But the huge old cottonwood tree and its leafy branches protected practically the entire garden patio from the heat of the afternoon sun. Summer sun was the most intense, but spring and fall afternoons were delightfully warm. The café tables were situated in the shady, greenest section, leaving the side edging the driveway as the sunniest part.

Kelly sat in one of the table's wrought iron chairs, while Lisa settled in opposite her. "So, what did your friends tell you that required privacy? I'm curious now."

"Well, it's a sad story. Sad, because if the accusations were true, a young woman was

71

assaulted by a professor while she was in his office asking questions. It's also sad, because if the accusations were false, then a wonderful professor's reputation was ruined and his career harmed."

Kelly leaned over the table. "Whoa, ruined his career? Now I feel like we've been lying to Barb."

"Universities are a different career environment. I imagine that a young doctor starting out could survive accusations if he was never actually charged. If he kept doing excellent work as a doctor, hopefully other patients would recommend him to friends. His practice would continue to grow." Lisa took a long drink from her iced coffee. "However, academia is different. Young professors join a faculty after they receive their PhD degrees. Then they have to teach classes and do their research and counsel students. And they have to publish lots of scientific journal research articles. You know, publish or perish. If they're good, then the senior faculty in their discipline will vote to grant them tenure status, and they move from an assistant professor position to an associate professor position. If they continue doing good research and teaching classes and counseling students and doing it well, then the senior faculty will vote that they be raised to full professor. Then, they become part of the senior faculty."

A different world, indeed, Kelly thought. "Wow, that senior faculty sounds like the Court of Inquisition in the Middle Ages," she joked. "Black-robed men who vote in secret."

Lisa smiled. "Well, it's not that dreadful. But their decisions definitely affect professors' lives and their families. And from what my friends learned, it sounds like that's what happened in this professor's life."

"What area was he in? What did he teach?"

"He taught anatomy and physiology in the School of Natural Sciences. Several of my friends either had him as a professor or had friends who did. I heard nothing but rave reviews about this guy as a professor. He was smart and diligent and clearly cared about students' learning the subject. He always scheduled exam prep study sessions for students and taught them himself, not handing it off to teaching assistants."

"Had your friends heard about the incident three years ago?"

"Ohhhhhhh, yeah." Lisa nodded. "It was three years ago. Professor's name is Paul Smith. Apparently a female student in one of Professor Smith's anatomy classes accused him of groping her when she went to his office to ask questions about the exam. The student reported the assault to a campus police officer. The campus police handed it over to Fort Connor police, of course, and the police department followed up on the complaint. They questioned the student and the professor. Apparently the professor was shocked by the student's accusations and denied them. But the student insisted he had 'groped' her and tried to do more in his office. She ran away and found the campus cop. That was her story. The professor denied everything. He said she'd come to his office to ask about an exam grade." Lisa sighed. "Anyway, an official complaint report was filed with the police. Apparently the student didn't want to press charges and go to trial, but the complaint was still there. And my friends said Professor Smith's career started going downhill after that."

"What happened? Was it gossip?"

"Oh, yeah. Universities are societies unto themselves. Beehives. Gossip spreads like wildfire across campus, especially if it involves a professor. And especially if someone does something against the law. Professor Smith never made full professor after that, and apparently he was on the fast track to making it before the incident. One of my friends said that other professors in his department stopped including him in professional studies. That alone can really harm a professor's career. They also said he started having personal problems. One friend said he started drinking. Even his wife left him." Lisa exhaled a long breath and sipped her iced coffee.

Kelly was stunned by the litany of bad things that happened to Professor Smith. "Good Lord! It sounds like that man's whole life imploded after being accused."

"That's a good way to describe it. I tell you, it depressed me just listening to it. I've never had Professor Smith for a class, but I'd heard many good things about him. Of course I'd seen him around the campus and the School of Natural Sciences. But I have to admit I'm conflicted now. If the student is telling the truth, then the professor has been exposed. But if those accusations were false, then a good man's career and life have been destroyed. And we'll never know the truth, because like Tommy, this is a situation of 'he said, she said.' "

"It makes me glad I'm not involved in academia. It sounds like a medieval caste system. And your teaching assistants and research assistants are the serfs. Tilling the soil, hoping the nobleman doesn't swoop down and lop off your head."

Lisa laughed out loud this time. "Whoa, it's definitely not that bad. No one's going to lop off our heads."

"But careers are fair game."

"Yeah . . . that's true."

Kelly looked around the patio garden and saw every table filled with lunch customers enjoying Pete's good cooking. "We should probably go back inside and free up this table. The lunch crowd is heavy," she said as she rose from the chair.

"Yeah, you're right."

As they left the shady corner, Kelly noticed Mimi hurrying down the café's front steps and heading in their direction. "Hey, Mimi. Getting tired of air-conditioning?" Kelly teased.

"Goodness, no. I saw you girls out here talking. I'll bet you were talking about Tommy."

"Actually, Lisa was telling me about a similar incident a few years ago when a female student accused a professor of groping her in his office. A sad, sad story, no matter how you look at it."

"A professor?" Mimi's eyes got wide.

"Yeah. The incident is similar to Tommy's but the worlds are so different," Lisa said.

"In academia and university life, careers can be tarnished a lot easier than in the real world."

Mimi rolled her eyes. "Lord, yes. I was never comfortable in that world."

Lisa glanced at her watch. "How about I tell you what I learned while I'm getting an iced coffee, Mimi? I have a physical therapy client in an hour."

"And I need to return to my client accounts," Kelly added, checking her watch.

"Well, then, let's all get out of this heat," Mimi suggested as the little trio hastened up the front steps and into the blessings of air-conditioning.

FIVE

Friday morning

Kelly polished off the last bit of egg yolk with the last bite of pancake. Yummmm. Nothing could beat one of Eduardo's breakfasts. Every now and then she had to succumb. Succumb to the Call of the Grill, Kelly thought with a smile as she sipped Eduardo's strong brew. Glancing around her small table beside a window in Pete's Café, Kelly noticed Cassie bussing tables close by.

"Hi, Cassie. How'd you guys play against Wellington last night?"

Cassie looked over at Kelly and broke into a big smile. "Oh, we beat 'em. Beat 'em bad," she bragged. "I hit a triple!"

Kelly laughed softly at the sound of young teenage exuberance. "That's great. Steve and I were both working in Denver so we couldn't see the game."

"We're playing Longmont tomorrow,

Saturday morning at Rolland Moore Park." Cassie gave the table a thorough wipe. "Where are you guys playing?"

"Steve's playing a morning game at Rolland Moore, and my team will play in the afternoon game at City Park ball field. So I'll definitely be able to catch your game. I'll just hop between fields at Rolland Moore."

Cassie emptied another table of dirty dishes onto her tray. "I love City Park. It is *so* pretty. I hope we play more games there. All those tall trees. Pete says they're oak trees, and they're really going to be pretty in the fall." She wiped the table, then hefted the trayful of dishes.

"Can you carry all that?" Kelly asked, pointing to the tray. "It looks pretty heavy."

"Oh, sure," Cassie said. "Funny, but it doesn't feel that heavy anymore. I remember last summer I couldn't carry a tray like this, the way Jennifer and Julie do." She shrugged. "I guess I'm stronger now."

"That's because you've had two summers and a fall worth of batting practice," Kelly said with a grin. "You worked hard with the ball machine. You're batting really well now because you've gotten stronger. Funny how that works together. No wonder you hit a triple."

"Do you think I can ever hit a homer like you do?"

"Sure, you will. In time. You've got a lot more growing to do. Look how much you've grown in the little over a year since you've been here. Must be three inches."

"Three and a half," Cassie corrected, a wide smile lighting her deep blue eyes.

"Three and a half. And I predict you'll probably grow another inch before this year is over."

Cassie's eyes popped wide. "You think so! *Awesome!* I hope you're right."

"Your legs have gotten a lot longer, too. That's why you can run so fast. You run almost as fast as I do, I think."

"No way!" Cassie scoffed.

"Oh, yeah. You're like a jackrabbit racing around those bases."

Cassie gave a giggling laugh that made Kelly laugh just hearing it. "Jackrabbit. I love it. I gotta tell Eric."

"Well, you can tell him that he looks like a really tall, skinny jackrabbit. And he runs even faster."

"He'll love that," Cassie said, shifting the tray. "Talk to you later, Kelly."

"If it's Friday, then you're going with Lisa to the sports clinic. Bring back some of Lisa's PT secrets, okay?"

"Lisa's secret is she's got magic hands," Cassie said as she headed toward the kitchen area.

Magic hands, huh? Kelly recalled how skilled Lisa had been when she helped Kelly recuperate from a broken ankle years ago. Cassie was one smart kid, she thought as she pulled her laptop from the briefcase bag.

The sound of her cell phone's music playing cut through Kelly's financial spreadsheet concentration. The phone screen flashed the word "Unknown" as Kelly clicked on.

"This is Kelly Flynn," she said in her business voice as she leaned back in the wrought iron chair outside in the café's garden patio.

"Kelly, this is Cathy Craig. Your e-mail said to give you a call. What is it exactly that you're researching?"

"Researching" was such a formal word, Kelly immediately switched into friendly, conversational mode. "Cathy, thanks so much for calling. I wouldn't really call it 'research.' I'm simply trying to find out as much as I can about what happens when someone is accused of sexual assault. Police procedures and all that. The son of a friend of ours here at Lambspun knitting shop was recently accused of sexual assault." Kelly deliberately didn't say more. She wanted to see how Cathy Craig responded.

"Well, I only know the basics of police procedures in that situation. But I can definitely attest to the personal devastation complaints like that can do to the person accused. Basically, the police have to question the person who's claiming assault. And they question the person accused of committing assault. Then police file an official report. If the accuser chooses to press charges, then there's a trial. But even when there are no formal charges pressed, that official police report is still on file. And it's available to employers."

Kelly noticed Cathy Craig's voice had hardened. "Elizabeth said that you were friends with a professor who was accused and his family."

"Yes, and I got to witness firsthand how a good man and his career are destroyed. Professor Smith is a family friend, and a good, honorable man. There's no way he could have done what that girl claimed. He told the police he was innocent, but the police can only take the information. Gossip started immediately. Paul denied that he'd done anything to that girl. She'd come into his office begging him to change her low grade on an exam. She wanted him to give her some extra credit assignment to do so she could raise her grade. Paul said he patiently explained to her that he couldn't do that. It wouldn't be fair to the rest of the students in his class."

"That's kind of arrogant. Asking a professor to treat you differently than the other students," Kelly couldn't help interjecting.

"Isn't it, though?" Cathy Craig's voice got harsher. "He told my dad and me that the girl got this funny look on her face after he'd refused her request. Kind of shocked. Like she was surprised he'd said no. Then she started begging him to reconsider. She wanted to get into a medical career and a low grade in anatomy could ruin her chances. Of course, Paul had to refuse her again. Then he said he ushered her out of his office. Office hours were over, and he had a meeting to attend. Paul said she was staring daggers at him as he locked up his office and left."

"Wow, she sounds like she'd never heard 'no' before. What happened then?"

"Apparently that afternoon the girl told a campus policeman that Paul had assaulted her in his office. That's when the nightmare began. Gossip spread immediately once the police were involved. Two officers actually came to Paul's office on campus to question him. Right in front of all of his faculty colleagues. Paul said it was as if he'd suddenly contracted a terrible contagious disease. Colleagues stopped chatting with him. No one wanted to join him for lunch. But worse than being ostracized was that colleagues no longer wanted to professionally collaborate with him or invite him to join professional societies. That is death at a university. You might be alive, but your career starts to die. Slowly. Paul was an associate professor and being considered for advancement to full professor. But when the senior faculty met, Paul no longer had their support. Not enough votes, so he didn't make it. A few months before, Paul had the full support of the senior faculty. It was *so* unfair."

"When my friend here at the shop explained the university system to me, I have to admit it sounds vaguely draconian."

"University politics is definitely another world. My father was a professor at the university for years." Cathy Craig's voice changed, sadder now. "After the incident, Paul's personality changed. He started drinking heavily at that bar near Old Town, Mason's. He even got into a fight at that bar one night. He told us some guy was giving him a hard time, and Paul hit him. They scuffled and the bartender and owner threw

Paul and the other guy out in the street." A long sigh came over the phone. "He even had an angry confrontation with that girl when their paths crossed on campus one day. In front of other people, too. Campus police said he'd been drinking and called Fort Connor cops. His wife Marcia left him after that. They didn't have any kids, thank goodness."

Kelly listened to the sad litany. "Good Lord, his whole world fell apart."

"Yes, it did, and it's been tragic to watch. Paul still hasn't gotten back to his old self. At least he quit drinking last year. Listen, I've got to get to another class. I wish I had better news for your friend's son, but bad things do happen to good people. Even if they are innocent."

"I'm afraid you're right, Cathy. I appreciate your taking the time to talk with me. I know how tight a student's schedule can be. Thank you."

"You're welcome, Kelly." Her phone clicked off.

Kelly stared out the window into the July afternoon. This was such a depressing story, Kelly felt sad just listening to it. How much of this depressing story she would share with Barb, she wasn't sure yet. But she would share it with Mimi and Burt. That way they'd be forewarned to help Tommy.

Later that day, Kelly walked down the corridor leading from the café into the knitting shop. Spreadsheets were finished early, so it was time for some relaxation. She could pull out the scarf she was knitting from ribbon-like yarns. Or, she could find a new distraction.

Kelly wanted to give a scarf to each of her five softball clinic girls. They could also use them as belts with jeans. She'd already finished two ribbon scarves. Kelly considered starting the next one, then the distracting idea beckoned to her again. The idea of trying out those new wet felting techniques had bounced around her head for a couple of days. Maybe this would be a good time to find out more about it.

Voices were coming from the workroom straight ahead, so Kelly continued into the room. There she saw Mimi and Rosa covering the worktable with white paper, taping it beneath so it wouldn't move.

"Hey, what are you two up to?" she asked.

"We're fixing the table for Mimi's Wet Felting class," Rosa said, glancing over at Kelly.

"Oh, perfect! I was thinking I might join one of those classes, Mimi. I keep thinking how pretty that blue scarf was that one of your students created."

Mimi burst into a grin. "Wonderful! I think you'll love it, Kelly. And it's really easy."

"I know you always say that," Kelly said as she dumped her briefcase bag on a counter holding several weaving looms. Mimi taught many weaving classes in the workroom. "But this technique doesn't involve knitting, so I'm hoping it will actually turn out to be easy."

Mimi gave her lilting laugh and a dismissive wave. "Trust me, it is easy. Here, let me show you the silk scarves I bought for the class to choose from. I'll give you first pick."

She beckoned Kelly toward a smaller table where several bags of recently dyed wool fleece sat. Kelly couldn't help but notice the variety of colors. A rainbow of colors.

"Is this the wool we'll be using to felt onto the scarves?" Kelly asked, fingering the royal blue wool in the bag closest to her.

"Yes. Each student will choose the colors they'd like to use on their scarves. Some people choose variations in the same color as their scarf. Others like to use contrasting colors. It's up to you." Mimi reached into a container where several silk scarves lay and

87

removed a cherry red scarf. "Here, you look great in red, Kelly. Why don't you use this one."

Kelly eagerly took the silken rectangle. She loved silk, the sensuous feel of it. Smooth, smooth. Her fingers stroked the deep red. Luscious. "It's beautiful, Mimi."

"I thought you'd like it. Now, why don't you hold up some of the wool fibers against the scarf and see which ones strike your fancy. People are different. There're no right or wrong colors." She pointed toward the bags filled with colorful wools.

"I fingered the blue one and it feels like the wool fleece Burt uses to spin, but before he spins it."

"You're right. And you folks in the class will also have to draft the wool into batten or roving, exactly like Burt and I do before we start to spin. That way the fibers are stretched and ready for the process." Mimi glanced at her watch. "Well, the class will start in half an hour, so I'm going up front to take care of customers. Stay here and play with the wools as long as you want, Kelly."

"Thanks, Mimi. It'll be fun." Mimi hurried off in her usual rushing fashion, but Kelly stayed beside the table, holding up the red scarf to the deep rose–colored wool.

Hmmmmm. That does look pretty, she decided. She skipped the royal blue fibers and the light green fibers and paused at the bag filled with light orange–colored fibers. She held up the red scarf, placing some of the orange fibers against it. There was a pleasing look to the combination. She pulled a handful of orange fibers free and held them next to the deep rose fibers. Nice, she thought, studying the strangely complementary colors.

Okay, time to see how they do next to the scarf, Kelly decided, and spread out the cherry red scarf on the smaller table, then took a handful of deep rose fibers and the orange fibers and placed them next to each other on the scarf. She was surprised by the effect. It was pretty. Very pretty to her eye. Of course, Kelly had always loved the color red. So, maybe that was why. Whatever the reason, Kelly made her decision. The deep rose and orange fibers for her.

Burt's voice cut into Kelly's fiber perusal. "Hey, Kelly. Mimi said I'd find you in here," he said as he walked over to her.

"Hi, Burt. I've decided to take Mimi's Wet Felting class, and she told me to pick the colors I want to use. See, I'm starting with this pretty red scarf." She held it up.

"Nice, Kelly," Burt said, fingering the

scarf. "Don't forget, you have to draft the wool into batten or roving before you start felting it onto the scarf."

"Mimi told me. So I can pretend I'm you, Burt, drafting away in the corner." She grinned at him. "Have you been out in that heat doing errands?"

"This morning, yes. But yesterday afternoon I took Barb to see her family lawyer. I tell you, she didn't look good afterward. Barb didn't say a word, just stared out the window. I figure the lawyer repeated everything that we've all heard ourselves. The complaint has to be investigated by the police, and they file an official report. I told her that Tommy needs to go see the lawyer, too."

"Did Mimi tell you what Lisa found out from her university contacts?"

"Oh, yes. And that professor's name rang a bell in the back of my brain. I remember two officers in the department investigated the complaint against that professor and made a report. Three years ago, as I recall."

"Yes, it was a real eye-opener about the harshness of university life. It seems your reputation can be ruined by rumors and gossip."

"Well, it takes more than rumors, Kelly. It takes an actual incident to start the gossip.

Changing the subject, Mimi and I thought we'd drop by the ball field tomorrow and see Cassie's team play. And whoever else is playing."

Kelly gave him a wide smile. "That's great, Burt. But you and Mimi will have to get off the 'repentance diet' and have a bag of popcorn like the rest of us."

Burt chuckled. "Sounds good to me, Kelly."

The sound of feet walking very fast echoed from the corridor. Mimi rushed into the workroom, eyes wide with obvious concern. "One of the customers up front said that she'd just heard on a radio news station that a young woman was found murdered in Fort Connor last night!"

Kelly stared at her. "What!"

"Where was it?" Burt demanded, former police detective persona appearing in an instant.

"In one of those large student apartment buildings near campus. Oh, Lord, she was probably a young college student!"

Burt hurried over to her and placed his hand on Mimi's shoulder. "I'll call Dan and see what he can tell me. Try not to worry."

"I can't help it!" Mimi said, her voice rising. "I have so many of those girls in my classes. This is *horrible*!"

Kelly dropped the scarf and wools onto the table and went to Mimi, placing her arm around Mimi's shoulders. "Don't jump to conclusions, Mimi. There are thousands of students in those huge apartment complexes."

"I know, I know. It's hard not to worry. I've known some of those girls since they were in grade school."

"I'll call Dan and see what he knows so far. If it happened last night, they may still be trying to notify next of kin." Burt hurried from the room.

"Here, Mimi. I've already chosen my wool colors," Kelly said, guiding her over to the paper-wrapped worktable. "Why don't I help you get set up for class. It should be starting soon."

Mimi blinked. "Oh, yes." She glanced at her watch. "Class starts in ten minutes."

"What do the students need? I can gather it for you and you can set it up."

"Yes, yes . . . go ask Rosa where she put the new bottles of liquid dish soap. And the sponges. We have to have them out in the middle of the table. Then everyone finds a spot around the table."

Routine duties were calming, Kelly had found. When her father was in the hospital dying of lung cancer, Kelly kept her account spreadsheets open on her laptop, ready to dive into whenever the nurses and doctors had to do tests and treatments on her father. Kelly had always hated that feeling of helplessness. There was nothing she could do to keep her father from dying. All she could do was to be there by his bedside, holding his hand and talking to him — while he could still talk.

Just then a young brunette woman stepped into the room. She looked around at the bags of wool fleece, then at Mimi and Kelly. "Is this the class on wet felting?" she asked.

Mimi gave her a big smile and walked toward her, welcoming. "Yes, it is. And what's your name, dear?"

Kelly moved back toward the bags of wool fleece. Mimi would be fine. Routine duties helped.

Six

Saturday morning

"Wooooo hoooooo!" Kelly yelled from the bleacher seats at Rolland Moore ball fields. Cassie's team's opponents had just gotten the third out and were headed back into the field. Cassie's Fort Connor Blue team was up to bat.

"Way to go, Fort Connor Blue!" Megan shouted, then let out one of those ear-piercing whistles Marty had taught her.

Kelly shrank away, hand over her right ear, at the sound. "Man! That goes straight through my brain and rattles around." She shook her head.

Megan grinned. "Yeah, it's super bad, isn't it? I love it. Marty said the secret is where you put your fingers on your front teeth." She put her fingers to her teeth.

"*Ack!* No more!" Kelly held up both hands in stop position. "Too early in the morning for that many decibels."

Megan laughed then pointed toward the ball field where Cassie's softball team was playing. "Cassie's getting to the ball faster. It's good she's playing right field. We need speed to run down those long balls."

"Yeah, I was telling her yesterday that since she's grown so much, her legs are a lot longer, and she's running faster. I said she looked like a jackrabbit running around those bases. And she'll be running as fast as I do pretty soon."

Megan chuckled. "I'm not so sure about that. You're even taller than she is and your legs are super long and strong. You lap those bases pretty fast."

"She hit a triple at their Thursday night game. I told her that's because she's had two summers and a fall of softball batting practice. And a whole year of tennis classes. She's got arm muscles she didn't have before."

"That'll do it." Megan grinned and pulled up the sleeve of her team tee shirt and flexed her muscles, arm bent in "weight-lifter" style. "Ya gotta be strong. Put it up there, Kelly," she challenged.

Kelly rolled her eyes but succumbed to the challenge. How could she resist? She shoved up her tee shirt sleeve and flexed her arm muscles like Megan. "Beat ya," she taunted, noting that her muscles were bigger than Megan's.

"Just a hair," Megan replied, unfazed.

"What are you two doing? Getting ready to square off?" Lisa said as she stepped over the bleachers, hot dog and soda can in hand. "I'll put my money on Kelly. She's bigger than you, Megan."

"Ah, the bigger they are, the harder they fall," Megan said, grinning. "And I'm tougher."

Lisa and Kelly laughed. "She's right, you know," Kelly said. "Megan is just one big muscle. Not an ounce of fat on her." Kelly glanced at Lisa, who had taken a big bite of fully loaded hot dog. "Matter of fact, there's none on you, either, skinny one. Let's see what the hot dog does."

Steve appeared at the foot of the bleachers. Hot dog and two pizza slices on a plastic plate, plus fries and a soda. "Hey, make room. I want to eat lunch early before we have to shift fields." He easily stepped over two bleacher risers at a time as he climbed toward Kelly and friends. Long legs to the rescue.

"Did you guys see that article in the paper this morning?" Megan asked. "About the college student who was found dead in one of those huge apartment complexes near campus?"

Lisa's blue eyes widened. "Good Lord, yes! Police said it was a homicide but didn't say how she was killed. Terrible."

"I know," Kelly said as Steve settled on the higher bleacher row next to her. "Police are probably still contacting next of kin. They don't want to put out too much detail until the family has been notified."

"That's gonna scare a lot of coeds into making sure their ground-floor apartments are locked, windows, too," Steve said, then took a big bite of hot dog.

Kelly eyed the fully loaded hot dog and her stomach growled. An early lunch sounded like a really good idea.

"Well, let's hope this scares some coeds into being more careful," Megan said.

"Mimi was really upset and worried yesterday when the news came on the radio," Kelly added. "Burt and I had to calm her down. Thank goodness she had a class to teach."

"Mother Mimi," Lisa commented. "She worries about all her chicks."

"I'm gonna go get one of those hot dogs," Megan said, stepping over a bleacher row. "Steve's looks way too good to resist."

"Listen, would you get me one, too? Just like yours, fully loaded, and a soda," Kelly asked, pulling a ten-dollar bill from her back pocket. "We'll have a bleacher lunch. Not the first time, and it certainly won't be the last."

"That's for sure," Lisa said. "We're still on for Jennifer and Pete's tonight, right? Are we ordering out? Let's do Chinese. I can't look at another pizza." She took a big bite of hot dog.

"Chinese works for me," Kelly agreed, watching Cassie's team batting lineup move along. Cassie stood in the next batter's circle, practicing her swing while her teammate was at the plate, ready to bat.

"Yeah, me, too," Steve said, then glanced to the side of the bleachers. "Hey, Eric. How'd your game turn out?"

Eric smiled. "We beat 'em by five. I got a couple of doubles, too."

"Good job!" Kelly congratulated Curt Stackhouse's grandson. Same age as Cassie but taller and skinnier. Thirteen going on high school.

"C'mon up here and join us," Steve beckoned. "Cassie's gonna bat next. Meanwhile, you can catch us up on what you've been doing."

Kelly watched the even skinnier and faster jackrabbit Eric step effortlessly over the bleacher rows. Way longer legs. Clearly in a growth spurt like Cassie's. "Your parents keeping you busy over at their ranch?"

"Oh, yeah. And I've been helping Grandpa Curt every day, too. Learning the cattle business, he says." Eric settled on the bleacher bench beside Steve.

"Boy, you're gonna be a heckuva rancher some day," Steve said, grinning at Eric. "Alpaca and sheep business with your mom and dad, and the cattle business with your grandpa. I'd say that's a dynamite combination."

Eric flushed just a little with Steve's praise. "I like it. Tell the truth, I like working with the cattle even more than sheep and alpacas. But they're good, too."

Kelly thought she spotted Eric's quick glance toward Steve's pizza slices sitting on the plate. Steve must have noticed, too, she figured, because he spoke up.

"Listen, Eric. I can't finish that pizza. This hot dog is doing it for me. Why don't you take the pizza?"

Eric's eyes lit up. "Really? Wow, thanks! I'm getting pretty hungry but I wanted to see Cassie bat first."

Steve handed over the plastic plate with pizza. "Go for it. You're in a growth spurt, I can tell."

Eric fairly inhaled the pizza, half a slice

disappeared in ten seconds. The second half went like the first. Gone. Much to Steve's and Kelly's amusement.

"I was about to ask for a bite," Kelly teased.

Eric stopped then swallowed. "Um, sorry. You want some?" He offered the last bite.

Steve held up his hand. "Nope. You're a teenage boy in a growth spurt. You need it. Megan's bringing Kelly a hot dog. Besides, she's teasing you."

Eric screwed up his face. "How can you tell? I can never tell when girls are teasing. They're weird." He wagged his head in the manner of boys growing to be men. It was an age-old question.

"You'll learn. And, yes, girls are definitely weird. They're inscrutable." Steve took a deep drink of soda to chase the last hot dog bite.

Kelly smiled and kept her mouth shut during this "man-to-man" exchange. Man talk. Also as ancient as time.

Eric looked out toward the field. " 'Inscrutable.' That was one of our vocabulary words. It means 'hard to figure out.' "

Steve gave Eric a pat on the back. "That's for sure. See Kelly there?" He pointed. "She's smiling. But you can't tell if she's smiling because she's watching a starving teenager eat, or if she's secretly laughing at us and our inability to figure out girls. Inscrutable."

Kelly just held her inscrutable smile, and pointed to the field. "Cassie's up. Let's all hope for a triple."

Cassie gave another practice swing, then settled into her batter's crouch. Pitcher let fly. Ball one. Cassie held still.

Good girl, Kelly thought to herself. *Wait for it. Wait for the right one.*

Ball two and Cassie held. "Way to read the ball, Cassie!" Lisa yelled from her spot farther to Kelly's right.

The next ball was a faster, low-dropping pitch. Cassie swung — and missed. *"Steee-rike one!"* yelled the umpire behind home plate. Cassie gave another practice swing and went into her crouch. The next ball was right in the zone. Cassie swung and popped the ball foul. Ball three. Another fast low-dropping pitch, and Cassie swung and missed again. *"Steee-rike two!"* bellowed the umpire.

"Uh-oh," Eric said.

"Yeah, tighten up, Cassie," Lisa advised.

Everyone leaned forward, waiting for the next pitch. High and over Cassie's head. Ball four. She dropped the bat and loped over to first base, long legs covering ground.

"Whew!" Steve said. "That was a close one."

"Now I know what I have to work on with the girls in clinic next week. We've gotta practice hitting those balls."

"They're hard," Eric added, waving to Cassie on first base. She waved to everyone and got several waves in return. "I've struck out a lot on those low balls that drop at the end."

"I'd be glad to coach you, if you can find time in that busy ranch schedule of yours," Steve said.

Eric's face lit up. "You're serious? Whoa! That's great."

"Let me talk to your grandpa. I don't want to interfere with your parents' schedule, so let's see if your grandpa Curt can loosen up some time for you. They've dropped in to watch some of your games. And Cassie's, too."

Just then a tall older teenage boy strutted up to the bleachers and looked at Steve and Kelly with a big cheesy grin. "Hey, Coach Flynn! Coach T! Did you come to watch us play? We're gonna annihilate Longmont Blue tonight."

Kelly looked down and saw O'Leary, the mouthiest of the Three Wise Guys she and

Jennifer tried to whip into shape for a Christmas church pageant a few years ago. "I thought I smelled trouble, O'Leary!" Kelly taunted. "You guys are Fort Connor Red team, right?"

"You betcha, Coach." O'Leary grinned and took a practice swing. Muscles flexed and he swung the bat in perfect form — smooth and powerful. "Outta the park!" he bragged, grinning. "Thanks to you and Coach T, I'm hitting everything they throw at me."

"Yeah, but are you hitting it deep or fouling out?" Kelly deliberately taunted, wondering if she could prick that huge O'Leary ego.

O'Leary's cheesy grin melted across his face. "Like I said, Coach. Outta the park!" He swung again, powerful and smooth, then kissed his fingertips and pointed over the fence.

Kelly, Steve, Eric, and Lisa laughed out loud. Steve nodded to Eric. "Kelly worked with O'Leary first, then I worked with him. And now you see the results." Steve laughed at O'Leary's swagger.

"Perfection," O'Leary bragged and strutted a few feet away, swung at an imaginary pitch again. Three young teenage girls from another team watched him, then giggled, and grinned in his direction.

"O'Leary, you haven't changed a bit. You're bigger and stronger, but you're still a rooster strutting around, impressing the girls," Kelly teased. The three teenage girls giggled and walked away.

O'Leary grinned, unfazed by Kelly's scolding. "Love you, too, Coach Flynn," he teased. "See you later." And he sauntered away, leaving behind a cloud of teenage boy ego and confidence all wrapped together. A fascinating mix of things to come.

"He's pretty sure of himself," Eric said, watching O'Leary swagger away.

"O'Leary was born with ego," Kelly observed. "He's a great kid beneath it all, but that mouth of his is gonna get him into trouble some day."

Megan climbed back over the bleachers, hands filled with hot dogs and soda cans. "Here you go," she said, handing Kelly a hot dog dripping with condiments and a can of soda.

"Thanks so much, Megan," Kelly said, taking the fully loaded dog and soda. Her stomach growled loudly now. No more need to wait, Kelly took a big bite of the juicy ballpark staple. *Yummmm.* Nothing like a ballpark frank with everything. She closed her eyes and savored.

"How'd Cassie do at bat?" Megan asked before taking a bite.

"She got four balls. See, she's on first base." Lisa pointed.

Another small group of young teenage girls, who looked junior high age to Kelly, paused a few feet in front of the bleachers. They scanned the bleachers, then one of them pointed to the top row where Kelly and her friends sat. Then they clustered together and started talking and smiling, then laughing, glancing back at the bleachers once more before they moved on.

"See, there's another thing about girls I can't figure out," Eric said, watching the girls walk away. "They're always in little groups, and they whisper and look at you and start to laugh." He wagged his head. "You don't know if they're making fun of you or what. Gotta be that inscrutable thing you're talking about."

"Who's inscrutable?" Megan asked, licking some escaping ketchup. "Not us."

Lisa started to laugh. "Megan's never had an inscrutable day in her life. She always tells it like it is. So does Kelly. Now, me . . . I have to be more careful around all those university egos." She leaned back against the bleacher row behind.

"It was the same when I was your age,"

Steve said with a smile. "It took me a while to figure them out. They're not making fun of you. The reason they're pointing and whispering and laughing is because they like you. Girls don't mess with guys they don't like. They ignore them." He leaned back against the bleachers.

Eric looked skeptical. "Really? That doesn't make any sense."

Steve, Kelly, Megan, and Lisa all smiled. "Girls don't need to make sense. We're inscrutable, remember?" Lisa teased.

Eric rolled his eyes. "That is so weird."

"Like I said, girls are weird," Steve advised sagely, then drained his soda.

"He's right, you know," Kelly added. "Girls do not tease boys they don't like. Now, I never teased boys. If I didn't like 'em, I ignored them."

Eric got a little smile. "What'd you do if you liked them?"

Kelly grinned. "I let them know."

Steve spoke up. "Don't believe it. She couldn't stand me when we first met years ago."

"True that," Lisa said, laughing.

"You're kidding," Eric said, eyes alight.

"We all thought something was wrong with her," Megan joined in. "Here was this great guy who was also cute paying attention to her, and Kelly wouldn't give him the time of day."

Clearly incredulous, Eric demanded, "Why? Why didn't you like Steve?"

"Yeah, why?" Steve teased.

"Because he was so sure of himself. Like O'Leary."

"No way!" Eric retorted.

"Thank you." Steve grinned.

Kelly laughed softly. "Not as bad as O'Leary. But he reminded me too much of my old boyfriend in college, who dumped me after I'd tutored him through all his accounting classes."

Eric screwed up his face. "What a jerk."

"Yeah, I thought so. Anyway, it took me a while to see Steve's good qualities, shall we say." She gave Steve her best inscrutable smile.

Steve just laughed. "It took forever. She wouldn't go out with me. She let me take her up to Rocky Mountain National Park to watch the elk rut. That took months."

Eric laughed. "Wow."

"I had trust issues."

"That's for sure," Megan said authoritatively.

"I still remember what she said to me when we first met. I was trying my best to get a smile out of her. Something. She gave me that look and said, 'You must spend a lot of time hanging around the golf course. What are you, a caddy or something?' "

This time Kelly laughed along with Eric, Megan, and Lisa, and Steve, of course. Hard to believe she'd taken so long to warm up to Steve. Another memory pushed forward from those earlier days.

"You know, your grandpa Curt got to see Steve and me after we first met. He knew my aunt Helen in high school, and I was trying to find out information that might help me learn who really killed her. I figured it might be someone from her past."

Eric's eyes nearly bugged out of his face. "You thought Grandpa Curt killed your aunt!"

"No, no, not at all," Kelly said, waving her hand. "I already knew he was a friend of hers, and I just wanted to ask him some questions about who she knew in high school."

Steve spoke up. "Kelly wanted to go up to Curt's ranch alone and ask him questions. Well, I didn't know your grandpa then, and I didn't think it was a good idea. So, I invited myself along."

"Which just annoyed me no end," Kelly chided.

"Turns out she needed my help —"

"Did not."

"We had to follow Curt from the Wool Market in Estes Park all the way to his ranch. I figured my truck would be less conspicuous on the road than her red car."

"What happened then?" Eric asked.

"Yeah, you never told us exactly what happened up there, Kelly," Megan said, leaning forward. "You said Curt was a nice guy and was really helpful answering your questions about Helen."

Steve smiled. "Next time you see your grandpa Curt, ask him if he remembers Barbie and Stevie."

Kelly started to laugh. "I figured we needed a reason to show up at Curt's ranch, so we posed as Barbie and Stevie, who were engaged and wanted to get into the alpaca business. Of course, Curt didn't have alpacas, but it gave us an excuse to show up in his ranch yard."

"I decided to make it realistic while we were talking to him, so I put my arm around her shoulders while we talked to Curt. Your grandpa was looking at us real funny-like."

Eric grinned. "I bet. I know that look."

"Oh, yeah," Steve continued. "Kelly didn't like having my arm around her, so when Curt's cell phone rang, she leaned over and said, 'Move the arm or lose a rib.' "

Eric let out a hoot of laughter; so did Megan and Lisa.

"That is *so* you, Kelly," Lisa cackled.

"Did you move your arm?" Eric asked.

"Oh, yeah. After a minute. I was having too much fun teasing her. Then she gave me a jab in the ribs, and I backed off." He laughed.

"I gotta ask Grandpa about that," Eric said.

"You do that. See what he says and tell us," Steve said. "Listen, why don't we get you a hot dog like Kelly's and Megan's. Those two slices of pizza aren't going to get you through an afternoon game."

Eric's eyes lit up. Teenage boy hunger calling. "Sounds good. Dad gave me money."

Steve stood up and stretched. "Naw. My treat. C'mon. Want anything else, Kelly?"

"I'm good, thanks." Kelly watched as Steve and Eric climbed down the bleacher rows and walked off.

"Steve's a good guy," Lisa said, watching them.

"And Eric's a good kid," Megan added.

Kelly nodded, watching them walk away, Steve's arm around Eric's shoulders. "True that."

Steve pulled his truck into a parking space

at City Park ball fields. "I'll be over at the Rolland Moore south field. Our game starts earlier than yours, so text me when you guys are getting close to finishing up. I'll come over as soon as I can."

"Will do," Kelly said, hearing her cell phone's music go off. "See you later." She grabbed her backpack with her first baseman's glove, water, walnuts for a snack, and her dad's old USS *Kitty Hawk* Navy hat.

Burt's name flashed on her phone screen as she stepped down from the truck to the ground. "Hey, Burt, what are you and Mimi up to? We missed you over at the ballpark yesterday."

"We're sorry we couldn't get there, Kelly. But Mimi had a private lesson scheduled for late in the afternoon, so we just went out to dinner after that. We needed to relax."

Kelly walked toward the north ball field. Bleachers were already filled. She saw Megan and Lisa on the field already, so she picked up her pace. "Oh, good. You two deserve it. Where'd you go?"

"We treated ourselves to your favorite place. Yours and Steve's. The Jazz Bistro."

"I'm so glad. As I said, you and Mimi deserve it."

"Listen, Kelly, I don't want to keep you from your game, but I wanted to tell you what I learned tonight. Dan called as Mimi and I were driving home and told me the name of the college student who was killed in her apartment the other night. I'd mentioned to him that Mimi was worrying the girl might be one of her students. And, sad to say, it turned out that the young woman actually did come to the shop for knitting lessons."

Kelly stopped at the edge of the bleachers. "Oh, no! Was she one of Mimi's 'girls' as she calls them? That's her worst nightmare."

"Actually, she wasn't. Mimi and I went back to the shop and checked the class registration files. She was a student in Barb's intermediate advanced knitting class. Name was Laura Brewster."

"I don't recognize the name, either, Burt. I only sat in on Barb's class once, and I never asked anyone's name. I was too busy trying to keep up with Barb's instructions. But I recall several college-aged girls there. Grad school, maybe."

"Well, this Laura was enrolled in graduate school at the university. But there's no record of her ever taking a class at Lambspun before, so none of us has any recollection of her. Mimi even called Rosa and Connie. The name didn't ring a bell with them, either."

"How's Mimi doing? Even though this girl wasn't one of her special ones, you know how Mimi gets when bad things come too close."

"Ohhhhhh, yes. She was shocked when she heard it. Then she felt even sadder that none of us remembers the girl at all."

"Sounds like Mother Mimi."

"Yep. But we sat and talked about it over a nice brandy, and now we're going to bed. I just wanted to let you know."

"Thanks, Burt. I'm kind of sorry I didn't take the time to meet some of those girls. I did talk to one of them, Elizabeth. She had the friend who knew that professor at the university who was accused of assault, remember?"

"No way I could forget that," Burt said with a sigh. "But right now, I want to join Mimi and finish off that brandy and go to sleep. Talk to you later, Kelly."

"Thanks, Burt. Give my love to Mimi and have a good night's sleep. Oh, did Dan say how this girl was killed? Was she shot?"

"Nope, she was strangled. And on that graphic note, I'm hanging up the phone. Brandy is waiting."

Kelly listened to the sound of Burt's phone clicking off. "On that graphic note,"

Burt had said. That was a good way to describe the murder. Strangulation meant the killer had to get up close and personal with the victim and literally choke the life from her.

A shiver passed over Kelly's skin even though the summer evening was still in the nineties. "Graphic" didn't begin to describe it.

SEVEN

Monday morning

Kelly stepped into the Lambspun foyer and looked around, hoping to see Mimi. She walked through the central yarn room and into the main room. To her surprise, Mimi was sitting in a back corner beside a window, spinning wheel whirring away.

"Hey, Mimi, I was looking for you," she said as she set her briefcase bag on the library table. "That was awful news Saturday."

"Yes, it was. Even though I didn't know the young woman, I couldn't help feeling sad. Her family must be grieving." Mimi didn't look up from her spinning while she talked. Her eyes were focused on the pile of lavender-colored fleece in her lap.

Kelly pulled a chair closer to the spinning wheel. She could sense Mimi's subdued mood. Once again violence had come close to Lambspun. "I know that must have been hard for you to hear. I know how much you worry about your 'girls.' "

Mimi didn't answer right away, simply kept spinning. The sound of the spinning wheel, turning, turning, started working its familiar magic. It was soothing. Kelly had always been drawn to the sound of the wheel as it spun fibers into yarns. She watched strands of the drafted lavender fleece, now turned into roving, slide through Mimi's expert fingers, joining the soft white mohair and a darker violet fiber already on the wheel, and wind around and around, then onto the fattening spindle.

The sound of the turning wheel was almost hypnotic. "An ancient art," someone had once said to Kelly in describing their craft. Kelly always relaxed whenever she was around the spinners. The rhythmic movements of the spinners' hands and feet, moving in separate motions yet at the same time, never failed to awe Kelly. She doubted she could ever master those motions — feet moving back and forth on the treadle, causing the wheel to turn.

At the same time, the spinner's hands moved through more delicate motions — allowing the drafted fiber to slide between the small opening between the spinner's thumb and forefinger and onto the wheel, forming yarn. "Not too much. Not too little," she remembered hearing Mimi admonish beginning spinners. Kelly also remembered what happened when a spinner's fingers opened too wide, and too much fiber passed through and onto the wheel. Suddenly, the spinner would find the fiber in her lap, twisting and coiling like a snake. That's the first time Kelly had ever heard spinners scream. Their neat piles of drafted roving turned into a mass of twisted fiber.

Kelly still remembered what she'd heard said to a class of beginning spinners — forewarning them of possible trouble. "Loosen your fingers a little, so the yarn twist will form smoothly. Not too much. If your fingers open too much, the twist jumps right through and winds the roving." Soon, several of those beginning spinners had a twisted mass of fiber in their laps rather than the fluffy roving they'd spent time drafting. It happened so quickly.

"Worrying doesn't stop bad things from happening, unfortunately. I wish it did." Mimi's movements with the wheel paused while she drafted more of the wool fleece in her lap, stretching the fibers so they became batten or roving. The better to spin with, as the fibers slid smoothly between her fingers and the wheel resumed its spin. Rhythmic.

Kelly watched in silence for several minutes. She loved to watch the spinners. She found it calming. The rhythm of the wheel, spinning, the wool sliding smoothly through Mimi's fingers and onto the wheel, turning, turning, and onto the spindle, fattening with newly spun twists of yarn. Yarn twists.

"I asked Burt to tell Barb it was one of her intermediate advanced knitting students who was killed. It's bound to be a shock to her. After all, she tries to get to know her students."

Kelly glanced at her watch. "She should be in pretty soon. Her class starts in an hour."

"Mimi?" Burt's voice called from the central yarn room. Mimi looked up for the first time.

"I'm in here, Burt."

Burt rounded the corner into the main room and, spotting Kelly and Mimi, his serious face spread with a smile. "Hey, I was wondering when you'd give in to the call of the lavender fleece."

Mimi smiled, the first smile Kelly had seen since she arrived. So unlike bubbly, enthusiastic Mimi. "Somehow it felt like a good day to spin the lavender."

Burt came over to her chair and leaned down. Mimi raised her face for his kiss. "How're you doing?"

"All right. The spinning helps. It always does."

"I know it helps me to watch you folks spin. It's relaxing, calming. I don't know how you two keep from falling asleep when you're doing it," Kelly joked.

Kelly was hoping to coax a laugh from both Mimi and Burt, and it worked. They both laughed softly.

"The mere thought of all that tangled yarn that would happen if we fell asleep is what keeps us awake," Burt said.

"Oh, my, yes," Mimi added. "What a mess that would be."

A loud voice came from the central yarn room as Big Barb rounded the corner. "Mimi? I'm going to use that turquoise yarn I found in a drawer downstairs in the basement. It was the last skein. Do you mind?"

Mimi looked up at Barb with a smile. *Coming back to herself,* Kelly thought thankfully. "Go right ahead, Barb. I don't have plans for it."

Rosa appeared beside Barb, standing in the archway between the two rooms. "Mimi, I have that distributor from Oregon on the phone. Do you want to talk to her?"

Mimi's feet and hands stopped their rhythmic movements and the wheel slowed to a stop. "Yes, yes, I do." She pushed back her chair.

"I'll bring in those other skeins in a few minutes, Mimi," Burt said as Mimi and Rosa headed toward the front of the shop.

"Well, I'd best go downstairs and retrieve that turquoise yarn before anyone else spots it. That dye lot was gorgeous." Barb dropped her oversize knitting tapestry bag onto one of the chairs beside the library table.

"Uh, Barb, could you hold off on that for a few minutes?" Burt said. "I wanted to talk to you about something. Something to do with your class."

Barb looked surprised. "Is something the matter? Has a student complained?"

"No, no, nothing like that. It's just something I heard over the weekend." Burt stood up, then glanced at Kelly.

"Kelly, why don't you join us in the café? It's between breakfast and lunch so there are some quiet spots to talk."

Surprised by Burt's request, Kelly quickly nodded. "Sure." She rose, to follow after Burt and Barb as they walked toward the café. The small alcove looked even cozier empty. Burt chose the corner table away from view of knitting shop customers on their way to the restroom facilities. Then he pulled out chairs for both Barb and Kelly and sat across the table from them.

"You've aroused my curiosity, Burt. What is it about the class you want to talk about?" Barb asked.

Burt folded his big hands in what Kelly recognized as his "settling in to talk" position. "Actually, it's not about the class itself. But one of the students in your intermediate advanced knitting class. I had a call last night from my old partner Dan at the department, and he said that they were going to release the name of the young woman who was killed at her campus apartment. He knew how much Mimi worries about her girls, as she calls them, so he gave me the victim's name. And . . . she was one of your intermediate advanced knitting students. I'm sorry, Barb."

Barb's eyes got wide. "What?"

Burt nodded. "Mimi and I came back to the shop after dinner and went through the class registrations. Mimi didn't recognize her, but we knew that you always get to know your students. Her name was Laura Brewster. Did you get a chance to know her when she was in your class?"

"No, she only came to one class." Barb peered at Burt. "What happened to her?"

Burt shook his head. "They don't know yet. Dan says it looks like an intruder got into her apartment, because things were pulled out all over. Drawers and papers. Who knows? Maybe this Laura came in and surprised the guy, and he strangled her."

Barb's eyes went wide again. "That's awful! Do the police think it was drug related?"

"The police may never know. It could very well be drug related. Or, it could simply be a violent intruder. Whatever, I'm sure the police will find out. And I'll make sure Dan keeps me updated. I'll let you all know anything I learn."

Barb glanced at her watch. "Oh, goodness. Time has slipped away on me. I'd better set up for my class. Students will be here in fifteen minutes." She pushed back her chair and rose.

Kelly and Burt followed suit. "Are you going to tell the students in your class, Barb?" Kelly asked as all three walked toward the hallway leading back to the knitting shop.

"Oh, Lord, I don't know," Barb said. "It's so awful. I'll see how the class goes." Barb strode faster and entered the workroom, then she turned and looked at Burt. "Thank you, Burt, for telling me. I appreciate it."

"You're welcome, Barb."

Kelly glanced at her briefcase bag on the

library table. "I'm going back to the café and grab an iced coffee. Do you want some?"

"I'll pass right now, but thanks anyway. I'm going up front to see if Mimi needs any help." He turned toward the front of the shop.

"Talk to you later, Burt," Kelly called behind him, then she headed down the hallway toward the café. Her cell phone jangled suddenly. Lisa's name flashed on the screen.

"Hey, Kelly. Just wanted to remind you of practice tonight."

"Already on my daytimer. Are we at the Rolland Moore Park fields or elsewhere?"

"This week we're using Lincoln Junior High fields. A little farther north and west."

"Yeah, I've been to that school for a coaching class. By the way, Burt's old partner from the police department told him the name of that grad student who was killed in her apartment the other night. He knows how Mimi worries about her students. Well, it turns out the girl was taking Barb's intermediate advanced knitting class."

"Oh, no. I'm sure Mimi is taking that hard. Did she know her well?"

"Actually, no. Mimi never met her, and

Barb said she didn't get to know her because the girl only took one class. Rosa and Connie didn't meet her, either. Naturally, that made Mimi sad, too."

"Of course. Mother Mimi. Oooops. Another call is coming in. See you tonight."

"Tonight," Kelly echoed as she clicked off her phone and headed for the café. A cozy corner table and a steady supply of coffee were the perfect partners for complex client accounts.

"Hey, there, Kelly!" a familiar voice called as Kelly walked along the sidewalk bordering the café's garden patio. Kelly glanced around the garden but all the tables were filled with customers enjoying one of Pete's delicious lunch selections.

"Over here, girl!" the voice called again.

Then Kelly noticed a hand waving between the cars parked along the far side of the café's garden patio. Colorado cowgirl Jayleen Swinson smiled broadly as she strode toward Kelly on the flagstones that provided a pathway through the garden. Clad in jeans no matter how hot the summer, the most deference Jayleen ever paid the hot weather was to switch from denim shirts to tee shirts complete with bandanna around her neck. Her Stetson was in place as usual.

"Hey, Jayleen, how're you holding up in this July heat?" Kelly said as she walked to meet her friend.

"Fair to middling," Jayleen answered. "A whole lot better than that gawd-awful heat last summer. C'mon over here and join me for a cup of coffee." Jayleen beckoned Kelly toward the patio garden.

Kelly followed her friend to a table in the dappled sunlight and shade. Last summer was the Summer of Fire for Northern Colorado. The High Park wildfire raged for two weeks. Jayleen and all her neighbors had been chased away from their ranches by the fire in Bellevue Canyon. Kelly and the Gang and other friends of Jayleen drove through the smoke last year to rescue Jayleen's alpacas and take them to safer surroundings until the wildfire was put out.

"Are you doing errands and such? I spotted you at the ballpark a week or so ago, but didn't get a chance to come over and talk." Kelly settled into a wrought iron chair across from Jayleen.

"We'll try and get over there this weekend. Both Eric and Cassie will have games. So, if your team is playing or maybe Steve's, then we'll try to catch that, too." Jayleen grinned. "Now that we're keeping up with grandchildren's sports, our weekends are busier than ever."

"I hear you. Say, Eric came over to our bleachers last weekend while Cassie was playing. Steve, Megan, Lisa, and I were there, and we got a chance to catch up with what he's doing. I hadn't had a chance to talk to him since the holidays. He's a great kid. And boy, does he have a busy schedule with all that ranch stuff."

Jayleen grinned even wider. "Eric's a fine boy. We're real proud of him. And he's picking up the ranching real easy. Born to it, you might say." She glanced toward the knitting shop straight ahead. "Is Cassie here or is she off playing tennis or working on computers at Greg's lab?"

"Uhhhhh, let's see. If it's Monday afternoon, then she's with Lisa at the sports clinic, watching the physical therapists work on patients."

Jayleen wagged her head. "I declare, that girl is busier than the busiest bee in the hive. But she's getting a whole lot of experience in a bunch of different things."

"She loves all of it, too. She tells us everything she's doing. It's really fun to watch her enthusiasm."

"Oh, yes. She tells Curt and me the same thing. And you should see her with the animals when she comes over. She just loves the alpacas. And she's even learned how to brush them. I swear, they come over to Cassie as soon as they see her." Jayleen chuckled. "She's got a knack with animals, for sure."

"It's another reason I'm so glad Cassie got to come and live with Jennifer and Pete after her grandfather had that heart attack. Her whole life seems to have blossomed once she came here. From the way she's always described it, she lived a very quiet and uneventful life with Grandpa Ben." Kelly gave a crooked smile.

"Sounds like you hit the nail on the head," Jayleen said, leaning back in the wrought iron chair. "And 'blossomed' is the right word. Cassie just thrives on doing all those different activities. I swear, she tells the funniest stories about going with Greg to his computer lab at the university. Those other people there, she calls them 'the geeks.' " Jayleen cackled. "I declare, she has Curt and me in stitches telling us what Greg gets up to over there."

"I have to admit, I was surprised that Greg took to Cassie so quickly. He's never been around a lot of kids, like Steve and I have. We teach kids softball and baseball every year. And we coach teams. Greg was a city boy and an only child. He always made it sound like he played with older kids growing up, not kids his own age."

"Well, Cassie has her own way of meeting people, I've noticed. She's a great listener, for one thing. Not many people know how to do that. Not really. They're always interrupting. But Cassie actually listens. So that's probably what Greg and those geek guys noticed."

"You know, you're right," Kelly said, nodding. "And she absolutely loves computers and putting them together and learning about them. Of course, that's right up Greg's alley. He really is a geek, himself. But he just doesn't admit it."

"I'll have to tease him the next time I see him," Jayleen promised. "Does Steve have a game this weekend? How about you?"

"Steve plays on Saturday, and I play on Sunday. So if you'll be at the ballpark to see the kids' games this Saturday, you can drop by our bleachers and give Greg a hard time in between games," Kelly teased.

"That sounds like a plan. And I'll check to see if Cassie wants to come up to Curt's ranch this Sunday morning and join us. We're taking a trail ride through the canyons with the grandkids."

Kelly grinned. "I think it goes without saying that Cassie will jump at the chance."

"I kinda hoped she would. She's getting to be a good little rider. I declare, the grandkids are so scheduled with other activities that Curt and I have to reserve time with them. Cassie fits right in."

Kelly spotted Jennifer walking over to their table. "Well, here's one half of the parenting team, so you can reserve Cassie's time right now."

Jayleen simply laughed.

EIGHT

Tuesday morning

Kelly paused in the central yarn room and admired the new display of yarns on the center table. With her mug-free hand, she stroked several of them. Cotton, bamboo, merino wool, mohair, and silk.

The front entry doorbell jingled, and Kelly looked up to see Burt enter the shop. "Hey, Burt. Are you escaping the noontime heat?"

"You bet, Kelly. I've been doing errands all morning," Burt said as he stood in the foyer. "If you've got a minute, I can tell you what I learned from Dan last night."

"Sure. You're stealing my line, though," Kelly said as she walked into the foyer.

Burt looked at her with a blank expression. "What?"

Kelly smiled. "I'm always asking you if you have a few minutes. Now, you're using it on me. Boy, not only can we read each other's minds, now we're starting to talk the same. I'm not sure what that means."

Burt chuckled as he pushed the front entry door open again. "Not sure if it means anything. Why don't we sit at this table here in the shade? We can pick up some of the breezes coming off the mountains and across the golf course."

Kelly followed Burt out the door and over to the open porch setback in the shade. A black wrought iron table and four chairs welcomed knitters and staff who wanted to knit or have lunch or simply sit and enjoy the colorful annual flowers that were planted in pots and flower beds dotted around the front entrance leading down to the driveway. The shaded areas had planters filled with purple and yellow and blue pansies that waved gently in the breeze. The sunnier flower beds were planted with brilliant red geraniums, sturdy enough to withstand even July heat.

Burt settled into a wrought iron chair beside the outdoor table and Kelly followed suit. "Dan called this morning and told me the name of the young woman who filed the sexual assault complaint against Tommy. It was Laura Brewster."

Kelly sat up abruptly. *"What!"*

Burt's gaze turned solemn. "Yes. She's the same young woman who was murdered in her apartment. Dan discovered the information as they were investigating Laura Brewster's background. They were searching for some connections to drugs. Something that might have caused a break-in at her apartment."

Kelly's mind started racing as she stared out at the foothills in the distance. *Laura Brewster. She's the one who accused Tommy. And now she's dead.* "Good Lord!" Kelly whispered.

"My thoughts exactly. Dan said they'd be questioning Tommy tomorrow. Naturally."

"And, naturally, Tommy becomes a suspect."

Burt nodded. "Since Laura Brewster recently filed a sexual assault complaint against Tommy, it makes sense that he'd be questioned. The police will take a look at anyone who might have had a grudge against her. So they'll also ask around the university and her neighbors."

The word "grudge" caught Kelly's attention. It had a darker sound to it. It made her feel uneasy, so Kelly switched subjects. "How'd Mimi respond when you told her?"

"Shocked. And saddened, of course. I told her last night when I got off the phone with Dan. She understands the police have to question Tommy. Laura filed a complaint against him. But we both know that Tommy works late nearly every night at the emergency clinic. So he's got a perfect alibi."

Hearing Burt sound so matter-of-fact and confident made Kelly feel better. "Thank goodness for that late-night job, right?" Kelly attempted a smile, but her face didn't totally cooperate.

"Amen to that."

A dark car came down the driveway just then. Kelly recognized Barb as the driver. "You'll have to tell Barb, you know."

Burt sighed. "Yeah, I'd better. Dan has probably already contacted Tommy about going to see him in the late afternoon. Tommy would most likely be asleep during the morning and early afternoon. What with those night hours he's working."

Kelly watched Barb pull her car into a parking space in the Lambspun driveway. "I can leave, if you'd like me to," she suggested, watching Big Barb stride down the sidewalk leading to the front of the shop.

"You can stay. Having someone else here might help Barb stay calm." Burt smiled and called out to Barb as she approached. "Hey, there, Barb. You've got the last intermediate advanced knitting class today, don't you?"

Barb slowed her long stride and shifted the enormous knitting bag hanging over her shoulder. "Yes, indeed. They've made excellent progress. I'm proud of them." Glancing toward Kelly, she added, "I wish you had stayed, Kelly. You would have gained a ton of self-confidence."

Kelly had to laugh at that. No one had ever accused her of lacking self-confidence. But Big Barb was right. When it came to knitting and mastering complicated stitches, Kelly definitely lacked confidence in her abilities. "Maybe next time, Barb," she promised with a grin.

"Why don't you sit for a minute, Barb," Burt suggested. "I have some information from my old partner, Dan." Burt gave the chair between them a little outward push.

Barb's expression changed immediately. The worried pinched look that Kelly had noticed so much this last month appeared again. "What's happened?" she asked in an anxious voice as she sank into the offered chair.

"Last night Dan told me that the young woman who filed the sexual assault complaint against Tommy was the same one who was killed in her apartment last week. Laura Brewster."

Barb stared wide-eyed at Burt. "Wh-what?"

Burt continued, his voice softer. "Naturally, Dan and another detective will be questioning Tommy regarding Laura Brewster's death."

"WHAT!" Barb exploded, face flushed with color in an instant. "That's ridiculous! Tommy works at the clinic all night. Ten o'clock until six in the morning. He couldn't have killed her."

"The police will question anyone who had a connection to Laura Brewster. Her neighbors, fellow university students, people like that. And we have to be honest, Barb. Tommy had a complaint filed against him by Laura Brewster earlier this month. The police have to follow that up. They would be derelict if they didn't."

Barb scowled. "The whole suggestion is ludicrous. How could the police possibly suspect Tommy of killing someone? He's a *doctor,* for heaven's sake! He saves lives. He doesn't take them."

"I'm sure Dan and the other detectives will come to the same conclusions that we have. Tommy works every night for the medical clinic, therefore he couldn't possibly have committed murder."

Kelly noticed that Burt used a soothing

135

tone of voice when speaking to Barb, clearly trying to calm her down. Deciding she could help with that effort, Kelly spoke up. "I agree, Barb. It sounds like the police are simply following procedures. Interviewing anyone who had contact with Laura Brewster."

Barb turned her scowling face toward Kelly, but didn't say a word. Burt reached over and patted Barb's arm — Mother Mimi style. "Don't worry, Barb. I'm sure Tommy will do fine. He has nothing to fear. And neither do you."

Barb didn't reply, just kept scowling. Kelly's cell phone jangled to life then, so she quickly left the table. "Excuse me, folks. I'll take this interruption elsewhere," she said as she headed toward the driveway.

Steve's name flashed on the screen. "Hi, there," Kelly said after clicking on. "What are you up to?"

"I just checked with Jennifer. She's going to take me through some newer apartment complexes tomorrow afternoon after she leaves the café. One of them was done by that out-of-state builder who's been getting into the local scene the last couple of years."

"That's good news. Jen will make sure you see the best ones. She's a jewel," Kelly said as she walked down the driveway toward her cottage. Might as well give Carl a pat and an ear rub while she was outside.

"You buried in accounts?"

"Well, I was. But I took a short break with Burt. We were sitting outside in that front patio at Lambspun. Burt heard from his old partner Dan that they would be questioning Tommy tomorrow in connection with the death of that student, Laura Brewster. It turns out she was the one who filed the sexual assault complaint against Tommy."

"Oh, brother. That's definitely not good. But it does make sense he'd be questioned. After all, she accused Tommy of assault, so naturally he's a suspect in the cops' eyes."

Steve's no-nonsense summing up of the situation was refreshing. Of course, she could never use words as blunt as that with Big Barb. That's why Burt was trying to tactfully update Overprotective Mother Barb concerning police procedures involving her Beloved Son Tommy.

"You summed it up perfectly, Steve. Unfortunately, poor Burt can't be that straightforward with Barb. She hit the roof a couple of minutes ago just hearing that the police would question Tommy."

"Oh, boy. I get the picture."

"Let's just say that Barb brings new meaning to the term 'overprotective mother.' "

Steve didn't reply, but his laughter over the phone spoke volumes.

"You're *kidding*? The girl who was killed was the same one who filed a sexual assault complaint against Tommy after going to the clinic where he worked? *And* she took one of Barb's knitting classes?" Lisa's voice over the phone had the sound of incredulity that Kelly felt earlier in the day when first hearing the strange set of circumstances.

"Yeah. Weird, isn't it? It makes me wonder if she was targeting Tommy or something. Does that make any kind of sense, or am I being too suspicious?" Kelly sipped some of the iced coffee in the shadiest corner of the café's garden. Customers were all gone. Just the birds and the squirrels and the constant stream of departing and arriving customers for the knitting shop and cars parking in the driveway.

"No, I think it's a valid question," Lisa said. "Now that you've told me, I think I'll make a couple of calls to friends. See if any of them had a class with this Laura. Maybe they'd have a clue as to her personality. One of my old friends from high school works in the graduate school records office. She could tell me which graduate program curriculum Laura Brewster was taking."

Kelly had to smile. "Oooooh, that sounds like sleuthing to me, Lisa. I see I've corrupted you."

"Yeah, yeah. I won't try looking at her grades or anything. Don't want to intrude on privacy —"

"Privacy?" Kelly cut in. "She's been murdered. You can't invade her privacy. In fact, anything you learn might help find who killed her."

Lisa laughed low in her throat. "Boy, you can rationalize anything, can't you, Kelly?"

"It's that hard-nosed accountant attitude. We have to solve puzzles. It's part of our job."

"Well, my job makes me be a little more careful of stepping across lines. But I agree with you. Maybe one of my friends remembers this girl from class or something. Maybe they can shed some light on what was going on in her life."

"It's worth a try. Thanks, Lisa."

Lisa's phone beeped. "Got another call. Talk to you later."

"Later," Kelly said and clicked off. Relaxing against the wrought iron chair, Kelly savored the midsummer languor that was part of her favorite season. Hot weather, shady spot, lots of sunshine behind the trees. It would be a perfect night to sit outside with Steve and stare at the stars. Except for one thing — mosquitoes. Maybe if they both held one of those citronella candles, the bugs would leave them alone. Kelly had to laugh at the image as she pulled out her laptop and files from her briefcase bag. Summer coffee break was over. Work demands beckoned.

"Your client Arthur Housemann called me today," Steve said that night as he lay on the chaise longue next to Kelly's.

Kelly quickly propped herself up on her chaise longue. "That's great! He told me he was thinking of calling you. What'd he say?"

Both chaise longues were surrounded by four large mosquito-repellent candles, one at each corner. *So far, so good,* Kelly thought. She hadn't noticed any bugs biting. Several had buzzed past her ear, but hadn't landed. At least, she didn't think they had. She'd find out later when she changed for bed. Any red welts from bug bites would show up. Meanwhile, this spot on their backyard lawn was perfect for gazing up at the stars.

"He's thinking of building some apartment units, not far from the university. Not big buildings. Smaller ones. Like my town house apartments in Old Town. Minus the turn-of-the-century detailing, of course."

"Most of that land near the university is already taken or has buildings on it. Did he buy a parcel from someone?"

"No, this is a parcel Arthur owns that has an older rental house on it. He bought it years ago, apparently." Steve folded his arms beneath his head.

"Oh, yeah, I remember now. I bet it's one of those houses over on Pecan Street. He told me once that he might convert one or two of those houses into apartment buildings." Kelly lay back on the chaise, too, arms beneath her head. "The rents are lower in those houses because they are a lot older and a little smaller."

"He said he'd been thinking about doing it for a couple of years now, but the time wasn't right."

"That's for sure. So many people lost jobs in the recession, it was too risky to make a move then. Most people stayed put, even if that was in their parents' basements."

Steve gave a short laugh. "That's the truth. Boy, that was a rough time."

"At least you found another architect to share a Denver apartment. You were both working ridiculous hours, you said."

"Don't remind me. Many nights I slept in the truck just because it would take too long to drive from Sam's office to the apartment. I started leaving a change of clothes and an extra shaving kit in the truck."

Kelly stopped tracing the stars in Orion and turned her head toward Steve. "Where did you change in the mornings?"

"At the Colorado State University gym. Membership was cheaper for grad school alumni. They had good showers and locker rooms. You'd be surprised how many guys use those places every morning. Home away from home."

"Boy . . . that feels like it was ages ago, but it was only two years. And look what you've done in those two years. Partner in the business. Kaufman and Townsend Construction."

"Two and a half." Steve grinned.

"Two and a *half*," Kelly emphasized, then looked upward into the stars once more. "How many apartment units does Arthur want in the new building?"

"That's what I'm figuring out. I can squeeze in four units in that original building footprint. But if I can expand that footprint, then we could have six. It depends on what Arthur wants."

"If it's that property on the corner of Pecan and Overland Trail, you could probably expand it."

Steve glanced at Kelly. "You've actually checked out Housemann's properties?"

"Oh, yeah. It was easy to do, since they're mostly in Fort Connor or Loveland. I wanted to be able to compare them to his other rental properties in the city. See what difference location made on rental revenue."

"Smart. Tell me, where are some of Housemann's Loveland rental apartment buildings? I checked out all of his properties in Fort Connor, but I'd like to take a look at those Loveland units, too. I'm already getting ideas."

"I'll bet you are," Kelly said, smiling up at the Big Dipper. "You started drawing yet?"

"Just a sketch or two."

"I've got an idea. Why don't you check with Jennifer. She could get you inside some of the newer rental apartments in town. That way you could see what some of the other builders have done lately."

"That's a great idea. I'll call her tomorrow. See? That's why I love you. You're smart."

"Yeah, yeah, yeah." Kelly grinned up at the dark sky. Another thought occurred. "A lot has changed these past two years. Jayleen's ranch is just about recovered from the High Park wildfire damage. You're now a partner with Sam. And Jennifer and Pete are parents of a thirteen-year-old."

"And it looks to me like they'll be raising Cassie all by themselves. From what Lisa says, Grandpa Ben will probably be an invalid the rest of his life."

"Sounds like it. You know, Jennifer and Pete both stepped up when Cassie suddenly needed a home. I think they have done a great job this last year. Cassie is a lucky girl."

"Cassie's a great kid, too. Some teenagers are a pain. I've seen too many like that. Always complaining about something."

"You know, Jennifer told me that Cassie asked them both about sexual assault. They were all three having dinner at home. Cassie had overheard several of the knitters talking about it at Lambspun. I'm sure they were probably talking between themselves, but Cassie has good ears." Kelly smiled. "And she pays attention."

"Wow, that's a big topic. How'd they handle it?"

"Really well, judging from what Jennifer told me. Cassie wanted more details than what she read in the Denver newspapers. Apparently she and Grandpa Ben read the newspapers together every evening."

Steve chuckled. "I wish I'd known Grandpa Ben. He sounds like a good guy. Cassie said he took her to every museum in the Denver area."

Old memories popped up in the back of Kelly's mind. "My dad and I used to go to museums all the time. In every city we lived in when I was a kid. Dad was in seventh heaven when we lived in Northern Virginia, outside of Washington, DC. Museums were everywhere." She laughed softly, remembering.

"I wish I'd met your dad, too. He sounds like a really good guy."

"He was," Kelly said in a quiet voice as memories filled her mind. Remembering.

NINE

Thursday morning

"What a good boy," Kelly said, rubbing that sweet spot behind Carl's right ear. "Carl's such a good dog. Good dog, Carl," she chanted in the singsong fashion that her Rottweiler recognized.

Carl, for his part, joined in the song with a little doggie moan of ear-rubbing pleasure. *Yes, yes, right there!*

Kelly gave her dog another rub on the opposite ear and watched Carl sing along in pleasure. "You're a silly dog. Yes, you are. There you go." She gave Carl a couple of pats on his muscular shoulders, signifying that Ecstatic Ear Rub Break was over.

"Okay, you've got two big bowls of water, Carl. You're set for the morning. Go get those squirrels!" She pointed toward the corner of her backyard where Carl's nemesis, Brazen Squirrel, had just landed on the top rail of the chain-link fence and was headed east. No doubt aiming for the hanging branch of a maple tree that was outside the fence.

At the mention of the word "squirrel," Carl's head swiveled to the left, spotting Brazen.

"And he's off!" Kelly said with a laugh, watching her dog aim straight as a bullet for the scampering Brazen. Carl hit the fence with both front feet, barking furiously as the wily squirrel jumped straight to the ground outside the fence and scampered to the nearby maple tree. Escaped, yet again!

The sound of her cell phone's music enticed Kelly inside her cottage again, as she slid the patio screen door shut. Lisa's name flashed on the phone. "Hey, there. Are you at the university or the sports clinic?"

"I'm on the way to the parking lot to drive over to the clinic, so I thought I'd give you a call," Lisa said. Kelly could hear outside noises coming over the phone. "I talked to my friend in the graduate programs office, and she was able to tell me that Laura Brewster was enrolled in the graduate program that's offered in the Anatomy and Physiology Department. The second year of the three-year program."

"Okay, anatomy and physiology. Sounds

like she was working toward a master's degree."

"Possible. Anyway, I called another friend, Sandy, who's also taking courses in anatomy and physiology and working on the master's program. I asked Sandy if she knew this Laura Brewster, and she did. She even had classes with her."

"Did she get to know her well?"

"I don't know. They shared a couple of classes, and Sandy said she was also in a study group with Laura. Said she was 'really intense.' Those words exactly."

"Hmmmmmmm, sounds interesting."

"Yeah, well, here's the *really* interesting part. My friend Sandy went on to say that this Laura had some problem with one of the anatomy professors. Sandy knew because she was outside in the hallway one time when Laura came out of the professor's office. Sandy said it sounded like Laura was arguing with this professor."

"Even more interesting."

"Apparently there's more. Sandy said you can call her or e-mail her if you have more questions. I'll text you her phone and e-mail after we hang up."

"Thanks, Lisa. I appreciate that. I'll send her an e-mail and see if she wants to meet for coffee."

"Oh, and there's something else that makes it really strange. The anatomy professor Laura was talking to was the professor who was accused of sexual assault by one of his students. Sandy said she always wondered if the student involved was Laura Brewster."

"You're kidding!" Kelly said, her little buzzer inside going off.

"Nope."

"That's one heckuva coincidence, don't you think?"

"Agreed. But you can find out all the details from Sandy yourself. Then you can tell me. Gotta run. See you at practice tonight."

"Tonight," Kelly promised before Lisa's phone clicked off. She shoved her phone into the back pocket of her summer white capri pants and returned to loading accounting files into her briefcase bag.

"Strange" didn't begin to describe what Lisa told her. Neither did "coincidence." Kelly had always been suspicious of coincidences.

Her cell phone buzzed with a text alert, and Kelly checked the screen. Lisa's text with her friend Sandy's e-mail. Kelly didn't waste a moment. She clicked on the e-mail address and quickly keyed in a brief message. *Meet outside in the University Quad for coffee?*

Kelly's curiosity was bubbling, urging her to find answers. And her little buzzer was definitely going off. She had questions. Lots of questions.

"Do you need a refill, Kelly?" Julie asked as she approached the café table where Kelly was working that afternoon.

Kelly looked up from the computer screen, which was filled with multiple spreadsheets. "No, thanks, I'm still good. Another benefit to working inside in the air-conditioning." She smiled at Julie.

"Well, let me know if you need anything. We'll head into the midmorning slowdown in a while." Julie raised her pitcher of iced coffee before she scurried back to the main part of the café.

Kelly glanced around the café alcove where she had settled in at the small table in the corner. Not as many customers seemed to use it. Smaller than the other tables and tucked into a corner, it seemed to be isolated. However, those same qualities which made regular customers shun the table made it attractive to Kelly. It was the perfect size for her to spread out her laptop and a file folder and settle in to work on client accounts. She was about to return to recording utilities expense onto a spreadsheet when her cell phone buzzed. A text message coming in.

Kelly checked the screen and saw an unfamiliar name. Sandy Atkinson. That had to be Lisa's university friend. Kelly clicked on the message and read it in full. Sandy could meet tomorrow afternoon at 2:30 P.M. in the University Student Union café and lounge, first floor. Kelly mentally checked her daytimer to make sure she was free that next afternoon, then she texted a reply to Sandy. *I'll meet you there at 2:30 P.M. Coffee, lattes, whatever are on me.*

She sent the text message on its way through the invisible connection of electronic cyberspace that they'd all become dependent upon, then returned her attention to Don Warner's construction spreadsheets once again. Warner had lots of projects, so there were a lot of spreadsheets.

Several minutes passed, then her cell phone buzzed again. Another message from Sandy. *Great. I have a weakness for those caramel macchiato lattes. Thanks.* She'd concluded the text with that familiar little combination of keystrokes called a "smiley face." It worked. Kelly smiled as she returned to the expense spreadsheets and her more plebeian iced coffee.

Kelly stood up from her chair beside the library table in Lambspun's main room the next morning and stretched — a long, deep stretch. A big yawn escaped then. *Funny how yawns sneak up on you,* she thought. *That's it. Time for a coffee break.* She grabbed her mug beside her open laptop and headed for the café. Midmorning, and the delicious breakfast aromas were floating down the hallway enticing Kelly forward. Eggs, bacon, cheese. All those delicious combinations that grill cook Eduardo created.

As she walked into the café, Kelly spotted Jennifer loading several tempting dishes onto her tray. "Hey, Jen, can you give me a refill once you take care of the hungry customers?"

"Sure thing, Kelly. Be back in a minute," Jen said as she walked over to a nearby table.

Kelly moved out of the way so the waitstaff could move freely. The café was packed and Jen, Julie, and part-timer Bridget bustled about serving all the hungry customers. Kelly checked her watch. Ten thirty. Maybe she could justify half a cinnamon roll. She could take the yummy snack and her coffee outside and sit on one of the cement benches in the garden. No need to occupy an entire table when hungry customers were showing up at the door.

Sure enough, two people opened the front door of the café then. Standing just inside the door, they did what everyone does: They looked around first, then stared at the large dry board on the wall which showed the daily specials for breakfast and lunch. Plus special coffees and lattes. Chocolate raspberry. *Yummmm,* Kelly thought. She had to try that.

"Hey, Kelly." Burt's voice came over her shoulder. "You here on coffee break, I bet." He walked over to stand beside her, out of the path of busy waitresses.

"Yeah, the yawns were attacking. We had a long game last night, so did Steve. So we slept like logs and almost didn't hear the alarm this morning."

Burt chuckled. "I know that feeling."

Kelly leaned over closer. "How's Barb doing? Have you seen her?"

"No, I haven't. I've been out since early this morning doing errands. But I'm hoping she's calmed down. After all, the girl was murdered only days after she'd accused Tommy of sexual assault at the clinic." Burt gave Kelly a knowing look. "Of course the police are going to consider Tommy a suspect. Barb may not like it, but she has to understand police reasoning."

"Barb's a smart woman. She's just being overprotective as usual. Boy, has she always been like that? Did she hover over him when he was a kid in Little League baseball and stuff?" Kelly joked.

Burt gave a good-natured shrug. "Actually, Tommy never got to play ball or any of those regular sports like the other kids. Barb was afraid he'd break something or lose a tooth. Tommy did learn how to play chess and joined a club when he was in elementary. And he liked puzzles. Loved solving puzzles, as I recall."

"What about Tommy's dad?"

"Apparently he and Barb divorced when Tommy was real little. Barb said he started 'running around' with other women." Burt rolled his eyes. "Age-old story, I guess. I didn't know Barb then, and neither did Mimi."

"Well, that explains Barb's overprotective tendencies," Kelly said. "But Tommy should be okay with the police because he works every night 10:00 P.M. to 6:00 A.M. at the clinic. That should eliminate him as a possible suspect."

"I sure hope so, Kelly. One thing I learned as a police detective was to always expect the unexpected. When it comes to people, anything is possible."

"Well, let's hope there's nothing unexpected in Tommy's questioning."

"I've asked Dan to give me a call after they interview Tommy and let me know how it went. I'll let you know as soon as I hear something."

Jennifer walked up to both of them then. "Two birds gossiping on a wire. That's what you two look like," she said with a grin. "Kelly, do you want a coffee refill? Iced or regular? What about you, Burt?"

"Iced for me, please."

"The same for me, Jennifer, thanks," Burt said.

"Would you please add a warmed cinnamon roll to my coffee?" Kelly asked. "I think I've found the perfect person to share it with." She smiled at Burt.

He groaned. "Only if we go outside. I don't want Mimi to see me."

"You read my mind," Kelly said as Jennifer walked away, laughing.

"Thanks for meeting me, Sandy. I appreciate it," Kelly said, setting a medium caramel macchiato on the table in front of the plump blonde with ruddy cheeks. She pulled out a chair at the café table in the midst of the central lounge of the Student Union building. Students filled every table in the large area. Kelly had deliberately chosen this smaller table that was slightly separated from the others. The better for private conversations.

"No problem, Kelly. This is my short interval between classes, so I wouldn't be able to get any real work done anyway." She took a sip of the sugary latte, closing her eyes in obvious enjoyment.

"Lisa always makes fun of me when I poke around in investigations. She calls it 'sleuthing around.' " Kelly grinned. "But I can't help it. I'm an accountant in real life and we solve puzzles for a living. So I guess it comes naturally to me."

Sandy smiled; her ruddy round cheeks gave her face a happy cherub appearance with her light blonde hair falling around her shoulders. "Lisa mentioned once or twice she had a friend who loved to solve mysteries. So I'm glad to meet you, Kelly. I'm a devoted Sherlock Holmes fan."

Kelly laughed out loud. "Well, I'm definitely not in the master's company. I'm just a nosy but focused accountant. We keep asking questions and poking around until we find some answers."

"Well, I have to admit that little scene I witnessed three years ago has stayed with me. And I often thought that it was Laura Brewster who lodged the complaint against Professor Paul Smith." She took another sip. "I didn't have Professor Smith's anatomy class, but I heard from other friends that he was an excellent teacher."

"Did you know her well? Lisa said you'd had some classes with Laura Brewster. And a study session, I think."

"That's right. But I wouldn't say I *knew* Laura. She gave the impression of being a very private person. A little standoffish, actually. She didn't sit around and talk with other students after class, like people are doing now." She gestured around them at the variety of students sitting and talking, eating and talking, or studying alone.

"Did she have any particular friends you noticed?"

Sandy shook her head. "Not that I ever saw. Laura was always alone. She'd come to class and sit and take notes and ask a lot of questions. But once, I remember her pointing to another girl in that class. Laura said she went to high school with her. Westgate High in Denver, I think she said."

Kelly filed that tidbit of information away for scrutiny later on. "Tell me about that time you saw her outside the professor's office. Professor Smith. What did you see exactly?"

Sandy took another sip of her sugary drink. "I was sitting on the floor outside my physiology professor's office, waiting for him to finish with a class so I could ask questions on a project he'd assigned. I had my book open and was reading the next day's assignment when I heard voices across the hall. Professor Smith came out of his office and Laura was with him. They obviously didn't notice me on the floor across the hall, because Laura kept talking to him. And her voice got higher. I remember her saying, 'Please, let me do some extra credit project so I can raise that grade.' Something like that. I just remember how upset she looked. Anyway, Professor Smith shook his head and said, 'No, that wouldn't be fair to the other students who took the exam.' Then he locked his office door. Laura kept pleading with him, her voice getting higher as Professor Smith started to walk away. She looked like she was going to follow him, but Professor Smith kind of waved her off then hurried down the hall and left."

"What did Laura do? Did she follow after him?"

"No. I remember she just stood and stared at his closed office door. At first, I thought she was reading the notices on the bulletin board next to it. But she kept staring for several minutes. I remember because it was weird. I was trying to read that chapter assignment, but I kept looking up at Laura and she was still standing there." Sandy took a longer drink of latte.

"Did she do anything else? Did she leave finally?"

"I thought she was going to because she started walking down the hall. But she didn't go down the stairs. Instead she went into the ladies' restroom. I went back to reading my assignment. Then a couple of minutes later, I heard this crying sound. A woman's voice. I looked up and saw Laura, crying loudly and running down the hallway right past me. Her hair was suddenly all messed up, and the top of her blouse was open. She really looked upset. I wondered if there had been some guy, you know, some weirdo hiding in the women's restroom and he made a move on her or something. Anyway, she kept crying all the way down the hallway and down the stairs. I guessed that she went outside. It wasn't until a couple of days later that everyone heard about a woman student accusing a professor of sexual assault. I never even thought of Laura until we all learned the professor accused was Professor Smith." Sandy looked into Kelly's eyes. "From that moment on, I had this bad feeling about Laura. I just knew in my gut that she was the one who charged Professor Smith with assault."

"Did you ever tell anyone else about what you saw?"

"I told a study group friend what I'd seen, and she said not to get into it. After all, I hadn't seen anything. Not really. Just a conversation between a student and a professor, then a girl running out of the restroom crying." Sandy shrugged. "My friend was right. I hadn't really seen anything. So I never told anyone else. But, you know, I have never been able to forget it." Sandy gave Kelly a wry look. "It always bothered me for some reason."

Kelly met Sandy's clear gaze and nodded. She wanted to give her affirmation. "I know how you feel, Sandy. Sometimes we see things that look kind of everyday normal on the outside, but something about it bothers us. I call it my gut or my instinct. If it keeps poking me about something, I've learned to follow it up. There's something I need to know."

Sandy smiled in acknowledgment. "I know what you mean. I live by my instinct all the time. Trust it implicitly."

Kelly returned her smile. "Thank you so

much for sharing that story with me, Sandy. Now maybe my gut can help me find some answers to who killed Laura Brewster."

Sandy's smile disappeared. "I sure hope it isn't Professor Smith. I heard lots of stories about how his career took a nosedive after those charges of assault."

"Well, I'm sure the police will find out who did it, Sandy. And my money is still on the violent intruder who broke into Laura's apartment. That makes a lot of sense."

Sandy gave a little shiver. "Brother, I think I need to warm up this coffee after hearing that."

Kelly joined her at the coffee bar once again.

Afternoon of the next day
"Hi, Lisa. How's your PT workload coming?" Kelly said, looking up from the yarn on her needles. "You're usually booked solid."

Lisa dumped her bag on the long library table. "That's for sure. I swear, today has been frustrating. Every client was late. Only about five minutes, but that adds up, and totally screws up your schedule." Lisa settled into a chair across the table from Kelly.

"I hear that." Kelly finished her knit stitch

161

before glancing up at Lisa.

The simple garter or knit stitch was the mainstay of Kelly's knitting repertoire. In the garter stitch, she would slip the knitting needle in her right hand into the left side of the last stitch on the needle in her left hand. Then she would wrap the yarn around the needles, and slide the stitch off the end of the left-hand needle onto the needle in her right hand. *Slip, wrap, slide.* The purl stitch, however, was different. The motions were slightly opposite, and if she didn't do it often enough, Kelly could make mistakes.

"Tell me, how did your visit go with Sandy yesterday?"

"Boy, was that ever informative," Kelly said, letting the ribbon yarn and needles drop to her lap. "Sandy told me that she was sitting across the hallway next to another professor's office door, waiting for him to finish a class. So she got to witness what went on between Laura Brewster and Professor Smith. She said they both came out of his office and she was pleading with him to give her an extra project to raise her exam grade. Sandy saw Smith shake his head. Then she heard him say, 'No, that wouldn't be fair to the other students who took the exam.' She said Laura kept pleading with him, her voice getting higher."

"Uh-oh, sounds like Laura was on the brink of losing it," Lisa said, arms folded on the table.

"Yeah, I thought so, too. Anyway, Sandy said the professor walked away and Laura just stood there staring at the office door for several minutes."

"That sounds a little weird. What happened then?"

"Sandy said Laura walked down the hall and went into the restroom. Then a few minutes later, Sandy heard loud crying and saw Laura run out of the bathroom, hair all messed up and the top of her blouse open. She ran down the hall and down the stairs, crying loudly the entire time."

Lisa met Kelly's gaze. "Oh, boy. Definitely not good. Did Sandy know if it was Laura who went to the campus police and reported a sexual assault?"

"She doesn't know, but ever since then Sandy said she's had a feeling that Laura was the student who accused Professor Smith of assault. She told only one friend, who advised Sandy not to say anything because she didn't really *see* anything."

"Wow," Lisa said, looking out the front windows. "That definitely arouses my suspicions, too. I'm inclined to believe that Laura Brewster made the complaint about

Professor Smith three years ago, given what Sandy said. I trust her opinion. She's levelheaded."

"I agree. Laura clearly had a grudge against Smith. And it appears that was her way of getting even. But there's no way to prove it." Kelly took a sip from the mug of coffee sitting beside her elbow. "Sandy also said Laura mentioned she had a friend from high school in that same class."

"Did Sandy mention a name?"

"No, Laura simply told her she went to high school with this girl. Westgate High in Denver, she thinks."

"That's one of the older high schools in the north of Denver, if I remember correctly."

"I wonder how close that high school friend was to Laura." She turned to Lisa. "You're familiar with university records. Is there any way I can access enrollment records for that particular anatomy class?"

Lisa gave Kelly a stern look. "Hold on, Sherlock. Only university personnel can access those records. So don't even think about it."

"But you're university personnel, right?" Kelly said with a sweet smile.

Lisa laughed. "You can turn off the charm. I can't help you. Grad students don't have that kind of access."

Kelly screwed up her face. "Drat. I guess I'll have to see if I can tempt Megan with a potential . . . uh, how shall I phrase it? Software breach?"

Lisa's blue eyes popped wide. "You mean hacking into the university system?" She threw up both hands in the "stop" position. "Not another word. I don't want to hear about it."

"Don't worry. I won't compromise your sense of ethics. But perhaps you might bend them just a little by scribbling down the department's log-in code. Pretty please?" Kelly smiled slyly. "In the interest of criminal investigation, you understand." Kelly slid a small scrap of paper across the knitting table to Lisa, along with a ballpoint pen.

Lisa rolled her big blue eyes and released a huge sigh, then she tossed her long blonde hair over her shoulder in what Kelly recognized was a gesture of impatience. Lisa took the pen and scribbled on the scrap of paper and shoved it across the table to Kelly. "There. I expect her to get in and out and only check enrollments. Promise?"

Kelly crossed her heart then held up both fingers. "Scout's honor," she said with a big smile.

Lisa frowned at her. "Were you even a Girl Scout?"

"But of course," Kelly said with a big smile. "Or maybe it was the Camp Fire Girls. I can't remember."

Lisa stared at the ceiling and exhaled another huge sigh. "You're impossible, you know that?"

"I'll take that as a compliment."

"Well, hi, you two," Megan said as she walked into the main room. "What are you talking about? Lisa's got that weird expression on her face."

"Oh, we were discussing Ethics and Moral Equivalency. Stuff like that," Kelly said, returning to her ribbon scarf.

Megan stared at her blankly. "Huh?"

"Kelly's teasing," Lisa said with a wave. "We were comparing notes about demanding clients."

"Oh, boy, do I know something about that," Megan said as she set her colorful fiber bag at the end of the library table and settled into a chair.

Kelly looked up from her stitches briefly. "Lisa's been complaining that all her clients were late today."

"Oooooh, that wreaks havoc on your clinic schedule."

"Tell me about it," Lisa said as she dug

166

into her knitting bag and removed a lacy yellow and white sleeveless knit top.

Megan reached inside her knitting bag and brought out a handful of black-and-white yarn attached to circular knitting needles. It looked to be knitted into a circle.

Curious, Kelly pointed to Megan's black-and-white yarn. "Is that a circlet? Are you knitting a neck warmer?"

"Yes, I am. Someone showed me a photo of a neck warmer in one of those knitting magazines, and I fell in love with it. It's a great design. So I checked to see if Mimi had a similar pattern." Megan pulled out a blue paper copy of a knitting pattern. "So I bought Lambspun's pattern instead of ordering one from a magazine."

"Good for you, Megan," Kelly said. "Shop locally. Keep the money in your hometown businesses."

"Spoken like a true accountant," Lisa added.

"I agree, so I'm doing my part and buying one of Lambspun's patterns," Megan said, picking up her stitches on the circular needles.

"Well, it's true. I like to see small businesses thrive. Over the years, I've watched too many of them start up, then struggle to make enough money to survive. The sad truth is the majority of the new businesses don't survive those first five years." Kelly gave a sigh. "Most of them don't have enough money to last through the lean months and still pay their bills. And their taxes."

"I think you told us that the taxes are what will get them most of the time." Lisa looked up from her fast-moving fingers. More of the lacy yellow yarn dangled from her needles now.

"Oh, yeah. That's the fastest way to get in trouble. With the Feds and with the state." Kelly gave a rueful smile. "They'll jump on you faster than fleas on a dog."

Lisa and Megan both laughed. "That sounds like one of Jayleen's sayings," Megan said.

"Close. It's one of Curt's. I love it. It's so picturesque," Kelly said with a laugh. "Which reminds me. I have to give Carl his monthly flea and tick medicine."

"Well, well, well, look at this. All three of you here at the same time," Burt said as he walked into the main knitting room, cup of coffee in hand.

"Welcome, Burt," Kelly said.

"Yes, sit down and visit with us for a while," Lisa added.

"I think I will," he said, settling into the

chair beside Kelly. "I get to see Kelly every day and Lisa lots of times, but I haven't seen you in a while, Megan."

Megan looked up at him with a smile. "This past week I was catching up on lots of scheduled things I'd forgotten about, like doctor's appointments. Eye appointments. Gotta change my contact prescription. I'm thinking of having that Lasik eye surgery so I can get rid of these contacts. Oh, and a dentist appointment, too. They were all scheduled in one week. I'd forgotten about them until I checked my daytimer."

Burt's expression turned serious. "Everything's okay, right? You did have a physical, didn't you?"

Megan gave him a daughterly grin. "Absolutely. I'm healthy as that proverbial horse."

Burt visibly relaxed. "Oh, good. Forgive me, I'm just being a dad."

Kelly smiled at her mentor and father figure. "We depend on that, Burt. In fact, we love it."

"The shop keeps both you and Mimi pretty busy," Lisa commented, looking up from the yellow and white yarn.

"Oh, yeah. That and some other stuff." He glanced over his shoulder toward the central yarn room. It appeared empty of customers at the moment. "Since you three are all here, I might as well share some disturbing news."

Kelly, Megan, and Lisa all stopped knitting and looked up at Burt. "Did you hear something from Dan?" Kelly asked.

"Yes, what did your old partner say?" Lisa leaned forward, looking at Burt.

Kelly leaned forward as well, paying attention. "Did Dan question Tommy, like you said he would?"

Burt took in a deep breath. "Yes, he did. He and his partner met with Tommy a couple of hours ago. They questioned him about the night that Laura Brewster was killed in her apartment."

"Kelly told us that Tommy always works nights at a medical clinic until six in the morning," Megan interrupted. "So, that means he has an alibi, right?"

Burt wagged his head slowly, his expression sad. "I'm afraid not. Tommy told Dan that he didn't work his usual shift at the clinic that night because he needed to study for a big exam in his family medicine residency program. He got another physician to substitute for him at the clinic. And Tommy said he stayed at home in his apartment all night and studied for the exam. So now, Tommy has no alibi."

Kelly stared at Burt in disbelief. She glanced at her friends, and their expressions mirrored hers. *Shock.*

"Oh, no!" Megan exclaimed, knitting sinking to her lap.

"Good Lord! That means no more alibi," Lisa said, staring at Burt.

"What did Dan say, Burt?" Kelly asked. "Are they considering Tommy a suspect now?"

"They have to. He had the Big Two — Motive and Opportunity." Burt's face creased with worry lines.

"Oh, brother," Megan said, brows furrowing as she picked up the black-and-white yarn once again.

"Have you told Barb yet?" Kelly asked Burt.

"No, not yet. I'm actually waiting for her to come in. She's checking on her class's last projects." Just then the sound of a cell phone text message came in. Burt dug into his pocket and pulled out the phone. "Okay. Mimi just texted me that she sees Barb parking her car right now." Burt pushed back his chair with a scrape. "I'll meet her outside so we can be private. Barb needs to hear this kind of news from a friend. I'll talk to you folks later." Burt turned and hurried through the central yarn room.

Kelly stared after him. *Not good,* she thought to herself. *Not good at all.*

"Oh, no. Now Tommy is a real suspect. Poor Barb. How's she going to handle this?" Megan said, staring into the central yarn room.

"Not well," Kelly said, frowning. "Barb is a super overprotective mother, and Tommy is her precious son. Clearly, the light of her life. She won't be able to accept it."

"Poor Tommy," Megan added sadly.

"I hate to be the one who says this, but what if Tommy is guilty?" Lisa suggested. "He did change his clinic schedule that night. Maybe he didn't use the time to study. Maybe he went over to Laura Brewster's apartment." Lisa glanced up from her knitting.

Megan stared at Lisa, clearly surprised. Kelly, however, looked over at her friend. "You're right, Lisa. There's always that possibility. I want to believe that Tommy's innocent, but we'll have to wait and see what the police learn in their investigation. Meanwhile, we can keep our doubts to ourselves as we support Barb. This is going to hit her hard."

Megan nodded, still looking at her knitting. "Like a stab to the heart."

Lisa shoved her knitting back into the bag

and rose from her chair. "I need to return to the university now. Besides, I think Kelly has something to ask you, Megan." With that, Lisa sped from the room.

"That was sudden," Megan said, staring after Lisa, then turned to Kelly. "What is it you wanted to ask?"

Kelly mulled over how best to present this suggestion to Megan. She figured she'd appeal to Megan's ever-present streak of curiosity. Plus, her penchant for risk taking. In that, she and Megan were alike.

"Let's just say I've been doing some sleuthing. Looking into this Laura Brewster. And it turns out she's an extremely complicated person. Holds grudges and is not above exacting revenge." Kelly paused dramatically.

"Revenge?" Megan's big brown eyes popped wide with obvious interest. "What did she do?"

"I went to see a fellow student of Laura's who witnessed an altercation between Laura and Professor Smith. He's the anatomy professor who was accused of sexual assault by a student. This other student saw the entire scene between Laura and the professor. Laura was pleading with him to allow her to do extra credit to raise her exam grade."

Megan screwed up her face. "What! Who does she think she is?"

"Exactly," Kelly agreed. "Anyway, Professor Smith refused and said it wouldn't be fair to the other students in class."

"That's right!" Megan emphasized in a righteous tone.

"Anyway, this fellow student, Sandy, said Professor Smith walked away but Laura stayed and stared at his office for several minutes. Then she went into the restroom. Sandy went back to studying. She was sitting on the floor across the hall and they never noticed her. A few minutes later, Sandy heard a woman crying, then she saw Laura run out of the bathroom and down the hall then down the stairs. Her hair was messed up and her blouse was all open at the top. Sandy forgot about it until she heard the next day that a professor was accused of sexual assault by a student. Then she learned it was Professor Smith, and she said she just knew that it was Laura Brewster who accused him. Falsely." Kelly leveled her gaze at Megan.

Megan stared back, her brown eyes huge, clearly shocked. "Good Lord! She lied! And smeared that professor!"

"And from what Sandy and others told me, Professor Smith's life pretty much fell apart after that. He didn't get promoted, nobody wanted to collaborate with him, and his wife even left him."

Megan screwed up her face again. "That's awful! Poor man!"

"I know. I felt awful hearing that, especially after learning that Laura Brewster is the one who accused Tommy of sexual assault. That's why I started asking questions."

"Oh, my gosh! She's the one who accused him?"

Kelly nodded. "So naturally I'm trying to find out as much as I can about this Laura. This student Sandy was in the same study group with Laura and said Laura mentioned there was a student from her high school in that class. She didn't get the person's name. But apparently it was Westgate High School in Denver. That's where I thought you might be able to help me. I wanted to check the university enrollment records to see who else went to Westgate High School and was also in that anatomy class with Laura." She gave Megan a smile.

Megan looked back at Kelly and slowly a sly smile spread across her face. "I get your drift, Kelly. You want me to help you 'sleuth around,' don't you?"

"If you would be so kind. Lisa already

gave me the psych department's general log-in code. She suggested we get in and out quickly."

"What's this 'we' business? You mean *me,*" Megan jabbed, then laughed.

"Well, yes," Kelly admitted and handed her the slip of paper. "Do you think you can do it? Find the information without causing a problem?"

Megan gave her a tolerant expression. "Piece of cake. This is my domain, Sherlock. So, leave me to it." She shoved her knitting bag aside. "I'll use your laptop for this. Slide it over here, please. You've got it in your knitting bag." Megan wiggled her fingers.

"You know me too well," Kelly said with a grin as she pulled out her laptop and pushed it across the table to Megan. No mention of Ethics or Moral Equivalency surfaced.

"Have you been keeping those squirrels in line? Have you, Carl?" Kelly said in the singsong voice her dog loved while she scratched behind his left ear. Carl leaned his front paws on the cottage fence and bent sideways, emitting a little doggie groan of pleasure as Kelly hit the sweet spots. *Oooooooooooooh, good!* He offered the right

176

ear for similar rubbing, and Kelly rubbed behind that ear, laughing as Carl crooned.

The sound of footsteps on gravel behind her caused Kelly to turn. Megan approached, knitting bag over her shoulder. "I'm heading back to my office. Got a conference call with one of my clients. I shut down your laptop and left it up front with Rosa."

"Thanks. You were successful, I take it."

Megan gave her a super-tolerant expression. "*Mais oui, mademoiselle.* I sent you an e-mail. See you at the game tonight." Megan gave a half wave and quickly walked to her car.

"I hope the e-mail's not in French," Kelly called behind her.

Megan shot Kelly a grin before jumping inside her car and revving the engine.

TEN

Sunday morning

Kelly headed toward the café, hoping to find Burt. She rounded the corner from the loom room and nearly ran into him.

"Whoa!" Burt said, jumping back, mug of iced coffee in hand.

"Oooops, sorry, Burt. I forgot to slow down," Kelly apologized. "Can you come outside with me for a minute? I've got to tell you something I heard the other day."

"Sure thing, Kelly. Now, you've got me curious," Burt said with a smile as he followed Kelly out the front door and onto the front step.

The intense July heat was a sharp contrast to the cool air-conditioned knitting shop. So Kelly pulled out a wrought iron chair in the shaded alcove at the front of the shop. She had old memories of seeing her aunt Helen sitting in that alcove, knitting on her lap, looking out into the pastures, watching the sheep graze. Burt settled into a chair across the wrought iron table from her.

There was no one else around, but even so, Kelly leaned forward a bit. "On Friday I went to visit one of Lisa's friends who had classes with Laura Brewster. I'd asked Lisa earlier to check with her friends to see if any of them knew her. Turns out, Lisa's friend Sandy was also a grad student in the Anatomy and Physiology Department, and she had an interesting story to tell."

"Okay. I'm listening," Burt said with a smile before sipping his iced coffee.

"It seems Sandy witnessed an argument between Laura Brewster and Professor Paul Smith. Sounded like Laura was trying to get him to change her bad exam grade. Smith refused and walked away. Sandy said Laura stared after him for a while, then went into the women's restroom. A couple of minutes later, Laura came running out, crying loudly, her blouse opened and hair messed up. She ran down the hall crying and raced out of the building. Sandy was sitting on the floor across from Professor Smith's office, so she saw the entire scene. She didn't think anything of it at first until she learned that Professor Smith had been accused of sexual assault by a student. Sandy had a feeling in her gut that the student was Laura Brewster." Kelly took a drink from her own mug of iced coffee.

Burt's smile had changed to a frown as he listened. "Did this Sandy tell anyone what she saw?"

"She told one study group friend who advised her not to say anything. After all, Sandy didn't really *see* anything. Just an argument and a young woman running from the restroom."

Burt gazed out onto the golf course greens, dark clouds starting to gather. "She's right. All that scene does is raise questions and suppositions. But it does catch you by surprise. It makes you wonder even more about Laura Brewster's motivation in accusing Tommy."

"It sure does," Kelly agreed. "It sounds like Laura Brewster was someone who held a grudge."

"I'll mention this to Dan when he gets back from Denver. He's down there for a meeting. Meanwhile, I wouldn't tell anyone else, Kelly," Burt advised, turning back to her.

"I've already told Lisa, since Sandy was her friend. And Megan, but no one else."

"Good. Let's just keep this particular bit of Laura Brewster's background to ourselves. Right now, it's simply supposition."

Kelly nodded. "Agreed. By the way, doesn't the department keep those official complaint files for officers to check? The complaint against Professor Smith should still be there."

Burt found his smile at last. "You're ahead of me, Sherlock. We'll have to wait for Dan."

Kelly snapped her fingers in a pretend gesture of impatience as Burt chuckled.

Early afternoon

"Now, wet down the entire piece again," Mimi said. "It needs to be thoroughly wet."

Kelly dutifully followed Mimi's instructions, shaking the plastic bottle of liquid dish soap and water and spraying it onto her fire-engine red silk scarf, which was stretched out over a worktable covered in plastic.

That morning, Kelly and the other three students in Mimi's Wet Felting class had pressed their chosen colored fibers onto their solid-color silk scarves by wetting the scarves and the fibers thoroughly by spraying them with the soapy solution. Then Kelly and the others methodically pressed the bunches and clumps of fibers onto their silk scarves with a sponge that was thoroughly wet with the soapy solution.

It had taken Kelly and her classmates over an hour to carefully apply all the fibers they'd chosen to add to their silk scarves. Kelly had stayed with her original inspiration of burnt orange and deep rose. She was really pleased with the effect those colors created once applied to the fire-engine red silk.

Once all the fibers had been carefully pressed into place on their silk scarves, Mimi instructed Kelly and her classmates to thoroughly wet down their creations with the soapy solution — not once, but twice.

Kelly held the spray bottle poised over her scarf. She placed her open palm gently on the fibers. They felt wet, not simply damp. Surely that was enough, Kelly thought. But she decided to check with the Sage Herself. Mimi.

"Mimi, this feels wet to me," she said, pressing her hand against the fibers again. "What do you think?"

Mimi walked around the table in the workroom and touched her fingers to Kelly's creation. "That feels right. Everyone, touch Kelly's scarf and make sure yours feels just as wet."

The two younger women across the table from Kelly reached over and pressed their fingers gently to Kelly's red and orange and rose fibers.

"Oooooooh, this is wetter than mine," the blonde said, then picked up her spray bottle and proceeded to spray her scarf again.

The young redhead with gaminelike features and shortcut hair pressed her fingers to Kelly's scarf and closed her eyes. "Hmmmmmm, mine feels just as wet. I think. Hmmmmm, maybe not. Yeah, this is a little wetter." She too went back to her side of the worktable and started spraying.

"Boy, this is going to take a long time to dry out," the older woman said as she felt Kelly's scarf, then touched her own creation. "Just about the same. What do you think, Mimi?"

Mimi obliged and felt the woman's dramatic royal blue and shamrock green creation. Those bright fibers against a soft turquoise silk scarf looked stunning to Kelly's eye. She'd always loved blues and greens together. She'd have to tell Megan to check out her class's creations once they were finished. Megan also loved bright blues and greens.

"I think yours feel just right, Sara. Exactly like Kelly's," Mimi said. "And don't worry about the drying. All of you still have a lot of prep work to do before you lay these pieces out to dry. In fact, you won't be finished today, probably. It may take until tomorrow." She smiled at them all.

"What kind of prep work?" the redhead asked.

"You'll be helping to dry out the scarves by wrapping them in a thick towel around a rolling pin, then rolling them over and over again to help squeeze out the water. The rolling also thoroughly presses the fibers into the silk so they completely join as one piece of fabric."

"Okay, I've gotta see that to understand what we're doing," the blonde said. "I can't picture it yet."

"I glimpsed one of your classes a few months ago, Mimi, and I watched those students rolling over and over and over again," Sara said with a smile. "They sure were rolling a lot."

Mimi's smile widened. "Oh, yes. It takes five hundred rolls to do one scarf."

Kelly and all of her classmates stared wide-eyed at Mimi. The blonde piped up. "Five hundred! Yeow! How long does that take?"

"Forever," the redhead opined, wagging her head. "Oh, brother. I'm gonna have arm muscles to brag about by the time this is finished."

Mimi laughed her little laugh. "Well, you might. Actually that's a good thing. Burt says you're stronger afterward, and that's always a good thing." She looked at Kelly. "This should be easy for you, Kelly, since you play softball."

Kelly smiled. "Probably. All those years of throwing the ball and batting. But, five hundred rolls is still a lot. We'd better break it down in segments." She glanced around at her three classmates. "Do fifty and see how that feels. Everybody is different."

"That's right. You'll need to get it all done by tonight or early tomorrow morning at the latest, while the fabric is at its dampest," Mimi advised, reaching over and touching the blonde's bubblegum pink and lime green fibers joined to an electric pink scarf. "This feels ready, Cindy."

"How about mine?" the redhead asked, giving her scarf and fibers one last spray.

Mimi reached over and touched the bright yellow and vibrant purple fibers on the young woman's dark gray scarf. "Yours, too, Melanie. Nice and wet. By the way, those colors are really going to pop next to your gorgeous red hair."

"Thanks. They're kind of shocking, and I like that," Melanie said with a grin. "Shake people up."

"Wake them up is more like it," the older woman teased.

Mimi clapped her hands together. "All right. You've all done very well. Now, grab one of those thick towels over there on the shelves. And grab a rolling pin, too." She pointed to the other side of the workroom where the wall was covered with yarn bins. On the bottom level, one bin held four towels. The bin next to it had wooden rolling pins stored.

"I'll get them." Kelly quickly walked over and grabbed all four of the towels. She also managed to gather two rolling pins. Melanie stepped up and carried the rest. Both Kelly and Melanie handed out towels and wooden rolling pins to their classmates.

"Okay, now you're each going to lay out the towel right beside your scarf." Mimi went to stand beside Cindy. She opened up the light blue bath towel and spread it on the table beside Cindy's electric pink scarf. "Carefully lift your scarf plus the plastic beneath and place them together on the towel."

Kelly watched as Mimi untaped the plastic layer from the table, where it had been fixed in place. Then she gently lifted both the layer of plastic plus the scarf on top and placed them on the outstretched towel.

"You're going to gently roll up the towel like you were taking it to the beach except you'll have a rolling pin inside," Mimi instructed. "Now, take the rolling pin and gently wrap the scarf, the towel, and plastic all together around the rolling pin."

"Okay, here goes," Melanie said as she started to remove the tape that held the plastic to the worktable.

"We might as well get at it if we're going to do five hundred rolls today," Sara said as she placed a rolling pin at the edge of her scarf. Slowly she started to roll all three — scarf, towel, and plastic — around the wooden rolling pin.

Kelly followed suit, gently placing the rolling pin at the edge of her scarf, then carefully, carefully wrapping the scarf, towel, and plastic around the rolling pin. Glancing up once, she noticed Melanie and Cindy doing the same.

Mimi hovered over them. Kelly took that as a compliment that Mimi no longer hovered over her and whatever project she undertook. Apparently, Kelly had moved up a notch on the expertise scale in Mimi's eyes. Who would have thought? Kelly smiled to herself.

Kelly carefully wrapped the last few inches of scarf, plastic, and towel around the rolling pin. It was no longer visible inside the thick roll. Only the red handles were sticking out of each end.

"All right, everyone. Now we can start our arm exercises. Get a chair if you want or simply lean over the table, and let's do these rolls together to start, okay? You're going to roll it out as far as you can without the towel roll opening up. Then you're going to roll it back. Out and back is one roll."

"Oh, darn," Melanie said. "I was hoping out and back would count as two."

"Dream on," Cindy joked.

"You guys are stronger than you think," Kelly said in an effort to encourage her classmates.

"Boy, I hope you're right," Sara said, rolling her arms out straight, then back. "That's one."

Kelly, Melanie, Cindy, and Mimi all laughed as they each started rolling.

A little later

"My arms are aching," Cindy said, rolling her wrapped towel a little slower. "And I've got two hundred to go."

"We'll take another break. Doing it in sets of fifty at a time then taking a break makes it easier," Mimi said. "I'll stay here with you all until you're finished."

Kelly started another set of fifty. She was starting four hundred. Clearly, all her years of sports, especially throwing softballs and swinging a bat, had given Kelly extrastrong arm muscles. Consequently, she wasn't tiring as fast as the other three. Strangely, Melanie and Cindy, who were younger, were tiring faster than their older classmate Sara. Kelly thought she knew why. With their sleeveless summer tops, Kelly could see whatever arm muscles they had flex every time they rolled the large towel roll. Kelly didn't see much muscle mass in either Cindy's or Melanie's arms. That told Kelly neither one of them exercised or worked out regularly. Building arm strength happened naturally whenever someone worked out a few times each week.

"Wow . . . my arms are sore now," Melanie said, dropping the rolling pin–towel setup. She rubbed her upper left arm.

"You know, doing this motion reminds me of those old Hollywood movies I saw as a child. There were a couple that took place in ancient Rome and had scenes of Roman galley slaves rowing those longboats."

"Oh, yes, I remember those," Mimi said. "The galley slaves were chanting as they rowed."

"That's right," Sara said as she continued

to roll beside Kelly. "They did it rhythmically in time with each stroke of the oars. Like 'Row! Row!' "

Mimi chuckled. "As I remember, there was also a slave master on the ship with a big whip who kept them all in line and rowing."

"Actually, they were all chained by the ankles, that's what kept them there. In fact if their boat was sunk in battle, they would go down with it," Sarah added.

"Oooooh, that's awful," Cindy said, rolling slowly.

"Life of a slave," Sara said. "Maybe these last rolls will go faster if we chant something like 'Row! Row!' " She grinned. "We even have a slave master watching over us." She pointed to Mimi then began to chant, "I must row. I must row," as she kept rolling.

Mimi chuckled. "Well, at least I don't have a whip, so that's good."

"Row or die," Sara changed the chant. "Row or die."

Kelly had to laugh. "Born to row, born to row," she chanted.

Sara and Mimi laughed.

Melanie frowned. "I don't like the slave ship image. Let's picture something else," she suggested. "So we can get this done. Maybe something funny."

"I don't know if I can finish now," Cindy said. "My arms are aching already."

"C'mon, you don't want to have to come back tomorrow," Melanie goaded.

"Believe me, your arms will ache even more if you come back tomorrow to finish," Kelly advised. "Your muscles will be really sore. Hang in there and finish now. Then you can go home and take a hot shower and relax."

"That's right. Oh, and buy some of that muscle rub cream at the drugstore. That will really help those sore muscles. After the hot shower, of course." Sara kept her methodical rhythm going. "Let's see . . . something funny, something funny."

Kelly was already up to four hundred and fifty, so she took a quick break, wondering if there was any other way to encourage her flagging classmate Cindy to keep going. It looked like Melanie was gritting her teeth and bearing it. But Cindy was clearly about to throw in the towel. Literally.

Sara spoke up again. "Hey, I've got a new chant. Since we don't like the Roman rowing chant, let's try this. Besides, it's funny. And it rhymes, too," she teased.

"Bring it. I need something to distract myself. I'm coming up on four hundred," Melanie said.

"Four hundred!" Cindy exclaimed. "I'm only on two hundred sixty . . . or something."

"Give it a shot, Sara," Kelly encouraged. "Cindy needs something to get through to the finish line."

"Okay, I just thought of it." Sara paused her motions for a second, then started another roll as she chanted: "I must, I must, I must increase my bust. I must, I must, I must increase my bust."

Kelly burst out laughing and broke her rolling stride. Both Cindy and Melanie joined in the laughter, and Mimi laughed so hard she had to sit down. Kelly and Melanie picked up the chant, and after a minute Cindy picked up the towel-wrapped rolling pin and joined her classmates.

Later that afternoon

"Hey, there," Megan said as she walked into Lambspun's main room. She dropped her new felted knitting bag onto the library table.

Kelly looked up from the blue and green ribbon yarns she was knitting into a scarf. "How's the workload going? Are you keeping those clients in line?" she teased.

"Kind of. One of my IT clients had his regular monthly panic attack, so I had to talk him down this morning. I swear, he's gotta cut back on the caffeine intake." She folded her arms on the knitting bag. "So, tell me. What were you able to find out from the information I sent you? There was only one student who went to Westgate High School the same year Laura Brewster did and was also in the same semester's section of Professor Smith's anatomy class. Nancy Marsted. So, it's got to be her, right?"

"That's what I figure. And thanks to you, O Mighty Master of Software Espionage, I had her e-mail. I sent her a message and asked if we could meet for coffee so I could ask some questions about that anatomy class. I haven't heard back yet." Kelly took a sip of coffee from her ever-present mug.

Megan grinned. "Mighty Master, huh? I like it. Maybe I'll put that on a tee shirt. Hey, what about Watson? You're Sherlock, and I can be Watson."

Kelly chuckled. "You got it. Nobody else is in your league. Watson, it is."

"All riiiiiiight." Megan gave a fist pump. "I will definitely put that on a tee shirt. It'll drive everyone crazy wondering what it means."

Kelly laughed out loud this time. "I love it. It's *so* you, Megan."

Megan pulled a bright pink knitted top

from her bag. It looked halfway finished.

"Oooooooh, that's a pretty shade of pink. Perfect for you with your coloring," Kelly said admiringly.

Megan smiled. "Thanks, but you could wear this, Kelly. You're just too conservative with colors."

"No, I'm not!" Kelly protested. "I wear red and bright blue."

Megan looked over at Kelly with a patient expression. "Everyone can wear red. And bright blue is easy. I'm talking about the other colors. The daring ones, like this. 'Bubblegum pink.' " She read from the label.

"The 'daring' colors, huh?" Kelly said with a wry smile. "I'll take that under advisement."

"You do that. It'll shake up your wardrobe."

Rosa walked into the room then. "Kelly, you were in Mimi's Wet Felting class today, right?"

"Yes, I was. Do you need me to move my scarf or something?"

"No, we're good. I already moved the four of them into the back room of the office to finish drying. They all look super. I love the colors you chose, Kelly. Deep rose and orange against fire-engine red. Striking,"

Rosa said before she scurried into the workroom.

Kelly looked over at Megan with a cocky smile. "Did you hear that, Miz Color Expert? *Striking.* So there." She made a face.

Megan chuckled. "Orange against fire-engine red? I'm proud of you, Kelly. There's hope for you yet."

Kelly gave an exasperated sigh and concentrated on knitting the shiny ribbon yarns. It was easy to make a mistake and suddenly find twelve stitches on the needles rather than ten. Kelly counted to make sure there were only ten. Suddenly she heard a distinctive beep on her cell phone, signifying an e-mail message just arrived. Pulling the phone from her bag, she glanced at the screen. "Good. Nancy Marsted didn't blow me off. She can meet for coffee tomorrow afternoon in the university plaza. Perfect."

"Aha," Megan said, looking up from the bubblegum pink yarn. "The game is afoot!"

Kelly laughed softly.

Kelly stepped down into the garden patio at the back of the shop late that afternoon. Empty now of café customers since it was four o'clock. Because of that, Kelly often chose to sit in the shade outside, surrounded by greenery, while she worked on client accounts. Choosing a shady table under the overhanging branches of the cottonwood tree, Kelly settled in for an afternoon's work. Tonight would be softball practice.

The familiar accounting spreadsheets came to life on her laptop, and Kelly checked her file folders for the appropriate column of numbers to update.

Suddenly she heard her name being called. "Hey, Kelly? Do you have a minute?"

She looked up to see Burt headed her way, holding a big white plastic drink cup emblazoned with Big Box's logo. "For you, Burt? Always." She pushed her laptop aside as her friend, mentor, and father figure pulled up a chair across the table from her.

Burt took a big sip of his drink and looked around the shady nook. "It's nice here in the shade. The late afternoon sun is behind the trees," he pointed out. "Cuts the heat, doesn't it?"

"Sure does. What's up? I can tell you've heard something."

Burt smiled and settled into a chair across from her. "You know me too well," he teased.

"Scary, isn't it? We can read each other easily now."

"Okay. First, let me update you on what

Dan said to me this afternoon before I told him about your visit with Sandy. Dan told me the medical examiner found traces of alcohol, rubbing alcohol, on Laura Brewster's neck. Now, he's found there were also signs that the skin on her neck had been rubbed hard. Dan figures the killer must have tried to eliminate fingerprints. And there were none found, which indicates the killer must have worn gloves."

"Does that throw a wrench into the violent intruder theory? I mean, how many people who break into campus apartments wear gloves?"

"You'd be surprised. Those break-ins aren't always spur-of-the-moment crimes. You know . . . they see an apartment patio door ajar and decide to sneak in and grab what they can then run off. Some of those break-ins are well planned. Some thieves are experts in stealing the expensive stuff and selling it in Denver. It's become a real racket."

Kelly looked out into the greenery. "And students are an all-too-inviting target. So many of them go out drinking with friends, then come home and forget to lock their apartment doors. Then they fall asleep on the couch in front of the television. That makes it all too easy for thieves. I can see someone sneaking in and stealing stuff while the students are snoring on the sofa."

Burt nodded. "Oh, yeah. And sometimes the thief is one of the victim's friends. They know where the good stuff is."

"So you think the police are leaning toward the intruder who turned violent? You said the apartment was ransacked. I can't picture Tommy taking time to pull out drawers and throw stuff around."

Burt gave her a wry smile. "True, there's the appearance that it was a break-in gone bad. Even her purse was found on the sidewalk a block away. But Dan and the department can't ignore that Tommy did take that night off from working at the clinic to study. And he has no witnesses to confirm that. So, I'm afraid Tommy is still very much in the department's bull's-eye."

"That's what worries me, Burt."

Burt sighed. "Yeah, me, too. Dan said they were going to question Tommy again tomorrow. So, I'm hoping he may remember something he did that can confirm his whereabouts. Like going out for pizza. Something. Anything."

Kelly looked at her dear friend. "Boy, that has the sound of desperation to it."

"Yeah, I'm afraid it does." Burt looked out into the greenery. "And Tommy had better take their family lawyer with him this time."

Once again, Kelly didn't have anything to say. Events were moving along at a faster pace now. A stray thought took her attention then. "By the way, was Dan surprised when you told him about the incident with Laura Brewster and the professor?"

"Ohhhhhhh, yes. He was definitely surprised. And he promised to get back to me. Don't worry. I'll let you know what Dan finds out as soon as I know."

"Thanks, Burt. I don't know if it will lead to anything, but maybe. I just have this funny feeling that there's more about Laura Brewster we don't know. In fact, I'm going to meet with a classmate of hers tomorrow morning and see what I can learn about Laura. This girl went to high school with her and was in that same anatomy class Laura was in. So let's see if I learn anything interesting."

Burt chuckled. "Now it's your turn to keep *me* posted, Kelly."

"Turnabout's fair play, Burt," Kelly teased.

Eleven

Early Monday Morning

Kelly heard her cell phone's music as she was pushing open the glass door to the grocery store. She glanced at the screen and saw Burt's name and promptly turned around and walked out of the store via the exit door, back into the early morning heat.

"Hey, Burt, what's up?" she said, walking around the corner of the store to find some shade.

"Hi, Kelly. It sounds like you're outside. I won't keep you. Just wanted to tell you that I heard from Dan. He left me a message. He checked those official complaint files, and the woman who lodged the complaint of sexual assault against Professor Paul Smith was Laura Brewster."

"I *knew* it! I could feel it," Kelly exclaimed, causing a shopper pushing a grocery cart to turn around and stare. Kelly walked farther away from the cart area.

"You already said that Dan was surprised when you first told him what Sandy observed. Did he say anything else now?"

"He sure did. Dan told me to thank you for that lead. He and his partner will pay Professor Smith a visit soon." Burt's chuckle came over the phone. "Good going, Sherlock."

Kelly just smiled as she watched the shoppers rush from their parked cars into the air-conditioned supermarket.

"I can get those interim statements to you tomorrow, Don," Kelly said into her cell phone. "But the numbers are going to change by the end of the month — you know that." She leaned against her desk in the corner of her cottage.

"I will bear that in mind, Kelly," Denver developer Don Warner said, the sound of a smile in his voice. "Don't worry. I don't plan to commit any capital until we've got the complete July statements. You'd have my head on a platter." He chuckled.

"You've got that right," Kelly teased her client. "Who're you meeting again?"

"That investor who wants to develop a strip mall on the northeast corner of the interstate and Route 7. You know that area is heating up."

Glancing outside the patio door into the cottage backyard, she spotted Carl stretched out on the grass. Snoozing in the morning sunshine. In another two hours, the July sun would be way too hot, and Carl would seek the shade of the cottonwood tree for his naps. Just like the café patrons who loved eating outdoors in the summer. Very few ever claimed the sunny table on the porch in July.

Slight movements in her flower garden to the right of the patio caught Kelly's eye. There was Brazen Squirrel digging away beside the salvia plants at the corner of the flower beds. The bright red spiky flowers jutted straight up, proclaiming their presence. Brazen ignored the flowers. He was searching for any nuts or seeds he'd neglected to dig up last winter. So far, Kelly noticed the busy little creature was coming up empty-pawed. Nothing. No seeds or nuts to be found.

The loud sound of a truck horn blaring on the busy street running between the shop and the Big Box shopping center caused Carl to raise his head briefly. Brazen quickly froze in place, squirrely attention fixed on Big Dog. Carl's head plopped down onto the grass again with a big doggie sigh. *All is well.* Nap time called again.

"It sure is. It's amazing to see that empty crossroads come to life. There's a gas station on the northwest corner already, so that investor will be getting in early. What's he putting up?"

"He hinted it was a franchise of a major national fast-food chain. But he knows he'll need that corporate approval before he moves forward. So keep your fingers crossed."

"Will do." Kelly heard the telltale sound of another phone call coming in. "And I'll send those interim statements later this morning. I want to look at them again."

"Thanks, Kelly. Talk to you later." Don Warner's phone had also sounded with an incoming call. It was a busy morning.

Kelly saw Burt's name flashing on her phone screen and clicked on. "Hey, Burt. Are you out doing errands already?"

"I sure am. Finished two stores and I'm getting gas right now. I wondered if you'd be at the shop later? I wanted to update you on what I've heard from Dan."

Kelly swished the last of the coffee in her mug. "Did Dan say how Tommy's questioning went?"

"I don't want to say more because I'm here at the gas pump, but I'll be back at the shop in a few minutes."

"Okay. Look for me in the main room. See you." Kelly clicked off and shoved the phone into her summer pants pocket then went to the kitchen. She drained the last of the coffeepot into her carryout mug, then gathered her laptop and files and shoved them into her over-the-shoulder briefcase. Glancing once more into the backyard, Kelly spied Carl's two big water dishes and saw that they were full. Big Dog was still asleep, and Brazen was skittering across the grass to the bushes along the side of the chain-link fence.

The summer morning was progressing on schedule, she thought as she headed for the front door of her cottage. Time to check those interim July statements. Working in Lambspun's main room and air-conditioning was a lot more comfortable in July.

"Hey, there, Kelly."

Kelly looked up at the sound of her name being called. "Hi, Burt, how're you doing?" She pushed her laptop computer to the side and settled into her chair at Lambspun's large knitting table.

Burt walked over and settled into the chair beside her. "I'm doing well," Burt said, his familiar smile missing. He folded his arms on the table and leaned closer to Kelly. "I'm glad there's no one else at the table, so they won't overhear. Gossip spreads in this town too fast as it is."

"Especially at the university, from what I hear," Kelly added and leaned closer to him.

Burt nodded. "I heard from Dan again and he said Tommy did not hold up well when he was questioned for the second time this morning. Apparently he stammered and repeated himself, couldn't finish sentences, and was clearly nervous trying to explain why he was at home studying that night."

Kelly shook her head. She had a bad feeling about this. "Not good. Not good at all."

"That's for sure. Dan was surprised and said Tommy actually looked frightened at times. Needless to say, Tommy's behavior definitely raised Dan's suspicions."

"Naturally." Kelly took a deep drink of her coffee. This was depressing news to hear. A stray memory poked up its head. "You know, I think I recall Barb saying that Tommy didn't hold up well three years ago when he was a suspect in his former girlfriend's murder. One of those detectives said he looked scared to death. Maybe Tommy has a pathological fear of police in uniforms or something."

Burt frowned. "Or something. But a

detective can't help but wonder why Tommy looked so scared if he was innocent of Laura Brewster's murder. It raises my suspicions, too."

Kelly considered Burt's statement. Burt had known Tommy since he was a child and had vouched for Tommy's character three years ago as well as now. If Burt was having second thoughts, that gave Kelly pause.

"Especially now that the medical examiner has found traces of rubbing alcohol on Laura's neck," Burt continued. "All over her neck. Like someone was trying to remove any trace of fingerprints. So Dan and the other detectives think that finding indicates the killer was someone who knew about medicine or worked at hospitals. Someone like that would think of cleaning prints off the victim's neck."

Kelly stared into Burt's eyes and saw the suspicions there. The same suspicions that rose inside her now. "And that points a big red arrow at Tommy."

Burt nodded gravely. "It sure does."

Kelly looked out into the adjoining central yarn room. Only one customer was browsing the yarn bins. "Poor Barb. This news is definitely going to hit her hard. Are you going to tell her?"

Burt sighed. "I really don't want to be the

one to tell her. Hopefully, Tommy will tell his mom."

The jingle of the shop front doorbell and the quick tap of footsteps sounded. Walking fast. Suddenly Barb charged into the main room. "Burt! I need to speak with you. I just heard from Tommy this morning, and he told me that a detective questioned him. *Again!*"

Barb's face was no longer flushed, but was pale, as if the blood had drained out of it. Kelly immediately pushed back her chair. "Here, Barb. Take my chair. I'm going to get more coffee."

"Thank you, Kelly." Barb looked at Kelly with a grateful expression. "It won't take long."

"You take as long as you need, Barb," Kelly reassured her, then she gave Barb's arm a pat. A Mother Mimi pat.

"Okay, a peppermint mocha with extra syrup," Kelly announced as she placed the specialty latte in front of the slender young woman seated on the other side of the outdoor café table.

Kelly chose one of the plaza tables that was slightly separated from the others in the expansive university plaza area. Students were everywhere. Walking back and forth from the two-story Student Union building, striding toward the various multistoried university buildings which held classrooms, sitting at tables talking to fellow students, slouched or stretched out on benches or on the concrete, dozing between classes. College students' habits hadn't changed that much over the years, Kelly noticed.

"Thanks a lot," Nancy Marsted said, smiling up at Kelly. Her light brown hair curled softly around her face and made her look younger than most of the other students.

"You're welcome," Kelly replied, settling into a chair on the opposite side of the table. "You're already in grad school, right?"

"Yes, I'm in my first year of grad school." Nancy took a sip of the sugary drink. She closed her eyes, obviously savoring, then looked up at Kelly. "So, you're thinking of taking that anatomy class?"

"Actually, I'm not going to take the class. But I know a student who did. Sandy Atkinson. Did you know her?"

Nancy shook her head before taking another sip of the latte. "No, that name isn't familiar."

Kelly continued. "Well, Sandy also knew another student in class who apparently indicated you were a friend of hers. Her name was Laura Brewster. Do you remember her?"

Nancy Marsted's brown eyes widened in obvious surprise, then a wary expression appeared. "I wouldn't say I was a friend of Laura's. More like an acquaintance. We went to the same high school and shared a college dorm room briefly. Why do you ask?"

Kelly decided to be completely honest. Hopefully, Nancy Marsted would respond in kind. It all depended on how close a friendship she'd shared with Laura Brewster. "To be totally honest, I'm trying to find out what I can about Laura Brewster. What kind of person she was —"

"What does it matter?" Nancy blurted. "You know she was the student who was killed in her campus apartment a couple of weeks ago, don't you? It no longer matters what kind of person she was."

Kelly chose her words carefully. "Actually, it does. A week before she died, she accused a friend's son who's a young medical doctor of sexual assault in his office."

Nancy Marsted's expression quickly changed. Kelly watched surprise replace the wariness. Then she closed her eyes and a different expression claimed her face. "Oh, God. Not again."

Kelly sat up straighter at that. "You're referring to Laura Brewster's sexual assault charge against Professor Paul Smith, aren't you?" Kelly asked quietly. The noise of passing students provided more than enough conversational privacy.

Nancy looked up at Kelly. "Yes. I was taking the same class with Laura that semester. It was the year we roomed together. I still remember how she acted after she'd gotten the exam papers back and Laura saw her grade." She closed her eyes. "I'd seen that look on her face before. Pure anger. She was enraged. She started pacing around the apartment, back and forth, mumbling to herself. I'd recognized that look before."

Kelly's buzzer went off. "Again? She'd gotten that mad before? Over what?"

"Oh, yes, several times," Nancy said with a weary sigh. "Over all sorts of things she considered slights or insults or instances when she didn't think she was being treated fairly in a class. Laura had come from a tough family life, and a college education was her way out. So grades were super important."

"How long would she stay mad?"

"Ohhh, the angry pacing and mumbling would go on for an hour or so, then she'd get real quiet. And she'd sit and stare out the windows and not say a word. That's when I knew someone was about to get payback."

"Payback? What do you mean?"

Nancy looked Kelly directly into her eyes. "Revenge. Laura was a master. She would choose the perfect payback for the guilty party. For instance, one professor was bragging about his new red sports car. So, when he gave Laura a lower grade in that biology class we were taking, she found out which car was his and went out late at night and keyed it on both sides. Really deep, she said." Nancy shook her head. "She'd checked the professor's schedule to find out which night he taught late and went out then."

"Wow, that was really mean," Kelly said, amazed at Laura's brazenly vicious behavior. "She told you every time she did something?"

Nancy closed her eyes again. "Ohhhhh, yes. Once I saw what kind of person I was rooming with that year, I figured I'd better stay on Laura's good side or she might start taking things out on me. Or things would start disappearing. I'd seen her bring home things she'd swiped from other students over petty little disagreements. A pretty scarf. A paperback book. Little things. So to protect myself, I'd say things like, 'Well, that'll show them,' whenever she'd tell me how she had gotten revenge on someone. That's what she liked to call it. Laura believed she was righting the scales of justice every time she exacted revenge. She got really energized from it. And since I had to stay in that housing contract with her until the end of the academic year, I decided to play it safe and stay out of her line of fire." She shook her head again. "I had only known her casually in high school, so I thought it would be okay to room with her that year. Boy, was I wrong."

"It sounds like the level of Laura's revenge increased over the years. By the time Professor Smith gave her a low grade, her revenge taking had become major league. Friends tell me Smith's entire career was ruined. Even his family life."

"God, yes. That really turned my stomach. I was counting the days until the semester's end. And I immediately signed up with a church group to share their housing arrangement. I told Laura that I'd joined a new church. Made it sound like I'd gotten really religious. I even started singing spiritual songs in the apartment. She seemed glad to see me leave in May." Nancy gave Kelly a sardonic look.

Kelly had to smile. "That was a smart move."

Nancy's expression sobered. "I'm sorry to hear about your friend's son. That's just awful. And it could ruin his entire career."

Kelly drained the last of her coffee in the cup. "Well, his career is the last thing Tommy's worried about now. Because of that sexual assault complaint that Laura filed with the police, Tommy has become the number one suspect in Laura's murder. You see, Tommy didn't work his usual shift at the clinic the night of her murder. He was home studying for a family medicine residency exam. No witnesses and no alibi."

Nancy Marsted's brown eyes widened. "Oh, no."

"Oh, yes." Kelly nodded sadly, then caught Nancy's gaze. "And we're all hoping something somewhere will help Tommy prove his innocence. I'll pass along all this information about Laura to a friend who was a detective, and he can pass it along to the cops. I have no idea if it will help or not. Tommy swears he did not touch her inappropriately during the exam, but like with Professor Smith it's a 'he said, she said' situation."

"I'm so sorry to hear that," Nancy said, her eyes clearly reflecting her concern.

Kelly looked out over the university plaza. "After listening to your description of

Laura's behaviors toward those who incurred her wrath, it makes me feel that her legacy of revenge has survived her. And it's still punishing people." She glanced back at Nancy and they both exchanged a look of sadness.

Mimi's blue eyes widened as she stared at Kelly. "Burt told me that alcohol removes fingerprints. Did you know that, Kelly?"

Standing beneath the portico near the front entrance of the shop to shade herself from the late-afternoon sun, Kelly took another sip of coffee. "I didn't know it until Burt told me." She shrugged. "Now the detectives think that indicated the killer knew something about medicine."

This time Mimi released a long sigh. "And that points right at Tommy."

Kelly continued. "What's worse is Burt told me Tommy didn't do well when he was questioned again. Apparently Tommy stuttered and stammered and acted nervous. Now you know how that looks to detectives. Dan's suspicions had to be aroused. Even Burt admitted he was getting suspicious. It's understandable."

"Burt said that?" Mimi asked, clearly surprised. "Why, he's known Tommy since he was a child, like I have."

Kelly decided this was as good a time as any to present the unthinkable thought to Mimi. "I know, Mimi. But I have to tell you that some of us are having doubts about Tommy. We didn't watch him growing up like you did. At least I got to meet Tommy. He's a nice guy, and apparently a good doctor. Hardworking, studious. I'd like to think Tommy is innocent of the charges and, of course, the murder. But none of us knows for sure. None of us can really know how someone else is going to react in certain situations. We can't get inside their heads. Nice guys can do bad things."

Mimi's expression sobered immediately and she stared at Kelly for a moment.

Kelly continued. "I have to admit, it's made Megan, Lisa, Jennifer, and me think. We don't know if Tommy would take advantage of a patient like that or not. None of us really knows. And we certainly don't know if he killed Laura in a sudden burst of anger."

Mimi drew back in shock. *"Kelly!"*

Kelly gestured. "I know it sounds awful to think that. But who knows? Maybe he went there to ask Laura to drop the charges, and she refused. Maybe Tommy panicked and reacted out of fear. We don't know." Kelly gave another shrug.

Mimi shook her head. "I will never believe that. Never."

Kelly opened the front door and waited for Mimi to step inside the foyer, then followed Mimi as she headed toward the front room. No one else was about. Even Rosa wasn't up front. "Don't hate me for saying that, Mimi," Kelly entreated, feeling slightly guilty now for broaching the subject. "But I'm trying to look at this entire situation from both sides. I started out believing Tommy was completely innocent of the assault charges. But when Lisa started telling us about some of the college girls she's spoken with and helped over at the university, I admit, it did make me think." She stared at Mimi. "The truth is, none of us can be really sure what happened at the clinic. As for the murder, I never figured Tommy could do that until I learned that he cancelled his clinic schedule that night. And he had no witnesses to his studying alone. It doesn't look good, Mimi. And now, he's looking guilty under questioning."

Mimi stared at Kelly, eyes wide, clearly shaken by what Kelly said. For the first time, Kelly saw doubt appear.

Burt came into the central yarn room, walking toward the front where Mimi and Kelly stood. He looked dejected to Kelly.

"How're you doing, Burt?" she asked quietly when he approached them.

"How is Barb taking it? The news from the medical examiner and Tommy's additional questioning?" Mimi looked at Burt anxiously.

Burt released a long sigh and moved closer to the counter. "Barb didn't say anything, but her face spoke volumes. She got pale. Or paler. I swear, I haven't seen color in that woman's face for over two weeks."

"Oh, poor thing," Mimi said. "Ever since we heard that Tommy didn't work at the clinic that night, Barb has looked halfway terrified."

"It's understandable," Burt added. "He's her only child, and he's a suspect in a murder. And everyone assumed that Tommy would have an alibi because he works the night shift. None of us were prepared for the shock of learning Tommy had no alibi for that night. And with the finding of rubbing alcohol on the victim's neck, naturally detectives are convinced the murderer was familiar with medical procedures."

Kelly could tell Burt was thoroughly dejected. His tone of voice, his facial expressions, his body language all spoke to Burt's mood. His warm, friendly self was nowhere to be seen.

"You know, Burt, I think you and Mimi both need to leave right now and take a drive up into the mountains. Go up into Rocky Mountain National Park. Stay and have dinner in one of those cafés in Estes Park. You two need to get away from all of this for a while."

Burt looked over at Kelly and the beginnings of a smile appeared. "Kelly, that's the best thing I've heard all day. Mimi, grab your purse. Let's go throw some clothes into a suitcase and head up into the mountains." Burt pushed away from the counter.

Mimi gave Kelly a grateful smile, and retrieved her purse from beneath the counter. "Would you tell Rosa to lock up, Kelly?"

"I'll be happy to," Kelly said as she watched her dear friends Burt and Mimi walk toward the foyer.

"Hey, Burt. I hope you guys are parked at the hotel and not rounding a curve in the Big Thompson Canyon," Kelly said over her cell phone as she stood in the gravel driveway outside Lambspun.

Burt's chuckle sounded over the line. "Don't worry. We just pulled into the hotel parking lot. I'm unloading suitcases. Mimi's already gone inside to the ladies' room. Thanks again for that suggestion, Kelly. At the first sight of those mountains as we rounded the bend into Estes Park, my blood pressure dropped about twenty points."

Kelly laughed out loud. "That makes me feel good, Burt. Listen, I won't keep you. I just wanted to update you on a little visit I made earlier today. I went to the university to meet one of Laura Brewster's high school classmates, hoping to learn more about her. You know, try to figure her out."

"Some people are impossible to figure out, Kelly. Even for professionals."

"Yeah, well, I think this Laura is one of them. Her school friend actually roomed with Laura their sophomore year at the university. Nancy, the friend, said Laura was someone who specialized in taking revenge on people, like professors who gave her a bad grade. Nancy said Laura actually keyed a professor's new sports car because he gave her a low grade in a biology class. Stealing things from students who had slighted her. Stuff like that."

"It certainly sounds sad to me. Laura Brewster definitely sounds like a person who needed a lot of help and maybe she didn't get it."

"Or, didn't want it," Kelly countered.

"Anyway, I thought I'd tell you. There's nothing I found that could help Tommy, unfortunately. It's simply background information on Laura Brewster. A complicated person for sure."

"Agreed, Kelly. We'll see you in a couple of days. Thanks again for the suggestion."

"Anytime, Burt."

"Did Cassie and her friend want any more of this fried rice?" Lisa asked, looking toward the screen door leading into Jennifer and Pete's family room. Cassie and her friend could be seen sitting cross-legged on the floor with large plates of Chinese food in their laps.

"I checked with them a minute ago, and they're good," Jennifer said as she set a glass pitcher of iced tea on the patio table. "They've got fried rice, orange chicken, spicy beef, and Pete's salad."

"And I brought home blueberry pie for dessert." Pete grinned as he ladled more orange chicken onto his plastic plate.

Greg sat up straighter in the wrought iron patio chair, nearly empty plastic plate in hand. "Blueberry pie! How many? Please tell me you brought two."

Pete chuckled. "Yes, I brought two. There's eight of us without the girls, and both of them will want seconds."

Greg's hand shot up in the air. "And me. I'm putting my order in."

"You know, I think I'll put my order in for seconds now. Don't want to risk losing the chance," Marty said with a big grin. Then he reached over and spooned more spicy chicken and fried rice onto his plate.

Kelly took a sip of her Fat Tire ale and set her empty plate aside. "I almost wish Pete had only brought one pie, so we could hear Greg complain."

"Weeping and wailing and lamentations," Megan teased. "Marty would join in that duet."

"Lamentations? Is that a book in the Bible?" Greg asked innocently.

"I think you mean Revelations," Steve said, then tipped back his bottle of craft brew.

"If you want lamentations, you should read the book of Job in the Old Testament. Now, *he* had problems," Pete said with a sly smile before he returned to his spicy beef.

"And lack of blueberry pie wasn't one of them," Jennifer joked as she leaned back into the shade beneath their backyard patio.

"Oh, boy, the King and Queen of Trivia are in the building," Marty announced.

"We'd better be ready for action."

Megan looked at Marty with concern. "Why? What are you planning to do?"

"I'll think of something." Marty grinned then leaned over and gave Megan a kiss on the cheek.

Another thought drifted into Kelly's head. It was time to inform all of the Gang. "You know who's really got trouble. Doctor Tommy. Barb's son. Burt told me today that police went to question Tommy yet again —"

"Why again?" Greg interrupted.

"Remember, officers questioned Tommy a couple of weeks ago after that girl accused him of sexual assault in his clinic office," Kelly said.

"How could we forget," Jennifer said, pouring iced tea into an ice-filled glass.

"Then Dan and another detective questioned Tommy after the girl's murder. That's when they learned he didn't work at the clinic the night she was killed in her apartment. Tommy told them he stayed at home to study for a big exam."

"Uh-oh," Greg said. "That's not good."

"You're right," Kelly continued. "Tommy has no alibi. And what's worse, Burt told me that Dan said Tommy didn't do well in his questioning, either. Apparently Tommy stuttered and stammered and acted nervous and had trouble answering their questions."

"Oh, brother." Pete grimaced.

"It gets worse. Now, the medical examiner found alcohol on the victim's neck, so they think the killer knew medical procedures." Kelly took a long drink of her favorite ale.

"Oh, no." Jennifer's eyes grew wider than usual. "He's acting like he's really guilty."

Kelly nodded. "Burt admitted that Tommy has a big bull's-eye on him right now."

"Wait a minute," Marty said, holding up his hand. "I thought these two crimes were separate. You're making it sound like the victim in both incidents was the same girl. Is that what you're saying?"

"Yes, that's right. Burt said the girl who lodged the assault charge was the same one who was killed." Kelly deliberately didn't give more details. "So you can see why Tommy would be considered a suspect, especially since he changed his work schedule the night of her murder."

Jennifer wagged her head. "Wow. That is damning. Tommy always seemed like such a nice guy. Quiet, studious, and a really good paramedic, I heard."

"I have to say that's bizarre," Marty observed, staring out into the backyard. Summer sounds of neighbors enjoying the outdoors could be heard all around. "That's one hell of a coincidence that the girl who accused Tommy is strangled by a late-night intruder a week or so later."

"What if it's not a coincidence?" Greg said, dropping his licked-clean plate onto the patio table. "What if Doctor Tommy really is innocent of those assault charges? Maybe that girl targeted him. I know of a professor who was targeted by a student who charged him with sexual assault. So, it happens. Suddenly Tommy sees his future medical career go down the drain, and he panics. Maybe he simply lost it." Greg shrugged. "Who knows? Maybe he went to her apartment to try and get her to withdraw the complaint, and she refused. Maybe Tommy killed her in a surge of anger. A crime of passion, right, Marty?"

Marty nodded. "Killing her in a fit of rage, that qualifies as a crime of passion."

"Who was the professor that was accused of assault?" Pete asked.

Kelly exchanged looks with Lisa and Megan but didn't say a word. Neither did they.

"He was a professor in the department of anatomy and physiology. Professor Smith. I knew his teaching assistant, and he said the professor was convinced that girl targeted him. He swore he never laid a hand on her." Greg leaned back in his chair and tipped back his beer.

"So you're saying that the girl who accused Tommy of assault may actually have targeted him?" Jennifer asked.

Greg shrugged. "I don't know. But like I said. It's happened before."

"Yeah, but even if that's true, it's a big stretch to think of killing somebody," Pete observed.

"I agree," Greg replied. "But I remember what happened to that professor. Professor Smith. My friend said he hit bottom big-time after those charges. I remember seeing him at the bar over in Old Town, Mason's, and he was usually drunk. Friends would have to take him home. He was in bad shape. And I remember his cussing out that girl, too."

"Someone told me that he had straightened himself out," Kelly interjected. "Stopped the drinking and stuff. She was a friend of that professor's family."

Greg shrugged again. "Well, it must not have taken hold. Because I remember seeing him a couple of weeks ago back at Mason's and drunk as a skunk. He even got into a fight with a guy who taunted him about that stuff. The professor got lit up and swung at the guy. Then they went at it. Bartender had to throw both of them out. That professor's definitely got a short fuse and still has a whole lot of anger inside. You could tell just listening to him rant at the bar. That complaint really stopped his academic career."

Kelly stared at Greg. "That was a couple of weeks ago?"

Greg took a drink of his craft brew. "Yeah. That would have been right after Doctor Tommy was accused of assault. We all know what a negative impact that assault complaint will have on Tommy's medical career. Who knows? Maybe good, studious, hardworking Tommy got mad enough to kill."

"Whoa, that's positively diabolical," Pete said.

"Yeah, it is, actually," Marty said, nodding. "You been reading those crime novels again?"

"People have been trying to get away with murder since the beginning of time," Greg opined sagely with a little smile.

"Have you been working with him, Lisa?" Megan teased. "Greg's bordering on the philosophical."

Everyone laughed at that, including Greg. Then he spoke up again. "You don't have to believe me. Ask Kelly. Ever since she got here years ago, she's been sleuthing around in local murders. And if I'm not mistaken, she's always found the real killer. So, if not for Kelly, those people would have gotten away with murder. You can ask Burt, because he's the one who told me that." Greg smiled and raised his bottle of craft brew in a salute.

Kelly joined her friends in their laughter. But Greg's comments started rattling around in the back of Kelly's mind.

TWELVE

Wednesday morning

Kelly slowed down in the hallway as she approached the corner opening into the loom room. She'd collided with too many people in the six years she'd been coming to Lambspun knitting shop. Moving too fast was the usual reason.

Looking around the corner Kelly saw no one. Good. She took a sip of her coffee and browsed the shelves that lined two entire walls. Fat triangular-shaped spools of specialty fibers — mohair, bamboo, silk, cotton, and combinations — sat in neat rows on each shelf, ready to be added to other yarns and knitted into garments or woven into decorative shawls, table runners, and other decorative pieces.

Every color in the spectrum and combinations of color. Decorative trims also caught her eye as did the rainbow of threads. Lambspun had something for every fiber artist — seamstress to spinner. Kelly stroked the soft gray mohair strands. She'd used them several times over the years.

A woman walked into the room now and approached the large loom that sat in the middle of the floor. She set her large fabric bag on the bench of the loom. Kelly and friends called it the Mother Loom. The woman settled on the bench and reached into her bag. Kelly noticed that there was a twelve-inch-wide table runner on the loom at the moment.

"Is that your work?" Kelly asked the woman, pointing at the table runner. It didn't look like it was woven from wool.

"Yes, it is," the woman said with a smile. "I took one of Mimi's weaving classes last year and fell in love with the loom and weaving."

"I've heard that story several times over the years," Kelly said with a smile. "Sometimes people fall in love with the spinning wheel the same way." She walked over to the loom and leaned closer to the fabric there. "Ooooooh, this is so fine. May I touch it?" she asked.

"Of course."

"Table runner?" Kelly asked as she stroked the fibers several times. There was a differ- ent feel to this fiber. Her fingers could always tell if the fiber was different or exotic.

"Yes, I'm doing it for my mom's birthday this September." She pointed to the creamy beige expanse of woven fabric. "I've got another two feet to go, so I think I'll make it."

"It's beautiful," Kelly said, admiring the novice weaver's work. "You're doing a great job. I think you're a natural."

The weaver chuckled. "I wish."

Kelly couldn't resist stroking the fabric again. "I can tell this fiber isn't wool or silk or cotton. But I know I've felt it before. What is it?"

"It's linen. Made from flax," she said with a smile. "I love using flax. It's an ancient fiber and was one of the oldest fiber crops in the world. It was used seven thousand years ago. Spread from the Mediterranean areas like Egypt and Iraq into India and China. It's been spun and woven into garments for centuries."

"Wow," Kelly said, impressed by this woman's knowledge. "You've really learned about it."

"Well, I love reading about history and the people from yesteryear. It's easy to learn information when it's wrapped inside historical stories." She touched the cream-colored fabric she'd already woven. "Mummies were entombed, wrapped in linen back in ancient Egypt. The Phoenicians loaded Egyptian linens and traveled all over the Mediterranean. The Romans used linen for sails on their ships. Flax was introduced into North America by the colonists, and it thrived here."

Kelly pondered for a few seconds. "Are the flax seeds I buy at the grocery store in the health food section the same seeds that are used for growing flax?"

The woman nodded. "Yes. And flax fibers are stronger than cotton, too."

Kelly rubbed the fine fabric between her fingers again. It felt firmer, more substantial between her fingers than other fabrics. An ancient fiber would have to produce a stronger fabric and garment in those early times. Cold winds blew in the winter, and the only refuge people had was huddling around the fire in a hut or a stable and wrapping their cloak or garment about them. No overcoats to be found in those early times.

"I love the way this feels," Kelly said, rubbing the linen again. The woman's woven stitches appeared open and even. Precise, actually. Kelly was envious of the ability to make her stitches so even and smooth. Something would always come up in Kelly's knitting rows.

Mimi turned the corner into the room then. "Isn't that a beautiful piece, Kelly? Jackie only started weaving last year, but she's become quite proficient. One of my star pupils." Mother Mimi beamed.

"I think she's a natural," Kelly agreed. "This is beautiful work, and I just had a wonderful history lesson in this ancient fiber, thanks to Jackie." Kelly smiled and ran her fingers across the fine linen fibers once again.

Balancing her coffee mug, briefcase bag, and an almost-finished ribbon scarf, Kelly sought out a table in the late-morning shade of the garden patio. She scanned the other tables scattered among the trees and greenery. The café was in between breakfast and lunch, so the patio garden was peaceful and quiet with no one talking. On this cloudy day, temperatures had dropped to the eighties. Delightful. Kelly spotted a table in the back corner of the garden and headed straight for it.

Kelly wanted some quiet time to finish and bind off this ribbon scarf. She'd knitted four of them already and had one more to go. Since her girls' softball clinic sessions ended next week, Kelly knew she needed to hustle to get all five scarves for the girls ready on time. Part of their end-of-class lunch she was treating them to.

She also wanted some time to think. For the past two days, Kelly had not been able to get Greg's comments about Professor Paul Smith out of her mind. Greg had seen Professor Smith at a popular Old Town bar several times. Smith would drink too much, then get into arguments that sometimes resulted in getting into fights and being thrown out of Mason's Bar. Repeatedly. And this self-destructive behavior was probably due to Smith's deep-seated anger at the student who had charged him with sexual assault. Her complaint had thrown a wrench into Smith's academic career and advancement. Greg had said: "That professor's definitely got a short fuse and still has a whole lot of anger inside. You could tell just listening to him rant at the bar."

Listening to Greg detail some of these incidents he'd witnessed that involved Professor Smith, Kelly couldn't help but wonder if the anger and resentment Professor Smith still harbored toward Laura Brewster had led him into taking revenge. Had Professor Paul Smith given in to those vengeful emotions and taken action? Clearly, Smith was capable of violence, as witnessed by numerous patrons of Mason's Bar. Smith regularly got into physical fights with anyone who taunted him about the assault charges. Smith clearly had fallen off the wagon and begun to drink heavily again. Had he gone to Laura Brewster's apartment and choked her to death? Many bar patrons had heard him make threats against her while drunk. Did Smith follow up on those threats? Those thoughts had been bouncing around Kelly's head for days now. It was time to get some answers, and Kelly knew just where to start.

The lunch crowd was winding down, Kelly thought as she walked between occupied and empty tables at the back of the café. Glancing around, she spotted Jennifer at the counter loading lunch orders onto her tray.

"You want a refill, Kelly?" Jennifer pointed to Kelly's mug as she approached the counter.

"No, I'm still good. I just want to ask you something when you have a moment. I can wait outside. Don't want to take a seat away from a customer."

Jennifer gave a dismissive wave. "Lunch is slowing down, so no problem. Why don't you grab that smaller two-top table in the corner next to the windows? It's separated a little from the rest. I'll be there as soon as I get these last orders in."

"Sounds good," Kelly said and headed toward the corner of the café. Sure enough, the smaller table located beside the large front windows was empty. It was much smaller than the other tables and usually Kelly noticed only one person at a time sitting there.

Settling in the chair with its back against the wall, Kelly noticed there was more than enough room for one person to study, eat, work on a laptop, or simply stare out the wide window at what was once the front entry yard of Uncle Jim and Aunt Helen's farmhouse.

The entire area in front of the café's main entrance and the garden patio were enclosed by the original old Spanish Colonial beige stucco or adobe wall, rimmed with red brick. In the center, directly across from the steps that led up to Pete's Porch Café, was a wide arch, obviously the welcoming entry to the original farmhouse property. Kelly knew that the café was located in the original kitchen and dining room area at the back of the farmhouse. A couple of years ago, Pete had expanded the original enclosed patio room on the side of the café and created an outdoor patio deck perched on the level right above the garden patio. During warm-weather months, which were plentiful in Colorado, customers flocked to the outdoor tables on the deck and in the garden.

"Okay, I've got a couple of minutes," Jennifer announced as she approached. "What's up?" she asked, settling into the chair across from Kelly.

"I've been thinking about what Greg said the other night. You know, about Professor Smith at the university. I remember how one of Smith's friends told me that he had stopped overdrinking and had straightened himself out. But Greg said that he saw Professor Smith at Mason's Bar a couple of weeks ago 'drunk as a skunk,' as Greg put it."

"Yeah, I wish I could say that surprised me, but it doesn't. I've seen too many people swear off liquor over the years, only to dive right back into the deep end over and over." She gave a tired sigh and stared out the window. "It's sad to watch."

"I started thinking. What if Professor Smith was the one who killed Laura Brewster? I mean, Greg said Smith got into a fight at Mason's the night Greg was there. Some guy at the bar taunted him about that girl, and they started fighting. The bartender had to throw both of them out."

Jennifer looked back at Kelly, peered at her. "Where are you going with this?"

"Well, I wondered if you would join me in going to Mason's Bar early some evening when that same bartender is working. We could get there before the bar crowd comes in. I'd like to ask that bartender some questions. See what he remembers about that night. Maybe Professor Smith made some threat against Laura Brewster. Who knows?"

Jennifer stared out the wide window again. "Sure, Kelly. I'll go with you. In fact, let me check with Mason's and see which bartender it was. I might remember him."

"Would you? Thanks, Jen. If he remembers you, then I bet he'll tell us more." Kelly paused before continuing. "And for the record, I wouldn't dream of asking you this if I didn't already know that you were no longer tempted by that bar scene. Believe me, Jen, I would never do anything like that. Honest."

Jennifer glanced back at Kelly and smiled. "Well, for the record, I know that, Kelly."

"Let me check with Greg and find out if he remembers what night he was there at Mason's." She dug out her cell phone from her cutoff jeans and scrolled through the directory to Greg's number. "He's probably deep at work with the geeks, as Cassie calls them. So I'll leave a . . . Hey, Greg? It's me, Kelly."

"What's up?" Greg asked in a crisp voice. "Cassie's over here working on this new project I gave her. Do you need to talk to her or something?"

"No, I called to ask you something. Do you remember what night you were over at Mason's Bar and saw Professor Smith? I wanted to go over and ask that bartender some questions."

"Sleuthing, huh? I was hoping you might pick up on what I said the other night. Yeah, I remember exactly. It was Thursday night, three weeks ago. We didn't have a game that night, so I joined some of the guys from my cycling group at the bar."

"Thanks, that helps a lot. What have you got Cassie working on?"

"I was showing her some programming codes from years ago. You know, those early ones. Then I explained to her how those old programs worked. Next, I'm going to show her what we can do now."

Kelly chuckled. "From the Stone Age to the Space Age, huh? I predict she'll love it."

"Oh, yeah. She's digging into it right now. She really gets into stuff."

"Well, tell her 'hi' from me, and I'll see you tonight at the games."

"Will do. See ya." He clicked off.

Jennifer rose from the table. "Gotta get back to the customers. What did Greg say?"

"He remembers exactly. It was Thursday night three weeks ago."

"Okay, I'll check with Mason's and see who was working then and when they're on duty next. Talk to you later." Jennifer turned and hurried back toward the grill counter.

Kelly took one more look at the old-fashioned adobe walls and picturesque front yard, then pulled her laptop from her briefcase bag and went back to work. Silent client accounts were waiting rather than noisy customers.

"Way to go, Greg!" Lisa yelled from the Rolland Moore park bleachers.

"Nice hit!" Kelly joined in, clapping her hands as well.

Seated beside them both on the midlevel bleacher row, Megan put her fingers to her mouth and let out one of those high-decibel, earsplitting whistles Marty had taught her.

"Yeow!" Kelly ducked her head, covering her ears. "Jeeeez, Megan! You're gonna make us all deaf."

Megan just laughed and waved toward the

field. "Hey, Greg is waving at you, Lisa. Get your hands off your ears and wave back."

"Only if you promise not to let out another of those whistles for this game. I'm with Kelly. Our ears are still ringing."

Megan just laughed. "Don't be such sissies. You've forgotten our trips to Coors Field in Denver to watch the Rockies play. Remember how loud those noisemakers were?"

"Good Lord, I'd forgotten those," Kelly said with a frown. "I'd like to go down for a game this summer, but I don't want to come back impaired."

Megan gave a dismissive wave of her hand and took another bite of her hot dog with everything. Mustard, ketchup, bright green relish, and grilled onions spilled out of the bun.

Kelly spotted Steve walk over to the batter's box, awaiting his turn at bat. He took a practice swing. Powerful. "We could use a home run right about now. This Thornton team has improved a lot."

"I'll say." Lisa picked up her bottle of iced tea. "No way were they this good last year."

Megan swallowed her big bite of hot dog then offered, "It's the batters. They've taken on a couple of new guys, and boy are they good." She returned to her hot dog.

"Well, this is perfect timing," Curt Stackhouse's voice sounded beside the bleachers. "I see Steve coming up to bat."

"Hey, great to see you two." She grinned down at Curt and Jayleen. "C'mon up here and join us. There's plenty of room."

"Yes, join us, please," Lisa said.

"Good to see you two," Megan added, smiling at them.

"We're happy to join you folks. We've all been so busy lately, we haven't had time for a get-together. We need to schedule a barbecue before summer is over," Curt said, offering Jayleen his hand as she climbed up the side of the bleachers.

"Put us down on your guest list," Megan said, raising her hand. "Marty and I would walk a mile for Jayleen's chili."

"Thank you, ma'am," Jayleen said with her wide grin.

"As I recall, you sure didn't ignore those steaks last time you were there, Megan," Curt teased.

Megan grinned. "I still have dreams about those steaks, Curt."

Jayleen cackled, then pointed toward the field. "Looks like Fort Connor Red is tied with that Thornton team," Jayleen said as Kelly scooted down the bleachers, allowing more room for Curt and Jayleen. Jayleen settled at the end of the row.

Curt climbed the bleachers from the bottom up, swung a long leg over a bleacher, and sat between Kelly and Jayleen. "We could use another run to take the lead," he said. "I hope Steve knocks one out of the park."

"Yeah, we need the big bat here," Lisa said.

Kelly watched the batter on deck hit a pop fly ball that was easily caught by the Thornton fielder. "Oh, boy. Two outs. We really need a run now. They've got both Greg and Marty on base."

"C'mon, Steve, hit one over the fence!" Jayleen yelled.

At that, Steve turned around and looked toward the bleachers. All of them waved. Steve grinned and waved back. Then he strolled to the plate, took another couple of practice swings, and settled into his crouch.

Kelly crossed her fingers and watched as the pitcher wound up and let fly a perfectly thrown ball. Right over the plate, and right there in the zone. Ripe for the taking. Steve didn't waste time. He swung and connected. Kelly heard that sweet sound of ball meeting bat. *Crack!* She watched as the ball sailed up, up, and away. Out of the park. Way out of the park.

She leaped to her feet. *"Way to go, Steve!"* she shouted and joined in as the bleachers exploded in cheers, watching Marty, Greg, and Steve round the bases home. Glancing at Megan, yelling loudly beside her, Kelly said, "Now you can let one of those fly."

"All right!" Megan grinned and put her fingers to her teeth.

Kelly already had her fingers in her ears as the first decibel pierced the air. Jayleen cackled and Curt let out a guffaw at the sound.

When all the noise settled, Curt turned to Kelly and said, "Tell Steve to give me a call next week. A friend and I have a building project that should be right up Steve's alley. My friend has the land and I've got the capital." Curt winked at Kelly and smiled. "We'd like to talk with him about it."

Kelly's accountant antennae sent out a signal. *Yes!* She returned Curt's smile. "I'm sure Steve will be more than happy to talk with both of you. In fact, Steve may very well give you a call tonight."

THIRTEEN

Thursday late afternoon

"Lucky we found parking in this block," Kelly said as she and Jennifer walked along Linden Street, one of the original streets in Old Town Fort Connor.

Linden and cross street Walnut were the two oldest commercial streets in the picturesque Old Town area. Both streets were lined with shops and cafés that spilled right into the Old Town plaza area, which was designed solely for pedestrian traffic. Outdoor cafés sprouted in warm weather like dandelions in new grass. They were everywhere.

"That's because we're here early. It's only five o'clock. Another half hour and the bar crowd will start to trickle in." Jennifer stopped on the sidewalk in front of Mason's Bar. Only a few outdoor tables were occupied. "Or, everyone is already inside in the air-conditioning," she said with a smile.

Jennifer walked over and opened the dark wooden entry door with the ornate brass knocker and stepped inside. Kelly followed quickly. She would appreciate the air-conditioning, too. The July sun was blazing down even at an angle. Hot, hot.

Glancing around, Kelly admired the bar's interior. Tall cushioned booths lined two walls, and tables dotted the dining room. Dark red cushions adorned both the booths and the dining table chairs. White tablecloths and dark red linen-looking napkins were artistically folded and rested on each plate.

"This is a nice place," Kelly commented as they paused to look around. "I thought it would have more of a sports bar look considering what I'd heard about people getting into fights."

"Actually, those kinds of altercations are pretty rare for this place. The owners are from Denver, and they've tried to cultivate a more sophisticated atmosphere for Mason's. They own another bar in Love-land, which is definitely a drinking man's bar." Jennifer began to slowly walk past the dining tables section and toward the back part of the restaurant.

"Nobody's here yet," Kelly observed as she followed Jennifer.

"Oh, they're here, all right. See? We're so early we've surprised the staff."

Sure enough, a young woman in a black skirt, white blouse, and black necktie appeared from the back and hastened toward them. "Good afternoon. Would you like a table?" she said with a cheerful smile.

"No, that's okay. We'll sit at the bar," Jennifer replied, returning her smile.

The young woman gestured toward the back. "Enjoy. If you'd like to have an appetizer, just tell the bartender and we'll bring it to you there."

"Thanks. We'll remember that," Kelly said, reassuring the young waitress that she'd done her hostess duties and alerted them to other options.

Kelly followed Jennifer through the archway, which opened to a Victorian-style decor, complete with long polished wooden bar, old-fashioned lighting fixtures adorning the walls and hanging from the ceiling, and an ornate mirror that stretched the length of the bar. Kelly also noticed the bar was completely empty.

"I've never been in here before, but I've heard it was pretty popular," Kelly said as she and Jennifer walked toward the bar.

"From what I've heard, it still is," Jennifer said as she sat in one of the red-cushioned bar chairs. "And it's so nice to no longer be recognizable to those young waitresses." She winked at Kelly.

Kelly slipped into the bar chair beside her and noticed a tall brown-haired guy walk toward them, big smile in place.

"Jennifer! Good to see you," he said with a bartender's grin. Glancing to Kelly, he added, "And your friend. What can I get you girls?"

Kelly smiled inwardly at the term "girls" as Jennifer spoke up.

"Just a diet cola for me, Manny. What are you having, Kelly?"

"Actually, I'll have a Fat Tire. It's hot out there."

"That it is, Kelly," Manny said, wiping invisible lint off the bar with his white towel. Then he looked at Jennifer and gave her a crooked smile. "I'd heard that you'd stopped drinking, and that's why we haven't seen you around."

"Oh, I'm still around, Manny," Jennifer said with her winning smile. "I'm just outside at the cafés having dinner with friends. We're usually out there in the plaza at Bollinger's because the pizza is so good."

"Well, you're right about that," Manny said. "But for the record, we miss you on the scene."

Jennifer gave Manny one of her most alluring smiles. "I was on the bar scene for ten years at least, Manny. That's long enough."

Manny nodded, with a smile. "If you say so. Anyway, it's good seeing you again." Glancing to Kelly, he added, "Now, let me get you that Fat Tire." And Manny walked down the bar to retrieve a tall glass, then proceeded to fill it from one of the tall draft beer dispensers on the bar.

"You handled that very smoothly." Kelly smiled at her dear friend.

"Thanks. It gets easier and easier, I've noticed."

Manny walked up, tall glass of amber ale in hand, crested by a frosty head. He set it in front of Kelly.

"Thanks, Manny," Kelly said, wondering how to start asking questions.

"There's another reason we stopped in today, Manny," Jennifer jumped in. "One of our friends said he was in here three weeks ago on a Thursday night, and a professor of his from the university got into a fight with a guy at the bar. Apparently they had to be thrown out, he said. Do you remember seeing something like that?"

Manny leaned both arms on the bar. No other customers in sight. "Yeah, as a matter of fact, I do. I recognized the professor because he used to come in regularly a couple of years ago. He'd always get drunk and sometimes get into arguments. Professor Smith was his name."

"Yes, that's his name." Jennifer nodded. "Another of our friends knew him and had heard rumors. She was concerned. Was he always drunk?"

Manny nodded. "Yeah, every time I saw him. And he'd get into arguments. Other guys at the bar would kind of goad him, though." Manny leaned forward over the bar. "Smith was the guy that student accused of sexual assault. One of the guys at the bar told me."

"Our friend said his career at the university took a nosedive afterward, too," Kelly said, lowering her voice. "That's probably why he drank so much. Our friend knew his family and said he was a great guy. She didn't believe he did it."

Manny looked over at the waitress who was taking a couple to a table. "Yeah, I heard stories, too. That was a raw deal if he was really innocent. Anyway, he must have sobered up for a while, because he hadn't been in here for a year or so. Until a couple of weeks ago. Damned if he didn't go back to his old habits. Getting drunk and getting into a fight." Manny shook his head.

"Was it the same thing as before?" Kelly asked. "Some guy giving him a hard time about the assault?"

"Yeah. Some guy really jerked his chain about that charge. Professor Smith started cussing the girl out and calling her a lying bitch. Stuff like that. Then he took a swing at the guy."

"That's sad," Jennifer commented. "Especially if he really was innocent. Sounds like his whole life was screwed up. Ruined."

"Pretty much," Manny said, glancing down the bar. A waitress was walking over. "Looks like I've got more customers. You girls enjoy." And he walked away, blue-striped long-sleeved shirt complete with old-fashioned garter around the arm.

Kelly looked over at Jennifer. "Well, that was certainly interesting." She took a deep drink of the Fat Tire. Her empty stomach sent a message. Food.

"Indeed it was," Jennifer agreed, sipping her cola. "I'm glad we took this excursion. That was pretty damning information concerning Professor Smith."

"I agree. It doesn't look like Professor Smith has been able to move on after three years. And he clearly harbored animosity toward Laura Brewster."

"That's putting it mildly."

Kelly took another drink and her stomach growled. "Hey, can you please pass me that bowl of peanuts? I'm going to need something to absorb the ale."

"Absolutely." Jennifer captured the bowl of peanuts and placed it in front of Kelly. "Eat up. I don't want to watch you weaving down the streets of Old Town."

The following Monday morning
Kelly walked down the hallway toward the shop, refilled mug of iced coffee in hand. She was ready to balance Don Warner's financial statements or die trying.

Approaching the workroom, Kelly heard Mimi's voice drift out the doorway.

"That's right. Now that you've pressed your fibers into the silk scarves and wet down the entire scarf, we'll turn the scarf over and wet down the back side of the scarf. See? Watch how Gemma is doing it. Get those sponges wet and press the fibers through the mesh covering. Yes, just like that, Janet."

"Why are we wetting the back side?" a woman's voice asked.

Kelly paused and smiled, standing for a minute to sip her iced coffee. Mimi was teaching another Wet Felting class.

"Because we need that soapy mixture to saturate the entire piece, front and back. Then you'll carefully roll all of it up, plastic and fabric, around a rolling pin and inside one of those thick bath towels you see over there."

Kelly heard a murmuring of surprised voices. They sounded exactly like her class last week.

"After that, you'll roll your piece in sets of twenty-five until you reach five hundred."

Kelly laughed softly, listening to the exclamations of shock, laughter, and protests of, "My arms will fall off!"

Mimi had heard it all before, and Kelly heard her tinkling laughter floating above the protests and exclamations.

"Why five hundred? What's so magical about that?" another woman's voice asked.

"Well, by that time your scarf will be thoroughly wet throughout. Once it's completely saturated and the fibers completely pressed to the silk, they become one piece. Then you can unwrap the towel, remove the plastic, and place the scarf over a wooden hanger. Then we can hang it in the bathroom shower down the hall for twenty-four hours to drip and dry."

Kelly listened to the various murmurings and comments for another minute, then continued down the hallway back to the main yarn room. Disobedient accounts were waiting.

Kelly speared the last morsel of chicken, finishing off the Caesar salad. Glancing about Pete's Café, Kelly saw that the late lunch crowd was starting to thin out. A couple of tables were empty already.

Jennifer approached with a pitcher of iced coffee in one hand and a pitcher of iced tea in the other. "Okay, what'll it be? Right or left?" She held out one pitcher, then the other.

Kelly lifted her nearly empty mug. "No contest. Iced coffee, please."

Jennifer obliged and poured a long stream of cold black coffee into Kelly's mug. "You really ought to give iced tea a try, Kelly. It's refreshing on a hot summer day. You might like it."

Kelly took a deep drink of cold black liquid. She could feel the caffeine seeping through her veins. "I have tried it." She made a face.

Jennifer gave her an incredulous look. "How can anyone dislike iced tea? It's mild."

Kelly shrugged. "Maybe that's what I don't like. It's not strong enough."

Jennifer smiled. "If you say so. Sometime I'm going to make you a glass of really strong iced tea. Just to see if you like it."

"I promise I'll try it, but don't hold your breath waiting for my squeals of delight."

Jennifer laughed. "You know, Eduardo is right to call you Crazy Kelly. Talk to you later." She walked away to another table around the corner.

Kelly sipped her iced coffee and looked through the large café window beside her into the patio garden. The late-July heat was tamped down a bit, caused no doubt by the dark clouds forming over the foothills. Soon they'd cover the entire sky and open up with the welcome rain.

The late-July monsoon season was finally upon them. The blazing heat from earlier in the month lessened as the monsoon clouds rolled over the foothills every afternoon. Rainstorms, mostly light but sometimes drenching, appeared for several days in a row, providing much-needed rain after a typical hot and dry July. Some years brought so much rain there was flooding, which was always a surprise.

And one year, Kelly was told, a five-hundred-year-old storm showed up during monsoon season in late July. The thunderstorms "hung up," as the locals say, right next to the foothills, the edge of the Rocky Mountains, and it rained for twenty-four hours straight. Even the smallest creek in Fort Connor overflowed its banks and came rushing toward the unsuspecting city. Three to four feet of water covered streets and rose higher in low-lying areas, even toppling railcars off their tracks. Homes were flooded, water pouring in through the ground-floor windows. Cars were lifted from driveways and floated down streets, bumping into each other and entangling in all manner of debris carried by the swift current. The newly built lower level of Colorado State University's library was inundated when the picturesque lagoon located nearby angled down, which allowed several feet of powerful current to gather and crash right through glass and steel, completely flooding the library's collections.

Homes destroyed, beloved pets carried off by the uncaring waters, and worse. Four people died in that frightening night, swept away by the fast-moving water.

So lost in thought and the stories she'd heard told by friends, Kelly didn't even hear her name being called at first. Finally Burt's voice penetrated her thoughts.

"Earth to Kelly," Burt teased.

Kelly jerked around. "Hey, Burt, I was

looking out at the monsoon rain moving in and remembering all those stories people told me about that terrible flood of 1997. I guess I was lost in thought, as they say."

"Oh, well, that's easy to understand, Kelly." Burt pulled out a chair across the table from her. "That flood was the biggest disaster Fort Connor ever experienced. And I know, because I was out there with the entire police department that night. It was a zoo, as you can imagine. I was out all night and the next day. All of us were. It was unbelievable."

Kelly listened intently. "Boy, I'm glad I didn't live here then. It would have been traumatic to watch all my favorite places covered by three and four feet of water."

"Traumatic, it was. Trust me." Burt took a drink from his oversize white plastic cola cup. "Back to the present. It was great to escape into the mountains for several days. Mimi and I really needed the break. Thanks for suggesting it, Kelly."

"You're welcome. I'm so glad you two got away. You have to do that more often. The Gang and I relaxed with ball games."

"How's your team doing? And Steve's?"

"Our team was beaten by Greeley, but Steve's team beat Thornton."

"Good going."

Kelly leaned back into the café chair. "You know, this is probably a good time to update you on some of the information I've learned since last week. And, yes, I was sleuthing." She smiled at Burt.

"By all means, Kelly. I've been away from all things criminal for a few days, so get me up to speed."

"You can tell Dan that Jennifer and I went to Mason's Bar the other day to ask the bartender some questions about Professor Smith."

Burt looked puzzled. "Why?"

"Greg told us one night when we were all together that he remembered being at Mason's Bar several times when Professor Smith was there. It seems Smith got drunk regularly and got into fights. All because of that incident with Laura Brewster. Some bar goer would taunt him with it, and Smith would light up. Greg said he saw the bartender throw Smith and other combatants out after they got into fights. Greg also said Smith did that regularly about three years ago then apparently sobered up. Until about three weeks ago when he showed up drunk again and resorting to his old belligerent behavior."

Burt stared at Kelly for a moment, then a little smile started. "Well, well, Sherlock.

You have been busy since I've been gone. I will definitely share that with Dan. Let's see what he can do with it."

Hearing Burt's praise always made Kelly feel good inside. "Tell Dan that I was poking my nose into other people's business. Again. Can't seem to stop."

"Keep poking, Sherlock. Keep on poking."

"Well, I am. I asked Jennifer if she'd accompany me on a trip to Mason's Bar to ask that bartender some questions. I figured Jen might remember him from those old barhopping days. Jennifer checked with Mason's, and sure enough, she knew the bartender on duty the night Greg was there and saw Professor Smith. Jen and I went over to Mason's in the late afternoon before the bar crowd moved in."

Julie walked up to them then. "I take it you'd like more iced coffee, Burt. Kelly just had a refill."

"That would really hit the spot, Julie. Thanks." He handed over his extralarge plastic cup.

Kelly watched Julie hurry off. Waitresses never walked slowly, she observed. They were too busy.

"So, did you and Jennifer learn anything?" Burt leaned both arms on the table in one of his listening positions.

"Actually, we did," Kelly said, pushing her laptop to the side. "The bartender on duty knew Jennifer from her barhopping days, so he was definitely chatty. He was tending bar that night when Professor Smith showed up. Manny, the bartender, said he hadn't seen Smith for a year and had heard that he'd stopped his drinking. He said Professor Smith had been a regular at that bar after he was accused of sexual assault. So Manny was surprised to see Smith back at the bar because he'd gone back to his old behavior of drinking too much and getting into arguments."

"What kind of arguments?"

"Manny said it was usually the same thing. Some guy would jerk Smith's chain about the assault charge and Smith would get angry. About three weeks ago, Manny said Smith started cussing out that girl and called her a 'lying bitch.' " Kelly looked Burt in the eye. "That caught Jennifer's and my attention. He was clearly talking about Laura Brewster."

"It certainly sounds like it," Burt said, his eyes narrowing a bit. "Did Manny remember anything else Smith said?"

"Not really, because Smith threw a punch at the other guy and they started fighting.

Manny said both of them were thrown out of the bar."

Burt made a disgusted face. "Brother. That's not good."

"Yeah, I agree. Jennifer and I both came to the same conclusion that Greg did. Professor Smith was still harboring a whole lot of animosity against Laura Brewster."

"Yeah, I have to agree." He looked at Kelly with a crooked smile. "I'll leave a message for Dan with this info and tell him you and Jennifer were both sleuthing. Dan will appreciate it. I'm sure he's taken a look at those assault allegations against Professor Smith a few years ago. And Dan already said he wanted to speak to that bartender as well. Good job, you two."

"Thanks, Burt. I'd like to think that this professor may get a deeper second look now, don't you?"

"You can depend on it, Kelly."

Fourteen

Friday morning

Kelly looked up from her laptop screen and the accounting spreadsheets claiming her attention. "Hey, Mimi," she called to her friend who suddenly appeared in the front of the café where Kelly was seated. Mimi had her familiar porcelain tea mug in hand. "Are you and Burt coming out to see some ball games this weekend? Both Steve's team and our team are playing."

"We'll have to catch the games next weekend," Mimi said with a smile. "This is the weekend we promised Cassie we'd take her camping again. So we'll be hiking on the Grey Rock Trail and cooking over our portable gas stove and sitting around a campfire instead of sitting on bleachers."

"Oh, wow. That's going to be way more fun," Kelly said. "I wish I could join you folks but our team is playing both Saturday and Sunday. Would you like Carl to come along and be a watchdog?"

Mimi laughed. "No, I don't think so. He'd be taking *us* for walks."

"Just teasing you, Mimi. Carl would be like having another kid. A wiggly one who barked."

Julie walked up then. "Do you need another cup of Earl Grey, Mimi?"

"I'd love it, Julie. Thanks." She handed over her mug. "I've already told Cassie. She and Pete are going down to Denver to see her grandfather this afternoon."

"He's still in the skilled nursing care facility, isn't he? Pete hasn't said anything different, and I know he would if his grandfather's situation changed."

Mimi's smile disappeared. "I'm afraid Grandpa Ben is going to be in that skilled care facility for the foreseeable future. From what I've heard about those severe heart attack patients, they're usually bedridden the rest of their days."

That was such a sobering image, it was hard for Kelly to picture. "That's so sad. I know Cassie must be disappointed to see her grandfather like that, but I can't help but think her life is so much richer and interesting now that she lives with Pete and Jennifer." Kelly gave Mimi a crooked smile. "I know that may not sound very understanding, but I'm thinking more about Cassie than her grandfather."

"I understand exactly what you mean, Kelly, and I agree with you. Cassie's life is just beginning, and she has so many more opportunities to develop all of her interests and abilities now that she's living here with Pete and Jennifer. And us." Mimi smiled. "That may not be charitable, but I don't care. I'm thinking about Cassie first."

"Me, too."

Burt walked into the café then, his own coffee mug dangling from his hand. "Oh, there you are. Getting a fill-up with Kelly, I bet." He smiled at them both. "Mimi, Rosa said to tell you that yarn vendor from Pennsylvania is on the line."

Mimi threw up her hands. "Oh, goodness. Would you get my Earl Grey for me, Burt? I've been trying to catch that woman for a week." And without waiting for an answer, Mimi hurried from the café.

"I wish I had a dollar for every time I've heard Mimi say that over the last few years," Kelly said with a laugh.

Burt pulled up a chair at the table where Kelly was working. "Dan said to tell you that you're one step ahead of him. He was planning to visit that bartender tonight or tomorrow. Bartenders' schedules are erratic.

Dan had already started looking at Professor Smith because of his past history with the victim. These past few days they've given him a closer look. Once they started asking questions of some university folk, they learned about Smith's erratic behavior at the bars three years ago. And more troubling, Professor Smith's recent lapse back into overdrinking at the bars in Old Town. One of his colleagues apparently hinted that there had been a recent confrontation between Smith and Laura on campus. No one went into details. So, that really got Dan's attention when I told him you and Jennifer went over to Mason's Bar. He was especially interested in your conversations with Manny the bartender, as you can imagine."

"I figured the cops were bound to hear the same gossip about Smith at the bars that we did once they started asking questions. It looks like the university crowd is its own little community, so everyone in that community knew about Professor Smith and his erratic behavior. It's kind of a closed-door society."

"Well, you're right about that, Kelly. It's always harder to get faculty to talk about other faculty, especially if it's less than flattering. So I imagine not many people were forthcoming with gossip about Professor Smith. But Dan said there were a couple of university folk who'd seen Smith drinking at Mason's Bar three years ago."

Julie approached them. "Here's Mimi's hot tea, Burt. I take it you'd like some more iced coffee."

"You read my mind." Burt handed over his mug.

"I'm still good, Julie," Kelly said to the busy waitress, watching her hasten off. The late-morning breakfast crowd was thinning out but Kelly saw Jennifer and Julie still racing between tables. "I wonder what kind of incident happened between Professor Smith and Laura Brewster on campus?"

"The way someone described it to Dan, it sounded like Professor Smith accidentally crossed paths with Laura Brewster on campus one day and lost it. Started yelling at her. Apparently she ran into the Student Union building to get away from him."

"Wow. I'd say that sounds like an 'inciting incident.' What do you think?"

"I agree. From what you said, this Manny has seen Professor Smith a lot over the past three years, and his comments about Smith's behavior were particularly telling. Especially his comment involving Smith's remarks about Laura Brewster."

"Oh, yeah. I'd say those remarks alone are damning. Of course, Dan will be the judge of that."

Burt laughed softly. "You got that right, Sherlock."

"Where is that land parcel Curt talked about?" Kelly asked Steve that evening as he turned his truck into the Rolland Moore ball fields.

"It's out County Road 10 just past the interstate." Steve eased his truck into a parking space.

"Man, I thought every inch of that was already built up between Fort Connor and Timnath."

"Curt's friend snagged that parcel a few years back and he's been waiting to build. That was a smart move." Steve scanned the surrounding ball fields. "Boy, these parking spaces are filling up fast. I bet the bleachers are gonna be full tonight."

"Friday-night full," Kelly said, gathering her small backpack and water bottle as she pushed open the passenger door. The sound of her phone caught her attention as she stepped to the ground. Spying Burt's name, she glanced over at Steve, who was gathering up a bag of baseballs, gloves, and a couple of bats. "This is Burt. You go on to your field. I'll talk to Burt as I walk to the bleachers."

"Okay. Better not be a long call, or you'll be standing," Steve said with a grin as he headed toward the separate ball fields scattered around the park.

"Hey, Burt, what's up?" Kelly said as she clicked on. She swung her small backpack over her shoulder as she slowly walked through the parking area of Rolland Moore Park.

"I just got a text message from Dan. He must be swamped if he doesn't have time for a call. The apartment complex where Laura Brewster lived had several video cameras installed around the property. Police were finally able to go through all of them, and one video shows a guy in a hooded CSU jacket walking near the victim's apartment building."

Kelly moved onto the grass. Surrounded by trees on two sides and a view of the mountains on a third, the ball fields served hundreds of student athletes as well as adults. Fort Connor had baseball and softball leagues for every age group. Rolland Moore Park sat in a picturesque location with a lake in the middle, where the resident and visiting populations of Canada geese paddled and waddled nearby, sharing the park with the ballplayers.

Kelly angled away from a family gathering up kids and sports equipment from the back of their van. Better to keep this conversation private.

"Really?" Kelly said, slowing her walk to better pay attention. "Maybe that's a clue that a violent intruder is the one who killed Laura."

"Maybe," Burt said. "But it could be anybody. Those hooded jackets really can hide someone's identity, especially at night."

Heading toward the middle ball field, Kelly peered ahead, searching for her friends. Steve's team was playing tonight and her team would play tomorrow, Saturday night. Sunday, both their teams had games scheduled. This was the start of end-of-season elimination games.

Kelly scanned another ball field and thought she spotted Megan and Lisa. "I have to admit Professor Smith is looking more suspicious. I'll be interested in what Dan has to say after he questions Manny. But whoever it was, violent intruder or someone else, he was definitely trying to disguise himself. It's July, for Pete's sake. Certainly not cold enough to wear a jacket at night, let alone a jacket with a hood."

"You got that right, Kelly," Burt said with

a laugh. "I'll let you know as soon as I hear something. It may not be until after the weekend."

"Don't worry about it, Burt. You and Mimi enjoy your weekend camping trip with Cassie." She clicked off and quickened her pace toward the bleachers where she'd spotted Lisa and Megan.

"Mega congrats to Steve on snagging his first building project as a partner," Marty said, holding his bottle of Fat Tire aloft.

"Great job, buddy," Greg chimed in, raising his craft brew aloft. "He's back, and he's building! Wooooohooooo!"

"Yay, Steve!" Megan added, raising her soda can on high. "Kaufman and Townsend rocks!"

Lisa and Pete and Jennifer joined in the congratulations and cheers, as did Kelly, who watched Steve color slightly and accept his friends' accolades as they relaxed on Megan and Marty's backyard patio after the game.

"Thanks, guys. I really appreciate that," Steve said with a little smile.

Kelly placed her hand on Steve's arm and smiled. "You deserve it, Steve."

"Well, I can't think of any builder who deserves this more than you, Steve," Pete said, reaching for a slice of pepperoni pizza. Pizza boxes from a favorite café in Old Town covered the tabletop. "You had to be willing to let go of everything you had here in Fort Connor and start again in a way more competitive market in Denver. Not many builders would risk that."

"I don't know of any of the smaller builders who even tried," Jennifer said, swishing the cola in the can. "Some of the bigger firms went to ground, regrouped, or merged with another firm to survive. But all of the smaller outfits like Steve's had to abandon building entirely and switch into remodels and rehabs. Even radon mitigation."

"Actually, that's not a bad idea," Lisa said, claiming a slice of barbecue chicken pizza. "Colorado has a lot of pockets of radon gas all over it. In fact, the other Western states have it as well."

"It's a viable way of staying in business," Jennifer added. "Of course, you have to take all of the training to become a certified radon technician, so there's some cost involved. Then you have to advertise your services. Not cheap."

"And join all the other people offering those services," Pete said. "I swear, when Grandpa Ben had his Denver house tested for radon gas a few years ago, those readings were all over the map."

"How'd you decide on which one?" Marty asked.

"He finally used a neighbor's recommendation for a certified technician who'd done a good job and charged a fair price." Pete took a drink of his bottle of Guinness.

"Personal recommendations. They work every time," Lisa said. "Half our business over there at the physical therapy center has come from former clients' recommendations. All hail, Recommendations." She lifted her hands.

Kelly chuckled. "I have to join in. That's how most CPAs get their clients. By recommendation of existing or former clients. They're worth their weight in gold."

"Amen," Lisa chimed in.

"All hail and amen? You're getting religious, and it's not even Sunday," Greg said to his girlfriend.

Marty gave an amused snort. "Spoken by the heathen among us."

Everyone, including Greg, laughed out loud at Marty's comment.

"All hail, Heathens! Isn't that a college football song?" Greg joked, then snatched a slice of pepperoni and another slice of barbecue chicken pizza.

"It may be," Steve said, laughing.

"All right, let's get serious for a minute," Marty said. "What is Curt thinking of building on that land?"

"Actually, Curt is the investor partner with this guy who owns the land," Steve said, setting his bottle of Fat Tire on his tanned knee.

"Where is that parcel again?" Megan asked.

"It's on the east side of the interstate, out County Road 10. The guy's owned it for years."

"Out Harmony Road?" Jennifer asked, sitting up straighter in her chair. "How far away from Big Box?"

"That's right. I don't drive that way too often, so I forgot they built a new Big Box right there at the interstate and Harmony," Lisa said.

Steve grinned. "The parcel is right next to the Big Box development. The corporation wanted this guy's land, but he refused to sell. And it really drove up the value."

"Ohhhhhhh, yeah. That's for sure," Jennifer said, nodding.

"Smart move," Greg agreed. "What's that guy want to build?"

Steve's grin widened. "A small strip mall with several storefronts and a fast-food restaurant. He's hammering out the franchise details now."

Kelly and all her friends stared at Steve for a few seconds then burst out in laughter.

"Fantastic!"

"Genius!"

"Right next to Big Box and all those hungry customers."

"And kids. Hungry kids and hungry parents."

"Gotta love it."

Kelly put her hand over her breast and declared, "That made my accountant's heart skip a beat."

"I'll bet," Pete said after he stopped laughing. "Talk about a savvy businessman."

Steve shrugged. "He's no different from anybody else who was willing to take a risk. He bought that land twenty years ago when it was still farmland, believing that those crossroads would attract more traffic and more people. And they did. Harmony Road is a major business thoroughfare on the south of the city. It's the main artery now."

"You know, twenty years ago we were already seeing development of stores and businesses and housing being built along Harmony. First, the section near College Avenue filled up, then development kept spreading east," Marty said.

"Because it had no place else to go," Jennifer jumped in. "The intersection of College and Harmony was already filled with shopping centers and stores. And going west on Harmony, it had become residential heading toward the foothills."

"Yeah, you're right. If you were paying attention, you could see the inevitable spread of the city toward the east. The eastern edge." Lisa reached for a slice of pepperoni. Only one slice left.

"We call that 'city creep,' " Jennifer said. "Most cities will creep over their boundaries, spreading wherever there's more room and land to buy."

"True, and Fort Connor is bounded by the foothills and the mountains on the western edge," Marty said.

"And by Landport on the north and Loveland on the south," Megan put forth.

"So, you see, the only direction where Fort Connor could spread or creep to was on the eastern edge of the city." Jennifer sipped from her cola. "Whoever Curt's business partner is, I lift my hat to him. Or, raise my cola can."

"He's gonna make out like a bandit," Greg observed, chasing the last of his two slices of pizza with his craft brew.

"Risk and return," Kelly opined. "The old investment adage. If you want a higher level of return, then you have to live with a higher level of risk."

"Well, I'm for another round of cheers and hurrays for our own risk taker, Steve," Jennifer said with a smile. "He took an even bigger risk when he gambled and jump-started his career all over again in Denver. Steve didn't have deep pockets or investors handing him money."

"Hell, no," Greg concurred.

Steve chuckled. "Most of what I had in my pockets was lint."

"So, I repeat," Jennifer continued, raising her cola can. "To Steve. Who's braver than any investor or builder or developer I've ever known."

"Hear! Hear!" Pete joined in.

"Huzzah!" Marty and Megan chimed together.

Kelly watched her friends congratulate Steve one more time. And she felt herself getting a little misty. Instead of reaching for a tissue, she leaned over and gave Steve a kiss.

FIFTEEN

Monday morning

"Hey, there, Cassie," Kelly said as she walked into the main knitting room. "I was hoping to see you here today. How'd the camping trip go with Burt and Mimi?" Kelly set her briefcase bag on the table.

Cassie looked up from the pile of rainbow-hued yarns she was piling onto the library table and grinned at Kelly. "It was great! We had such a good time!"

"Wonderful. I want to hear all about it." Kelly settled into a chair with her mug of coffee.

"Weather was perfect, too," Cassie continued. "It was cooler up in the mountains farther up the canyon."

"Oh, yes, that's another thing I love about going up into the canyons. It's cooler and beautiful and peaceful." Kelly closed her eyes and let out a sigh.

"Oh, I know. I just *love* that about the

canyon! You can walk in the trees, and it's so green and pretty. And the river is close by, and it makes so much noise." Cassie stared off into the room.

Kelly recognized that look. It came over people who had fallen in love with the Cache La Poudre Canyon and couldn't find the words to explain or describe it. "I know what you mean, Cassie. I feel the same way whenever I go up into the canyon. It's hard to explain. But something about it grabs hold of you inside and doesn't let go."

Cassie smiled at her. "That's right. You said it, Coach." Cassie took one of the fluffy lavender balls of yarn and tossed it to Kelly. "Catch!"

Kelly caught the really soft ball with one hand. Then she looked to the right side. "Aw, no one's on second base. Runner will score."

"I thought you got him out at first," Cassie played along.

"Nope, he got by me. He's on the way to third! Quick!" She tossed the yarn back.

Cassie snagged it out of the air. "Got him!" she cried, smashing the ball on the table.

Both of them laughed. "Which one was the tagged runner, the cookie or the scissors?" Kelly pointed to the table where the ball of yarn sat on top of a chocolate chip cookie beside a pair of scissors.

"I was aiming for the cookie," Cassie joked. She gathered the balls of yarn together and started to stack the new yarns into an empty bin on the wall of shelves behind her.

Kelly leaned back into her chair. "Mimi said you did all the cooking again. Both on the portable gas stove and over the campfire grill."

"Oh, yeah. I love cooking over the campfire." Cassie shoved the last lavender yarn ball into the bin, then picked up another packing box and set it upon the table. "The smell of bacon frying then frying the eggs. Love all that."

"You're making me hungry." Kelly took a big sip of coffee.

"And I use Mimi's way to cook toast in the pan."

"Which is?"

"She butters both sides and browns them lightly on each side in the pan." Cassie flipped open the box cutter knife on the table and sliced through the packing tape on the top of the shipping box.

"Divine."

Cassie looked up at her and smiled. "Do you want me to ask Eduardo for an order of bacon?"

"Don't you dare. I don't need it. My yogurt and fruit should be enough." Kelly protested, halfheartedly.

"If you say so," Cassie said, grin spreading. She opened the shipping box and lifted out a layer of baby blue yarn and dumped the skeins into a pile on the table.

They looked different to Kelly. The twist wasn't as thick or as fluffy. "That kind of looks like cotton, but I can't tell from here."

Cassie read the label. "Good guess, Kelly. Looks like some others we've got in those baby bins."

"Baby bins, that's funny," Kelly said, chuckling.

"That's what I call them because Mimi keeps all those baby yarns together in those bins in the workroom. Be right back." Cassie carried the box through the door into the workroom.

Kelly opened her briefcase bag and was about to take out her laptop, then decided she'd rather use the time to catch up more with Cassie. She reached beside the laptop and pulled out the last of the ribbon scarves she'd knitted for her girls' softball clinic. The others were finished, fringe and all. She'd already told Cassie what she was making, and Cassie had picked out her colors. Two shades of blue for the Colorado Blue team. Kelly decided she might as well let Cassie finish the fringe for her own scarf.

Cassie walked back into the main room and spotted the scarf on the table. "Hey, is that my ribbon scarf you said you were making for us? That is *so* pretty." She walked around the table to Kelly's side.

"It sure is. Turquoise blue and sky blue." Kelly held up the slender ribbon creation. "When I first started knitting at Lambspun years ago, I knitted up a couple of these scarves for myself. I used them as decorative scarves then someone showed me they worked equally well as colorful belts for jeans during the colder months."

"I love these colors!" Cassie's eyes lit up as she took the ribbon scarf and ran it through her fingers. "This is awesome. You used the knit stitch, right?"

"Yep. They're super easy. You just cast on ten stitches, then start knitting. One ball of ribbon yarn will make the entire scarf plus fringe."

"Fringe?" Cassie asked. "Is that hard?"

"Nope. Real easy. It's so easy, I'm going to let you finish your own by making the fringe."

Cassie's eyes popped wide. "Wow! Really? How do I do that?"

"Sit down, and I'll show you. You can always stack those yarns later. Yarns aren't going to get up off the table and run away." Kelly reached over to the center of the table to the accessory tray and found the scissors.

Cassie pulled out the chair beside Kelly and pushed aside several stacked books on knitting, crocheting, and spinning. Lambspun was an equal opportunity spot for fiber workers of all kinds.

Not only knitters and hookers, as crochet enthusiasts called themselves, but lace makers, lovers of tatting, felters, even those who specialized in custom dyeing of fibers, and, of course, the always-present spinners and weavers — everyone showed up at the shop. Some people would drive several hours a day from other locations to take one of Mimi's workshops or even a private class.

"Okay, I've already bound it off, so the ends are ready to attach the fringe." Kelly reached inside her bag for the remaining bunch of ribbon yarn. "So, you'll measure off how long you want the fringe at both ends of the belt or scarf. You can use it for either. Whatever you like."

Cassie examined the end of the scarf, fingering the yarn. "Hmmmmm, how long should I make it?" Cassie wondered out loud. Then she held out her thumb and forefinger about four inches apart. "That looks pretty good."

"Okay, that looks about four inches. Hold it right there while I mark it on this paper." Kelly reached inside her briefcase bag and withdrew a lined sheet of ledger paper, devoid of numbers. "You know, this paper looks about eight inches along the side. What do you think?"

"Yeah, that's about right." Cassie nodded.

"Let me measure it to be sure. Then you can use this to measure each ribbon strip to cut. That way they'll all be even."

"Eight inches? Why double?"

"Because you're going to thread each folded strip through the last stitches on the edge, one strip for each stitch. Then you'll slip the ends through the loop and tie it off. And, voilà! You have two layers of four-inch fringe hanging from the edge."

Cassie's eyes lit up again. "Hey, that's cool! And it sounds easy. But I want to see you do it first."

"Trust me, it's easy. If I can do it, you can." Kelly smiled. "Okay, let me mark this paper for you, then you can start measuring the ribbon yarn and cutting it into eight-inch strips." Kelly reached into the middle of the table again and snagged the tape measure. Then she measured one side of the ledger paper and marked eight inches with a blue pen. "Here you go," she said, handing the paper to Cassie. "I'll do the first strip of fringe for you so you'll know how to do it."

"Gotcha," Cassie said, imitating several of Kelly's friends who used the same expression. Cassie laid the ribbon yarn beside the ledger paper and began to cut.

"You'll need twenty strips in total."

Cassie snipped the yarn with the scissors then looked up. "Twenty? There're only ten stitches."

Kelly grinned. "On each end of the scarf."

Cassie closed her eyes and leaned her head back. "Duh," she said.

"I asked the same thing," Kelly confided. "Megan and Lisa laughed at me."

Cassie chuckled as she measured the next strip. "At least you didn't laugh."

"Well, well, what are you two up to?" Mimi asked as she walked into the main room. "Is that one of those scarves you've been knitting for your softball girls, Kelly?"

"Yes, indeed, and I thought I'd let Cassie do her own fringe, so she could learn how." Kelly leaned back in the chair and took a big drink of her iced coffee.

"I'll finish filling up the yarn bins after I finish this, Mimi. I hope you don't mind."

Cassie never looked up from her measuring and cutting while speaking.

Mimi grinned over at Kelly. "Don't even bother with the rest of that yarn, Cassie. I'll finish it up now. That way I can spend some time with you girls."

Kelly always had to smile whenever Mimi referred to her, Megan, Lisa, and Jennifer as "girls." A little past her midthirties, Kelly felt a long way from girlhood. Her friends were all around the same age.

Mimi walked over to the open box of cotton yarn and scooped up a large armload, then went into the workroom. Kelly looked over at Cassie. "How many have you got so far?"

"This is the sixth," Cassie said, keeping her eyes on the scissors cutting through the ribbon yarn.

Kelly had to admire her concentration. Not every thirteen-year-old could concentrate as well as Cassie. Kelly noticed Cassie had the same concentration whenever she was learning something new. Learning how to bat, learning how to throw overhand with correct form, even learning how to knit for the first time. She recalled when Cassie first came to live with Jennifer and Pete last year, she had taken to Lambspun and all things fiber right away.

And Mimi — being Mother Mimi — taught Cassie to knit within her first week at the shop. Kelly had noticed then how Cassie concentrated on everything Mimi told her to do, trying each stitch slowly.

Concentration was an admirable trait to cultivate early. That ability to focus would help Cassie not only in her subjects at school but also as she attempted to learn any new skill in life. Cassie already had a leg up, in Kelly's way of thinking.

Mimi returned to the main room and started on the last box. "What's the yarn in that box, Mimi? Cassie and I noticed the last box had cotton yarn for baby clothes."

"Right you are, girls," Mimi said with a smile. "And this box has a selection of frothy mohair and merino yarns. All colors." She slit the box open with an expert slice of the box cutter. Opening the flaps, Mimi lifted out an armful of multicolored froth.

Cassie looked up from cutting the strips briefly to glance at the mohair and merino colors and declare, "Oooooooh, pretty." Then back to the ribbon strips. "I'm on sixteen."

"Wow, you really are efficient," Kelly said. "Snip that one and I'll show you how to tie each strip through the yarn loops."

Cassie snipped the scissors, then handed

the strip to Kelly. "Here you go."

Kelly picked up the turquoise and blue ribbon scarf. "First, you use your knitting needle to open up those last bound-off stitches. Just enough so you can get a crochet hook through with the ribbon yarn."

"You crochet it?"

"No, you just use the hook to pull the ribbon through the loop." Kelly picked up the knitting needle and demonstrated how to widen each end loop by pushing the needle into each loop. "See? Now, each loop has a little more space."

"Yeah, it does," Cassie said, peering at the scarf.

Kelly picked up a crochet hook from the accessory tray and hooked the ribbon yarn over it. "Now, you insert the hook through the loop, then carefully pull the doubled end of ribbon through the loop." Kelly demonstrated, pulling about half an inch of doubled ribbon yarn through the loop with the crochet hook.

"About that much?"

"Yes. Now, watch. You carefully take that little loop of ribbon yarn off the hook, then put the hook down. Now, you can take the ends of the strip on this side of the scarf . . ." Kelly carefully did exactly that. "And you insert them through this little loop on the other side of the scarf like that." Her fingers demonstrated. "Now, you slowly pull the ends of the strip until it makes a little knot with the loop. And voilà! You have fringe at the end of the scarf."

Cassie blinked. "Hey! That's cool! I love it! Can I do one now?" She reached for the scarf.

"Be my guest," Kelly said, smiling at Cassie's enthusiasm. She leaned back in her chair and watched Cassie deftly imitate the simple technique. Meanwhile, Mimi beamed down at both of them. Mimi's girls at work.

"Is that one of Pete's Wicked Burgers I see?" Burt asked as he walked up to Kelly's favorite small table beside the windows that looked out onto the garden patio.

Kelly waited to swallow the delicious bite before answering. "Indeed, it is, Burt. And you, I have to say, are casting envious eyes upon it. So, you'd better order one, because I'm hungry enough to finish this myself." She took another big bite, and this time made all manner of savoring sounds and yums of delight.

Burt laughed, watching her. "You're a great advertisement, I'll say that. Okay, I give in. I'll order one if you promise not to tell Mimi."

"Burt, you know we never snitch on our customers' eating habits," Jennifer said as she appeared from the kitchen area. "One more Wicked Burger with everything, coming up," she said as she scribbled in her waitress pad. "Iced coffee to go with that or hot?"

"Actually, I'll switch to soda," Burt said, settling into the chair across from Kelly. "Boy, you weren't kidding when you said you were hungry. You're halfway through that Wicked Burger already."

"Told you," Kelly managed after swallowing. "I was buried for two hours this morning figuring out how to free up more funds for Don Warner's next project. So I figured I deserved a reward." She winked at him.

"You want more iced coffee, Kelly?" Jennifer said as she turned toward the kitchen once more.

"Sure, I can always use a refill in July." She took another bite.

"While you're finishing off that burger, I'll catch you up on my phone call from Dan early this morning." Burt placed both arms on the table and leaned forward, the "better to talk" position.

"Did he speak to Manny the bartender?" Kelly asked before she took another big bite.

288

"Yes, he did, as a matter of fact. And it sounds like Manny repeated everything he told you and Jennifer earlier. So Dan and his partner plan to interview Professor Smith today or tomorrow if they can."

Kelly swallowed the yummy burger bite and chased it with some iced coffee. "That definitely sounds like Dan and the department are seriously considering Professor Smith as a possible suspect. Just like we thought they would."

Burt nodded. "So, we'll see how that interview goes. I want to hear what Dan thinks of Smith after interviewing him. Dan can usually get a good read off people. They'll be asking about those assault allegations. It'll be interesting how Smith handles himself under police questioning. That's clearly an open wound with him, so we'll see how he reacts when Dan starts to probe around there."

Kelly wiped the last bit of Wicked Burger sauce from her mouth with her napkin. "Ahhhhh, three thousand calories of absolute wicked delight." She grinned at Burt. "I don't regret a bite."

Burt chuckled. "You just made a rhyme. I didn't know you were a poet."

"I only wax poetic about food. Sort of like Greg and Marty. And speaking about food, this morning Cassie told me about all the things she cooked at the campsite last weekend. Sounds like she's gotten really good with the camp stove and the outdoor grill over the campfire."

"She sure has. I didn't have to lift a finger making anything like I usually do. Cassie was on top of it all."

"Cassie told me everything she cooked at the campsite last weekend," Kelly said as Jennifer walked up with Burt's large soda. "Sounds like she had a blast."

Jennifer grinned. "You bet she did. She regaled Pete and me for nearly half an hour telling us all about it." Glancing over her shoulder, she added, "Better get back to the other customers. Pete and I will be at the ball fields tonight to watch Cassie's team play. Maybe we'll see you there."

"Mimi and I will be there," Burt said as Jennifer turned to walk away.

"I told Cassie it made me nostalgic hearing her talk about the camping trip. I remembered all the times Steve and I went camping. My favorite memories are of going to sleep listening to the Cache La Poudre River sing me to sleep with the sound of those waters rushing over rocks."

"There you go, getting poetic again," Burt said. Then he glanced up and his smile faded. "Listen, I'll talk to you later. I see Barb and I think I'll go and let her know that the police have now got a second suspect in the Laura Brewster murder. That will maybe ease her mind a bit." He scraped back his chair and rose.

"That's a great idea," Kelly said. "That poor woman hasn't smiled in three weeks. I've never seen her look so depressed." She looked across the café and spotted Barb standing beside the counter. "Good for you, Burt. I can't think of anyone more deserving of a good deed than Big Barb right now."

Later that afternoon Kelly tabbed between columns, entering some of Don Warner's expenses for the Denver shopping center he was renovating. Sometimes builders' initial estimate of project expenses are close to actual costs. When that happy coincidence occurs, everyone is happy: Don Warner and team, landowners, and accountants. But when the opposite occurred — project estimates were lower than actual costs — then the accountant was the one who had to balance the overspent accounts and delayed revenues and figure out how to solve the problems.

Sitting at the main knitting table, Kelly had been able to straighten out two of

Warner's disobedient accounts, but she was still knee-deep in the financial swamp of this project. The large room was empty and no customers were browsing in the central yarn room or the foyer. That was an unusual occurrence, but Kelly was grateful for the quiet.

Then a familiar voice broke into Kelly's concentration. "Hello, Kelly."

Kelly blinked out of the cloud of numbers and looked up to see Big Barb setting her huge tapestry knitting bag at the end of the table. "Hey, Barb, it's good to see you. How're you doing?"

"Thanks for asking, Kelly. I appreciate that." She looked over at Kelly with a brief smile. "I'm doing really well, actually." She settled at the table and brought out the baby blanket she was knitting. "Let me see if I can finish this blanket, so I can send it to my niece."

Kelly pushed her laptop to the side. She hadn't gotten to talk with Barb for a week and was anxious to see if her mood had improved. "I imagine you're relieved that the police have found a second suspect in Laura Brewster's murder."

Barb gave Kelly a look. "I'll say. Some professor at the university. And from what I've heard whispered around, this professor

had a past history with that . . . that girl."
Barb's proficient needles started to pick up
where she'd left off in the pale blue wool.

Surprised by Barb's statement, Kelly
wondered if Burt had revealed the connection between Laura Brewster and Professor
Smith. Either that, or Mimi had whispered
it to Barb. Kelly decided she couldn't feign
ignorance, since she was mainly responsible
for bringing that information to Burt's attention and subsequently the police's.

"Yes, I'd heard about their, uh . . . past
history. It certainly does make you think.
This professor has certainly gotten on the
police radar screen."

"I should say. If those police detectives
have any sense, they should be putting their
energies into building a case against that
man and leave my law-abiding, good citizen
son alone!"

Barb hadn't looked up from her knitting
during her passion-filled statement, but
Kelly could still feel the heat coming across.
"I think you make a very good point, Barb.
I certainly trust that Detective Dan and his
men will investigate this professor
thoroughly."

"They'd better. Or they'll have me to deal
with."

Kelly suppressed her smile. Big Barb had

morphed into Protective Mom once again. And the Fort Connor Police Department had better watch out.

Sixteen

Tuesday afternoon

Kelly shoved the cell phone into a pocket of her white summer pants and continued walking across the gravel driveway that separated her cottage from the knitting shop. The early-afternoon sun was bearing down, so Kelly was about to pick up her pace when she heard Burt call her name. She glanced toward the garden patio and saw Burt beckon her to join him at a shady table amidst the greenery.

"Good choice," Kelly said as she approached the retired detective. "If this wasn't in the shade, I would have pretended I didn't see you and kept walking toward the air-conditioning."

Burt chuckled. "I understand. I've been darting between air-conditioned car and air-conditioned stores all morning. It's hotter than hot today."

"Well, we've only had a couple of ninety-nine- and one-hundred-degree days, so you know we were due for more. This is still July, our hottest month." She settled into the chair across from him and signaled waitress Julie, who was clearing a nearby outdoor table.

"Don't I know it," Burt said, pulling out a folded white handkerchief and mopping his forehead. "I sat down here only ten minutes ago, but I swear I've downed two glasses of ice water so far. I look forward to August and the gradual drop in temperatures."

"Maybe we should go inside then," Kelly suggested, glancing around. "The lunch crowd is starting to slow, judging from the free tables."

"No, no, what I have to tell you requires more privacy than the shop or the café offer right now."

Kelly perked up at that. "Well, that certainly has aroused my interest. You must have heard something."

Julie walked up to them then, a glass pitcher of iced coffee in her hand. "Hey, you two. You both look ready for a refill. Poor Burt was parched when he got in a few minutes ago." She took Kelly's mug and poured a cold dark stream of iced coffee into it.

"I'm ready for some," Burt said, holding

out his empty mug, which Julie filled quickly.

"Okay, that should hold you two for a few minutes," Julie said with a grin before she walked over to some other outdoor diners.

Kelly took a deep drink of icy cold black coffee and leaned back into the wrought iron chair. "So, what's up? Did you hear something more from Dan?"

"He left me a message this morning about the medical examiner's report. The ME actually checked Laura Brewster's body a second time, Dan said. Apparently the ME had to use an assistant for the initial examination because of the schedule —"

"Bodies piling up at the morgue?" Kelly said with a devilish smile. "Forgive me, I couldn't resist."

"Yeah, yeah," Burt said with a wry smile. "Anyway, the medical examiner wasn't convinced that there were no traces of DNA found under the victim's fingernails. After all, the victim had been strangled, so it would be natural for the victim to try to resist by clawing or scratching at the killer's face."

"That makes sense." Kelly tried picturing that, but she couldn't really because she had no image of Laura Brewster in her mind.

"In other words, the examiner doubted

that assistant's work, so he examined the victim's fingernails himself. And he did find small amounts of human tissue underneath the nails on the middle and ring fingers of the right hand."

"Really?" Kelly felt a little buzz go off inside. She'd learned over the years to pay attention to the little warning signs or the buzz she felt occasionally. It always led to something important.

Burt nodded. "The medical examiner sent the tissue off to the crime lab for DNA analysis a few days ago."

"When do you think they'll hear back? That crime lab seems to be jammed a lot of times."

"Well, the logjams are being cleared up, thank goodness. So Dan's hoping they won't have to wait too long. Needless to say, he's enthusiastic about the medical examiner's discovery. It could bring a breakthrough on the case. Of course, both Tommy and Professor Smith would have to agree to submit DNA samples for comparison."

Kelly nodded. "What if the DNA sample doesn't match either of them? What then? Will Dan go back to the violent intruder theory?"

Burt let out a sigh and sank back in his

chair. "Yeah, I'm afraid so, and all we have is a parking lot surveillance video showing a guy in a hooded jacket walking into the building. No face, no identifying characteristics, nothing."

Kelly looked out into the deep green of the shade plants in the garden. "Wow. That's going to be next to impossible. Trying to find the killer, I mean. There's nothing to go on, really. That guy in the video could be a resident of the apartment. Completely innocent."

"Tell me about it," Burt said ruefully.

"Where would Dan start. If that happens, I mean?"

"He'll have to go back to basic police work. Interviewing anyone who knew Laura Brewster once again. Asking more questions, seeing if any relationship or situation turns up. Then questioning the people in that apartment building, hoping someone saw or heard something that night. Or noticed anything different. Anything at all."

Kelly watched Burt's expression turn pessimistic, as if he were still responsible for finding the killer in this case. "With cases like this, I bet you're glad you no longer have to find out whodunit."

Burt met Kelly's sympathetic gaze and nodded. "You got that right, Kelly."

■ ■ ■ ■

"Hello, Kelly. How are you this afternoon?"

Kelly stopped digging into her knitting bag and looked up to see Big Barb smiling at her as she entered the main room. Delighted to see a smile on Barb's face, Kelly exclaimed, "Hey, there, Barb. It's so good to see you looking like your old self again."

Barb set her enormous tapestry knitting bag on the long library table. "Thank you, Kelly. It's good to feel like myself again." She pulled out a chair at the end of the table and sat. Then she started pulling out several plastic bags of yarn from her oversize knitting bag and piling them on the table. Each bag held a different color yarn.

"Do you have a class today, Barb? I can't keep track of the schedule around here. Something different is happening every day."

"Yes, but it's not for over an hour, so I thought I'd come early and organize my thinking for the class. I may talk to them about felting. A couple of students asked me about it."

"I think that's a great idea, Barb. Maybe build some more interest in Mimi's next class. I really enjoyed her last class. Of course, I have to wait till fall to use the felted scarf I made."

"I believe yours was the striking red silk with orange- and rose-colored fibers felted onto it."

"Yes, that's mine. Megan was giving me a hard time about being too conservative with the colors I wear. So it was good to be able to flaunt my new creation. And it's certainly easier to do than some of the more advanced projects you're always teaching."

Barb wagged her head, still smiling. "Kelly, Kelly. How many times have we told you that you are much better than you think? Give yourself credit, my girl."

Kelly started to laugh as she pulled out the summer top she'd started knitting earlier, before the ribbon scarves. It was an easy pattern that she'd almost finished. Only a few more rows of the variegated royal blue and shamrock green cotton yarn to go before she could start binding off. Maybe she could chat with Barb and finally finish this piece. It seemed like every time she settled in to knit this top, something distracted her.

"Thanks so much for the boost in confidence, Barb. I think I'll sit right here with you as I try to finish this top. And for the record, I've tried to master some of those more complicated stitches you teach. But it didn't work. The yarn would get twisted as I was knitting, or I would mess up another stitch when I tried to do it. So I'd go back to the reliable old garter stitch and purl stitch with some yarn over stitches thrown in for variety. That's about as adventurous as I'll get in knitting." She grinned at Barb.

"You can do it, Kelly. Take charge. You need to make those stitches behave," Barb decreed in her old authoritative voice.

Kelly was so glad to hear Big Barb sound like her old bossy self, she willingly played along. "Yes, ma'am," Kelly replied, interrupting her knitting to do a half salute. Deciding to broach the subject that had been responsible for the improvement in Barb's mood, Kelly glanced around to make sure no one else was close by. "It's good to have the old Barb back," she said with a grin.

Barb glanced up from examining the bags of yarns and returned Kelly's smile. "Well, I've felt a lot better now that the police have located another suspect in the death of that girl."

"I'm sure you have. By the way, how's

Tommy holding up? Under all that stress, I mean."

"As well as he can, poor dear." A frown captured her face again. "I hope this ordeal can be over soon. I had a feeling something would come out of the girl's past. Burt confirmed the rumors I heard. She had made accusations against this other man in town, this professor, a few years ago. And it seems his career at the university had been severely affected. That sounds like a reason to kill to me."

Kelly was struck by the coldness of Barb's tone, so she chose her words carefully. Clearly, Barb was back in her role as Protective Mother. Super Mom. Ready to swoop down and wreak havoc on those who would threaten our children or families.

"It certainly sounds suspicious to me," Kelly agreed.

Burt suddenly appeared in the archway between the main and central yarn rooms. He glanced first at Barb, then at Kelly, and his familiar smile broke out. "Hello, you two. So nice to see the both of you," he said as he walked over to the table and chose a chair close to Barb.

Barb peered at Burt. "Have you heard any new information from your former partner?"

"No new information yet. But Dan did leave me a message that they had contacted Tommy early this morning and asked if he would submit a DNA sample for the medical examiner. Tommy readily agreed and went to the department downtown and submitted a sample. I thought you'd be pleased to hear that." Burt smiled at her.

Barb simply stared at Burt, not returning his smile. "What? He didn't tell me he was going to do that. Was our lawyer present?"

Obviously surprised by her response, Burt replied, "I don't know. Dan didn't mention a lawyer. But it's a simple procedure. Just a swab from inside the cheek. I'm sure Tommy knew that. He is a doctor, after all." Burt gave a half smile.

Barb didn't return that, either. Instead, she looked annoyed. "Still, he should have called me." She reached for her huge knitting bag and dug inside until she pulled out a phone. "I'm going to call him right now," she said, springing from her chair.

Kelly and Burt watched her hasten out of the main room and head for the foyer. Kelly glanced over at Burt. "Wow. I guess Super Mom wanted to be consulted."

Burt wagged his head, staring after his old friend. "I guess. Barb is used to being bossy, but Tommy's a grown man."

"I get the feeling he's never really cut those apron strings. In fact, I got that feeling years ago when he was temporarily a suspect in his girlfriend's murder."

"Really?" Burt looked surprised.

"Oh, yeah. Remember, I'm not an old friend of the family like you and Mimi are. I'm an outsider, so I saw that 'dominating mother, submissive son' relationship years ago." Kelly glanced into the room, remembering. "Wow. That was almost three years ago. Gee, time really does fly, doesn't it?"

Burt chuckled. "You're right about that, Kelly. It passes too darn fast for me. And I've got news for you. The older you get, the faster time passes. Lightning speed sometimes."

"I've heard that said, Burt, and I have a feeling you're right. It's hard to believe that it's been six years since I came back here for Aunt Helen's funeral."

"And you've been here ever since." Burt grinned. "And speaking for myself, Mimi, and all your gang of friends, we are mighty glad you came."

Kelly returned his warm smile. "So am I, Burt. So am I."

"Ooooooooh, is that buttered?" Megan

asked as she dipped her fingers into Marty's box of popcorn that evening.

"Of course," the redhead replied as he leaned back against the Rolland Moore ball fields' bleachers. Extending the box toward the bleacher row in front of him, he said, "Eat up, guys. I'm gonna go get some with jalapeño butter. I'm craving hot and spicy."

"Seriously?" Greg said, putting his half-eaten hot dog aside. "I'll pass it around. After I have some, of course." Greg scooped up a big handful of buttery popcorn and gobbled it up. Two or three kernels dropped down between the bleacher rows.

"Pass it along. You're still eating your third hot dog," Lisa said, taking the box and offering it toward Kelly and Steve at the end of that row of bleachers.

"Don't mind if I do," Kelly said, taking a sticky handful. "Want some?" She offered the box to Steve, who was leaning back against the bleachers behind them.

"Sure." Steve took a few kernels and tossed them one at a time into his mouth.

"Have you ever noticed how people eat popcorn?" Pete asked Jennifer, seated on the other side of Kelly. "Kelly took a small handful. Steve tosses them into his mouth one at a time. Then there's Greg's technique —"

"Gobble and gorge," Lisa said with a devilish smile.

Kelly and friends laughed out loud at that image.

Greg put both arms up in a wrestler's pose, flexing his muscles. "Hey, I'm carbo-loading. I've got a race this weekend."

"In Fort Connor?" Megan asked.

"No, Loveland. It's a short one. Just twenty miles. Charity event." Greg reached his long arm down the row where the popcorn box had landed — next to Pete — and scooped another huge handful.

"You know what I want?" Jennifer said. "I'd love one of those chocolate-covered ice cream bars on a stick. I haven't had one of those in ages."

"Ummmm, that does sound good," Kelly chimed in. "What made you think of that with all the popcorn talk?"

Jennifer pointed down to the front of the bleachers where Cassie and three of her softball friends sat, devouring popcorn, sodas, and ice cream bars. "Cassie's friend Judy got one and suddenly I remembered eating them as a kid in the summertime. Playing with friends in the playground."

"Running through the sprinklers," Lisa joined the reminiscing.

"The only time I ran through sprinklers

was when I was hot and sticky after ball practice," Steve said, crossing his arms behind his head as he relaxed.

"Well, it's been hot and sticky today, so I say it's ice cream bar time," Marty declared, rising from the bleachers. "I'll get more regular popcorn, some with jalapeño, and some ice cream bars. Anything else?"

"I'll come with you," Pete said, jumping up from the bleachers. "Anybody want another hot dog?"

Greg started to raise his hand.

"You must be kidding!" Lisa stared at him with a horrified expression.

"I just did it to see your expression," he said, giving her a wicked grin. Lisa rolled her eyes and made an exasperated sound.

Pete jumped to the ground and walked over to Cassie and her friends on the first row of bleachers. "You girls want anything? We're going to the concession stand."

Cassie and the other three girls chorused simultaneously in rousing replies of "Yes!" "Potato chips, please!" "Can you get ice cream, please?"

Pete grinned. "Then, c'mon. We'll need your help to carry all that," he said, beckoning to them. All four girls jumped off the bleacher row and followed after Marty and Pete.

"The magic words. 'Concession stand,' " Kelly said with a smile, watching the thirteen-year-old girls cluster together in a gangly bunch.

"That's for sure. When I taught that kids' tennis team at the recreation center, they all made a mad dash for the concession stand afterward. It's gotta be the age," Megan observed.

"They're all going through growth spurts," Lisa said. "I watched it with my younger sisters. They shoot up like weeds."

"Like Cassie," Jennifer added. "She's almost eye to eye with me now. And she's going to grow a lot more."

"She's going to be tall. That's for sure."

"We've never met Pete's sister," Megan said. "I wonder if she's tall. Pete is medium height, so his sister is probably shorter."

"But we don't know how tall her father is," Greg said, leaning back on the bleachers again. "Wonder who he was. Some student, Pete said."

Jennifer gave a little shrug. "That's all we know. Tanya was in the midst of her 'I wanna be a rock singer' phase. Pete said she was partying every night and sleeping around. All she remembers is the guy was probably a student because she was still taking classes at the university and everybody would flock to the bars in Old Town at night."

Greg closed his eyes. "Hmmmmm. Well, Cassie's tall now, and you guys say she'll keep growing. So the dude had to be tall. And Cassie's smart, so Tanya must not have been a roaring drunk."

"I asked Pete about Tanya, and he said she got a lot of nausea when she was first pregnant, so she quit drinking. It made her sicker," Jennifer said.

"Well, that was a blessing," Kelly said. She noticed Eric's team appear on the sidelines in their green uniforms, watching as the other game finished up. One more strike and that game would be over.

"Well, whoever the guy is, he's missing out on watching one great kid grow up," Steve offered.

"That's for sure," Megan added. Then she pointed to the side. "Hey, here comes Mimi and Burt."

"Hey, hey, you two," Kelly greeted as Mimi and Burt walked over to the bleachers. "There's plenty of room. Cassie and her friends have staked out that first row."

"Hello, everyone," Mimi said, climbing onto the second row.

"Hey, folks," Burt greeted with a wave. "Looks like we got here in time. That's

Eric's team taking the field now."

Kelly glanced toward the field and saw the other two teams heading off while Eric's green-shirted team claimed the baseball diamond.

"Where's Cassie?" Mimi craned her neck, looking around while Burt settled onto the bleachers.

"She and her friends are at the concession stand with Pete and Marty," Megan said. "They'll be right back."

"Well, howdy, folks," Jayleen's voice sounded right beside the bleachers.

"Hey, there, Jayleen, Curt," Steve said. "You want to climb up?" He offered his hand to her.

"Naw, I think I'll join Mimi and Burt down there for a spell." She strolled toward the front row.

"I'll join you folks," Curt said as he stepped onto a lower row of bleachers and climbed up beside Megan. "We were a ways down, talking to some rancher friends. Then I spotted Eric's team take the field."

Kelly peered at the field, looking for Eric's number 12 shirt. Spotting the tall gangly thirteen-year-old taking some practice swings with the bat, she noticed that Eric's form had improved.

"Eric's swing is looking smoother," she

observed out loud.

"Well, he's been doing the work," Steve said, staring out toward the field. "He's been practicing regularly with the ball machine."

"That boy's been hitting way better since you started working with him, Steve," Curt said, staring down at the field.

"Eric's a quick learner," Steve said. "Plus he's willing to work at it. Practices with the ball machine a couple times a week. That makes a whale of a difference."

"That's for sure," Kelly agreed. "Cassie uses the ball machine after every clinic session I teach. In fact, the rest of the girls do the same now. I had three machines going at once."

"No wonder she's improved," Lisa said.

"Practice will do it every time," Megan decreed. "I had a tennis pro instructor years ago who always told me to practice four hours for every hour of lessons. That's how to improve your skills. He swore by it."

"Whoa, four to one. That's a lot," Jennifer said.

"Makes sense. What you practice, you learn," Kelly added.

"Well, we have a couple of real good learners who're not afraid of doing the hard work," Curt observed. "Both Cassie and

Eric have got a heckuva good work ethic. They're gonna do great in life."

"Oh, yeah," Kelly and the rest of the Gang agreed.

Seventeen

Friday afternoon

"Hello, there, Kelly-girl," a familiar voice sounded, breaking through Kelly's spreadsheet concentration.

Kelly swiftly turned to see Jayleen Swinson stride across the empty café alcove toward her, broad smile in place. "Jayleen, it's great to see you here," Kelly said on sighting her old friend. "I've only seen you briefly at baseball and softball games, and we hardly got a chance to talk."

"Good to see you, too, Kelly," Jayleen said as she pulled out a chair across the table from her. Late afternoon and the café was empty. "You and Steve are going to have to come up to the ranch for a trail ride with Curt and me. It's been a while since you two have taken a ride."

Kelly shoved her laptop aside and leaned across the table. "You know, that sounds tempting. Getting outside in the woods up in the canyon. Peaceful. Steve and I could use some of that."

"You two work too hard. It's a good thing you both play ball. At least you're outside in the fresh air and sunshine regularly."

"Are you kidding?" Kelly joked. "This is late July! We're cooking in the sun."

Jayleen chuckled and leaned back in the chair. "Summertime in Colorado."

"It's been fun watching the kids' games this summer. It's also given us a chance to see you and Curt more often. We're down at the ball fields every weekend, either playing our games or watching Cassie's and Eric's." Kelly took a drink of her iced coffee.

Jayleen nodded. "It sure has been nice to have Cassie join us and the grandkids for all our adventures. She's become a regular member of the family ever since she came here last summer. Hard to believe a whole year has come and gone."

"I know what you mean. Cassie fits in so well with the Gang and at Lambspun, it's almost like she was meant to be here. And I know how well she's fit in with you and Curt and his grandkids, because I get to hear her tell all about those adventures." Kelly grinned.

"She's a jewel, that's for sure," Jayleen

said. "Not every young girl would be able to adjust and adapt so easily to a totally new home environment like she did last summer. New town, new family, new home, new school, having to make new friends. Cassie found her place in each one."

"Yeah. She has an amazing ability to fit in just about anywhere." Kelly smiled across at Jayleen. "And you two took to each other right away, as I recall. Like coffee and cream."

Jayleen glanced down with a smile. "I have to admit, she captured my heart from the moment I met her."

"I remember. It was here at Lambspun. You invited Cassie out to the ranch, and she fell in love with it."

Jayleen nodded. "And those alpacas."

A stray thought surfaced in Kelly's mind. Something she'd wanted to say to Jayleen if she ever got the chance. "You know, Cassie never knew her grandmother because she'd died. All she had was her grandfather Ben. And now he isn't able to be involved in her life like he used to. It seems like Cassie is sorely missing grandparents in her life. And you and Mimi have both become the grandmothers Cassie never had."

Jayleen met Kelly's gaze and smiled. "You're right about that, Kelly-girl. Cassie has filled a hole in my heart I never knew I had."

Kelly knew what she meant. *Jayleen's missing children.* Her drinking had cost Jayleen the custody of her school-aged children years ago. Her second husband raised them alone. Jayleen had told Kelly she'd tried to make contact after she'd become sober, but neither her son nor her daughter responded. They obviously weren't interested in meeting her. By now Jayleen's children probably had children of their own. Grandchildren Jayleen would never know.

"Well, I can't think of two women who deserve grandchildren more than you and Mimi," Kelly said, looking into Jayleen's eyes.

Jayleen glanced out into the empty alcove. "That's right. Mimi's son died in college. Way too young."

"And he was Mimi's only child, so I suspect Cassie is filling a hole in Mimi's heart as well."

Jayleen looked back at Kelly and laughed softly. "Perceptive as ever. Isn't that what Curt says to you?"

"I think it's Burt, but no matter. By the way, Curt and Burt aren't too shabby as grandfathers, either."

At that, Jayleen let out a bigger laugh.

"Well, you're right on that. And both of them have plenty of experience in that department, too."

Kelly joined her laughter as Mimi walked into the alcove. "Hey, there, you two. I thought I heard Jayleen's laugh," Mimi said with a grin as she paused at the edge of the alcove and the hallway. "I'm going to have to steal her away, Kelly. Jayleen and I need to talk about fleeces and such."

"Mercy sakes alive," Jayleen said, pushing herself out of the chair. "Kelly and I were having such fun talking I purely forgot about taking care of business. We'll talk some more at the next ball game, Kelly," she promised, then headed toward the hallway.

"No problem." Kelly waved them off. "I have to return to these wayward spreadsheets anyway."

"Oh, I think Burt was looking for you," Mimi said as she turned away. "I'll tell him you're here."

Kelly debated returning to the numbers that wouldn't behave, then decided to refill her coffee mug instead. Jennifer always left a full carafe of coffee for Kelly in the café kitchen. That way she could easily last until dinner without munching on anything. By the time she returned to her café table in the corner, Burt appeared in the alcove.

"Hey, Kelly, Mimi said you were here. Catching up with Jayleen."

"Yeah, I told her she and Mimi had become the missing grandmothers in Cassie's life," Kelly said as she settled into her chair.

Burt chuckled. "You're right about that. I've felt the exact same thing. Mimi has loved being a second grandma to my daughter's kids, but I have to admit, Cassie has got a special place in Mimi's heart."

Kelly nodded. "And the same with Jayleen. I told her I couldn't think of two women who deserved grandchildren more than the two of them."

"That's the truth." Burt's smile faded. "I wanted to let you know that the crime lab came back with DNA results."

That got Kelly's attention. "Really? That's been, what? About four days? Boy, they are moving faster. So, did they find any matches?"

Burt frowned. "Well, yes and no. Professor Smith had no matches whatsoever, so he's off police radar entirely. Dan said he would contact Smith today. But Tommy showed some similarities in certain markers, Dan said. No exact matches, just those similarities. But that was enough to draw police interest."

Kelly screwed up her face. "What? What kind of similarities are we talking about here? I thought you either got a match or you didn't."

Burt shrugged. "Most of the time, that's what you do get. But the medical examiner was being very, very careful. He only had a small example of skin tissue from under the victim's nails. So he's going to run the tests again. In fact, he may ask Tommy for another DNA sample, too."

Kelly sank back in her chair. "Good Lord. Does that mean Tommy is still a suspect?"

A pained expression crossed Burt's face. "I'm afraid so. Tommy hasn't been cleared by the police yet. Professor Smith has been. They won't be questioning him further because he's no longer a suspect."

Kelly stared at Burt for a minute. "Do you think Tommy will cooperate and provide another sample?"

"I have no idea, Kelly. That decision will be between Tommy and his lawyer."

Kelly shot Burt a look. "You forgot Barb. There's no way this decision is going to sit well with her. I can picture the storm clouds on her face right now. Lightning bolts."

"Oh, yeah," Burt nodded. "And I guess I'll be the first one to dodge those lightning bolts. I'm getting ready to meet her in the parking lot in a few minutes. It's better if I tell her before her class. So she has time to settle down."

"You hope."

Burt released a long sigh. "Yeah. I hope."

Kelly hoped that Burt was right. She was just glad she didn't have to be the one to tell Big Barb.

Kelly peered around the corner of the front room and saw Mimi at the counter next to the cash register. Rosa wasn't there, so Kelly hastened over while Mimi had a quiet moment, before another customer walked up.

"Hey, Mimi. How'd Barb take Burt's news about those DNA results? Have you spoken with her?"

Mimi's eyes went wide, and she peered into the central yarn room, clearly checking if it was empty. "Oh, Lord, yes. Barb is furious! She went outside to call Tommy right away and tell him to get over to their lawyer's office immediately." Mimi lowered her voice even more. "I told Burt that she looks mad enough to storm down to the police department and tell them off."

"Well, if anyone could do it, Barb could." Kelly could picture that scene right now.

Big Barb going toe to toe with Detective Dan.

"Lord have mercy, I hope you're wrong," Mimi said, worry lines gathering as her cell phone jingled with one of Mimi's favorite lighthearted tunes. "Excuse me, Kelly. It's one of those other shops I've been talking to."

Kelly raised her coffee mug to her and headed through the central yarn room. Now that she'd beaten those disobedient numbers into cooperation, Kelly decided she deserved a break. Besides, she was almost to the point of binding off her knitted top. Perhaps this would be a quiet time.

As she turned toward the main room, however, Kelly was surprised to see Barb holding class around the table. Almost every chair was taken. So much for peace and quiet.

"Oh, excuse me. I didn't know you were holding a class here, Barb."

"That's all right, Kelly. Take a seat. My class and I are having a catch-up session on their projects today. So, join us."

"Thanks. I promise to be quiet," Kelly said with a good-natured smile as she headed toward a chair at the end of the table closest to the windows.

"Okay, Barb. I have another question." An

older knitter on the right side of Barb spoke up.

"Just one?" said a younger woman across the table. "I have several." She glanced up briefly from her needles.

"Me, too," said the knitter on Kelly's right side. She didn't look up but kept her attention on her knitting.

"I don't think the police can charge Tommy with anything if there are no DNA matches," the older knitter beside Barb said. The light green sweater she was knitting looked close to finished. This woman didn't watch her stitches at all. She focused on Barb. Kelly always was in awe of knitters who could ignore their knitting and yet produce perfect stitches.

"I agree. I think the court would rule against them, right?" the knitter beside Kelly asked.

"I would think so," the younger knitter added. "There's no real match."

"Even if the police charged Tommy, wouldn't a jury consider that reasonable doubt . . . or something like that?" the younger woman spoke up.

"Ohhhh, don't even mention a jury trial," the knitter beside Barb said.

"Please, no. I don't even want to think about that," Barb said in a low voice.

323

Kelly observed Barb. There was no sign of the Furious Mom ready to give the police a piece of her mind, which Kelly pictured a few minutes ago. Nor was Bossy Barb in evidence. Barb sat quietly, concentrating on the sweater she was knitting. Kelly noticed her face was pinched with the same worry that Kelly had seen most of this month since Tommy's ordeal began.

"Have you spoken with Tommy, Barb? I mean, since those results came in?" another knitter asked quietly.

Barb didn't reply in words. She just nodded her head.

"How's he holding up?" the woman beside Barb asked.

"Pretty well. Confused, of course." Barb murmured so low, Kelly had to lean forward to hear.

The knitter beside Kelly spoke up. "Have the police ever considered the possibility that the victim was killed by someone who got into her apartment? I mean, she was in apartments near campus. I know how insecure those places can be. My son lived in a couple of different apartments while he was going to the university. And he and his roommates had break-ins several times. They had televisions stolen, laptops, anything valuable that was electronic. It was a nightmare."

"I know. My daughter's place was broken into twice. Once by a guy who tried to assault her roommate. A friend walked in and scared the guy away."

"Good Lord . . ."

"Did she identify him to the police?"

"She tried to, but he didn't match any of the photos they had. With an entire campus filled with students, it's way too easy for any one of them to be tempted by a patio door left open a crack."

"Or an unlocked lower-floor window."

"Or worse, an open lower-floor window. And no one in sight."

"So many of these kids just don't think," the older knitter commented.

"And so often the real reason is because the person inside is either drunk or close to it and doesn't pay attention," the younger woman observed.

The young woman's voice had the sound of experience. These comments were all too familiar to Kelly. Living in a university or college town was an educational experience in many ways. Plus, Kelly had quite a few acquaintances and business associates, so she was well aware of the relationship between the city and the university. College students had certain habits — like partying late on Friday and Saturday nights — that caused problems. If the students lived in university housing, it was more easily handled. If the students lived in single homes in the midst of older neighborhoods surrounding the university, then the partying issue became a bigger problem. Add to that mix a significant portion of those neighborhoods being inhabited by senior citizens, then the situation could turn volatile.

"That's definitely an issue that leads to these incidents. Someone enters an apartment through an open or unlocked door while the resident is drunk —"

"Or, asleep."

"Do you think that's what happened in this instance? I mean, with this girl who was murdered?"

"I think it's entirely possible," the woman beside Kelly added.

Kelly listened to all the comments swirling around the knitting table and decided she might as well add her two cents. "I agree. I've always thought it was possible that Laura Brewster was killed by some violent intruder. For all the reasons you folks have just mentioned." She picked up the stitches where she left off. Only a couple more rows and she could start binding off.

"That's entirely possible."

"What do you think, Barb?" the older knitter beside her asked. "Do you think it was some violent intruder like Kelly said who killed Laura Brewster?"

Barb didn't look up, just kept knitting her neat perfect rows of stitches as she spoke. "Yes, I think it's definitely possible that some intruder was responsible. All I know is Tommy didn't kill that evil girl."

Kelly looked up from her knitting. Barb's cold voice brought a chill to those words. No doubt everyone at the table felt it as well, because a silence enveloped the entire room now.

"Hey, Kelly!"

Kelly swiftly turned around and scanned the café patio garden at the sound of Megan's voice. She spotted her friend hopping along the flagstones, heading her way.

"I'm glad you're still here," Megan said as she rushed up to Kelly's table. "Would you and Steve like to buy some raffle tickets for charity? My business group is raising money for the Food Bank of Northern Colorado." Megan plopped her knitting bag onto the wrought iron table and dug inside.

"Sure thing. That's one of my favorite local charities," Kelly said, reaching into her briefcase bag on the ground beside her chair. "How much?"

"We're selling them for a dollar each, but most people are buying several." Megan grinned and waved her fistful of tickets.

Kelly laughed. "I'll take that as a hint. Here's twenty dollars. That'll be ten for Steve and ten for me."

"Thank you, thank you," Megan said. "I appreciate it more than you know. I had them shoved in the bottom of my bag here and completely forgot about them. Then I got a phone call from the organizer this morning reminding me I had to turn in the money tomorrow at our luncheon! I've been in a panic ever since. I'll be hitting up team-mates and families on the bleachers," Megan said, breathless, as she tore off the tickets and handed them over to Kelly.

"I can see that. Why don't you sit down and knit a little while? Get your equilibrium back." Kelly pushed one of the chairs toward Megan. "I was finishing up this last expense account, so why don't you catch me up on your clients. I haven't heard a rant for a while. Don't tell me they're all behaving themselves." Kelly closed off her spreadsheets and shut down her laptop.

"Most of them are, but there's always one who refuses to get his stuff to me in a timely manner, shall we say?" Megan said as she settled into the chair.

"Ohhhhh, yes. I can definitely relate to that," Kelly said, reaching into her bag and bringing out the knitted summer top she was finishing. She was in the midst of binding off the bottom stitches.

"This guy has only been with me six months, so I don't have him fully trained yet," Megan said as she pulled out a shamrock green sleeveless top she was knitting. Megan could finish three items in the time it took Kelly to produce one. Amazing.

Kelly snickered. "Fully trained. I love it."

"Everything he wants is a super rush. Expedited." She made a disgusted face. "When it happened last month, I had just had another client shift his schedule around. So that freed up some time to take care of Late Guy. And I warned him that I couldn't always get his stuff done at the last moment." She shrugged as stitches formed on her needles. "I guess he didn't believe me. Because he called this morning, all in a panic. He needed this project done today, absolutely positively. And I had to tell him that I would not be able to get his request done today. I already had two other clients' projects that I was finishing and they were due today as well. And both of them had

planned ahead and gotten on my *schedule.*"
She emphasized the last word.

"How'd he handle it?" Kelly asked, slipping another bound-off stitch from her needles.

"Not well. He got all hyper. His voice went up an octave, I swear. But I talked him down off the ledge. Promised him I could do it tomorrow. And he promised he'd get on the schedule on time next month." She looked up at Kelly with a crooked smile. "We'll see."

Kelly chuckled, picturing Take-No-Prisoners Megan soothing her client in her own inimitable fashion. Glancing over toward the driveway, she spotted Lisa. "Lisa! We're over here." She waved, then beckoned her friend.

"Well, perfect timing," Lisa said, smiling. "We're all so busy lately it's been hard to find a time when we can sit and knit for a few minutes." She pulled out a chair between Kelly and Megan.

"How come you're finished at the clinic early?" Kelly looked at her watch. "Normally you're booked solid, Cassie says."

Lisa dug into her large felted knitting bag and pulled out the lacy knit lemon yellow top. It looked almost finished to Kelly. "One client called in sick an hour ago. And another client called right after that and changed his appointment. He'd forgotten he had another appointment scheduled somewhere else." She gave a dramatic sigh. "So, I decided to grab this unexpected gift of free time and come over here and visit for a few minutes."

"Megan was entertaining me with her naughty-client story. She has one who isn't 'fully trained' yet, as she put it." Kelly gave Megan a wicked grin.

"It's my newer guy. Swears he'll get his stuff in on time the next month, then calls in at the last minute and begs me to help him. This month his luck and my patience ran out. I had to tell him he'd have to wait behind my other clients. Much wailing and complaining." Megan's needles seemed to move even faster with her description.

"Oh, yes. Some clients simply refuse to conform. Obedience is simply not in their DNA. They'll do the normal things like pay their taxes and their rent on time, show up at their jobs on time, but they will rebel by being late to everything else. Social occasions, clubs, meeting friends, and especially appointments." She looked over at them with a weary expression. "Some clients are so bad, they've lost their appointment slots entirely. The clinic has a strict schedule and we have to stick to it. So, those always-late patients mess themselves up. All our PTs are so booked, a patient may have to wait over a week to get a missed appointment rebooked. Believe me, most of them only show up late once."

"Your mention of DNA reminds me," Kelly said. "I spoke with Burt earlier today and he said the DNA tests came in at the crime lab and Professor Smith had no matches. So he is completely off the police radar screen. Unfortunately, Tommy had some markers that were similar to the sample found under the victim's nails. Not a match, but some similar markers."

Both Lisa and Megan stopped knitting and looked up at Kelly, clearly surprised. "Oh, no," was all Megan said.

"How can there be no match but still have some similar markers?" Lisa asked, puzzled.

"I have no idea. That's all Burt learned from Dan. Oh, and detectives asked Tommy for another DNA sample to do another test. Whatever. It doesn't sound good."

Kelly glanced at both her close friends and saw the same feelings on their faces that she felt inside. Not good. Not good at all.

EIGHTEEN

Saturday afternoon

"Mimi, is it all right if I settle into this corner and work?" Kelly asked as she walked into the front room. "Rosa has a beginning knitter's class going in the main room and the workroom is full of spinners."

"Sure, Kelly," Mimi said, looking up from the cash register. "The shop is pretty busy this afternoon."

"It's surprising for a late July day," said the customer who was standing at the counter, a skein of fire-engine red yarn in her hands along with a set of knitting needles and a familiar yarn instruction book.

Kelly glanced outside to the gray clouds gathering over the golf course, even darker ones hovering over the foothills. No sunshine to be seen. "Well, it's the very end of July. Still monsoon season. So, more rainstorms will feel good if we get them."

The middle-aged customer standing at the counter turned to Kelly with a puzzled look. "Monsoons? Don't they happen in India?"

Mimi laughed lightly. "Yes, they do. But monsoons also happen in other areas of the world. If the ocean temperatures are warm enough and the air currents are moving in the right direction, they will bring torrents of rain sweeping from the Pacific, over Mexico, and up through Arizona, New Mexico, and Colorado."

"Really?" The woman looked shocked to learn that. "Every year?"

"Just about. Usually in late July but they can show up earlier or later in summer."

"She's right," Kelly said from her spot in the comfy corner chair.

She was about to pop open her laptop when another woman stepped down into the front room of the shop. A large tapestry knitting bag over her arm, the middle-aged brunette woman paused to stroke a finely woven shawl that was draped along the wall beside Kelly. Kelly thought she recognized the woman from Barb's advanced knitting class session yesterday.

The woman fondled another woven item displayed, then glanced toward Kelly's corner. "Hi, there, Kelly. It looks like you've found a perfect spot to work."

"It sure is. I squirrel in here whenever those monsoon clouds appear."

" 'Squirrel in.' I love it," the woman said, smiling.

"I don't want to be stuck in the cottage during a drenching monsoon." Kelly gestured to the large window beside her looking out toward the driveway. Her cottage was visible in the back. "I left the patio screen door open enough so my dog Carl could escape inside if thunder rumbles. You know how dogs hate thunder and lightning."

"I know what you mean. My cocker spaniel hides under my bed whenever there's a thunderstorm." Her smile left, and she glanced to the side. "That was a sobering session we had yesterday, wasn't it? I mean the one around the knitting table with Barb."

"Ohhhhh, yeah," Kelly said, nodding. "I have to admit, it left me feeling depressed."

The woman walked over closer to Kelly. "I know what you mean," she said, her voice lowered. "This whole situation is depressing. To think that a young man who worked so hard to become a doctor and save lives may be guilty of actually taking a life. That's more than I care to think about. And I can see what it's doing to Barb. I'm worried about her."

Kelly closed her laptop and pushed it beside her in the chair. "I'm sorry, but I forgot your name."

The woman's smile returned. "I'm Patty. I've been taking Mimi's and Rosa's classes here at Lambspun for maybe four years now. And I've seen you in the shop off and on. Sitting in on Mimi's classes. We were actually in a felting class together years ago. It was up in the mountains, remember?"

The image of the beautiful mountain lodge where Kelly and friends and other class members had stayed radiated in her mind. "Yes! That was wonderful, wasn't it? What a picturesque setting up there at the lodge."

"Oh, it was glorious. One of the best mountain getaways I've ever taken." Patty pulled out the metal chair at the nearby winding table.

Once Patty had settled, Kelly leaned forward, lowering her voice as well. "What did you mean when you said you've been worried about Barb? Has all this stress over Tommy and the allegations caused health problems?"

Patty shook her head. "No, no physical changes that I'm aware of. And Barb and I have been friends since forever. So we talk regularly. We've known each other for years.

We're the same age. Her son Tommy played with my two boys Brian and Donald. We're even in the same bridge group." Patty smiled. "What I meant was I'm worried that she's been under a heckuva lot of stress these past couple of years. First, with that guy who swindled her family. And she was under suspicion for his death, remember? And now, all this with Tommy."

Kelly watched Patty's face as she recounted the shocks that Big Barb had undergone these past two years. Kelly remembered every one, having been right in the middle of it all. Sleuthing around. "You obviously know Barb a whole lot better than I do. Have you seen changes? Clearly, something is worrying you."

Patty looked toward the windows again, as if gathering her thoughts. "It's little things. She seems short-tempered more often. And distracted. Sometimes I'll be talking to her and ask her a question, and she'll look at me, kind of startled. She hadn't heard a word I've said. And, she's forgetting things. Like our bridge club a few weeks ago. She's never missed our monthly bridge club. Heck, I remember her coming in one time wearing a white nose-and-mouth mask that you get at the hospital. She had a bad cough and didn't want to spread the germs. But she wasn't going to miss a class." Patty gave a little laugh.

"I have to admit, that is quite a litany. I was here to witness it all, but hearing you go through it like that . . . well, it does give you pause," Kelly said.

"Doesn't it, now? And I'm not the only one. Another friend, Susan, the weaver who usually comes in on Saturdays to weave? Well, she's worried, too. And she's known Barb longer than I have. Since she and Barb were little kids here in Fort Connor."

Kelly sought to recall the face of that weaver. So many knitters, spinners, weavers thronged to Lambspun. "Does she have straight gray hair, shoulder length, kind of?"

"Yes, that's Susan. I knew you'd seen her. Anyway, we were both concerned when Barb didn't show up for bridge club three weeks ago. Susan told me later that she'd actually driven over to Barb's house to see if she was all right."

Kelly smiled. "Susan definitely sounds like a good friend. I take it Barb was okay. Maybe not feeling good or something. Maybe coming down with a flu?"

Patty shrugged. "No. Susan told me when she drove over to Barb's house, the lights were on, but Barb wasn't there. And her car was gone. That's really unusual. Barb usually keeps regular hours."

Kelly's smile disappeared. Instead, her little buzzer went off inside. "That *is* strange. Did you see Barb the next day or something? Was she all right?"

"Susan told me she called Barb that next day and said Barb was all right. Said she was out, that's all."

Kelly felt her little buzzer again. But what was it buzzing about? Just because Barb broke from her usual schedule? Everyone does that from time to time. Her buzzer quieted down a bit. "Well, I can understand why you two were worried. But it sounds like Barb just got off schedule. Everybody does, you know." She gave Patty a reassuring smile.

"Yeah, that's what we figure. But I still notice how distracted Barb has been lately, and I figure it's stress." Patty glanced toward Mimi, who was passing by them, several magazines in her hands. "Mimi, haven't you noticed that Barb's more distracted lately?" she asked over her shoulder.

Mimi glanced toward them both, clearly surprised by the question. "Distracted? Now that you mention it, I have noticed that. Barb's not her old hard-charging self." Mimi's expression changed to concern.

"You know her, Patty. Is she having a health issue?"

"Not that I know of, Mimi," Patty replied. "I was just telling Kelly that these past two years have been pretty stressful for Barb. I guess it's just now taking a toll."

Mimi's blue eyes went wide. "Oh, my goodness, yes!" Mimi rolled her eyes and continued up the steps to the loom room, magazines in hand.

"I guess that about sums it up," Patty said with a rueful smile. "Speaking of schedules, I guess I'd better get back on mine before I get behind."

"I know what you mean, Patty," Kelly agreed as she pulled her laptop onto her lap once more. "Time to get back to those pesky client accounts."

"Keeping track of the money, right, Kelly?" Patty said as she rose from the chair.

"Oh, yes. Someone has to make sure those dollars stay where they're supposed to," Kelly said as she popped her laptop open. Spreadsheets were calling.

The next morning

"I'm meeting with a lumber supplier at four this afternoon, but I should be finished by five," Steve said over the phone.

Kelly held her cell phone with one hand

while she tried to open the front door of Lambspun with the other — while holding her coffee mug at the same time. "Okay. I'll pick up something from that new place on the corner of College and Jefferson. That way we can eat before heading for the ball fields."

"Sounds good. See you later. Love you," Steve added.

"Love you, too," Kelly echoed as she hooked one finger around the door handle and yanked it open. She clicked off and dropped her phone into her over-the-shoulder briefcase.

The Lambspun foyer was empty and the shop was quiet. Summer-morning quiet. It was now August. Vacation month for most families, if they hadn't already had their family escapes before.

Colorado schools finished at the end of May, so all students were free to head on family vacations, summer resident camps, or the many sports camps hosted by the university during the summer months. The university's grounds and facilities were extensive enough to host several different kinds of summer camp experiences as well as a dizzying variety of educational and recreational retreats and workshops.

Soccer players would spread across the

athletic fields and into the various gyms dotted around campus, while church groups
would fill the auditoriums and lecture halls
to hear speakers and gather for discussion
groups. Motivational workshops would
alternate with those on meditation, and
charitable organizations would mingle with
chamber of commerce executives. The great
melting pots were the different dining halls
scattered around campus in the dormitories,
Student Union, and various cafés dotting
the campus. Everyone all mixed together.

Kelly walked slowly through the central
yarn room, fingering some of the yarns.
There was a striking combination of colors
in a skein of raw silk fiber from India. She
hadn't noticed that one before. A slight
movement from the main room caught her
eye, and Kelly turned to glimpse Barb at
the end of the library table. However,
instead of knitting on the lavender-colored
sweater that gathered in her lap, Barb was
staring to the side into the alcove. No one
else was to be seen.

Curious as to her friend's mood, Kelly
fixed a bright smile on her face as she
entered the room. "Hi, Barb, how're you
today?"

Barb jumped as if startled, and stared at
Kelly for a second. "Uhhh . . . I'm okay."

Picking up her stitches on the sweater in her lap, Barb resumed knitting.

Kelly set her briefcase bag on the table, pulled out her laptop computer, and settled into a chair along the side. Since Barb hadn't ventured any other comments, Kelly decided to see if she could start a conversation, even if one-sided. "I've bound off that cotton top I've been working on. Now I'm wondering what project to start next," she said, expecting Barb to jump in with suggested projects.

Instead of her usual helpful or instructive comments, however, Barb made no reply at all. She concentrated on her knitting, her hands swiftly moving through the motions. Wondering at Barb's sudden attack of quiet, Kelly sought for some subject she might suggest that could provoke a reply.

Just then Mimi stepped into the room. "Barb, the workroom is clear for your class today. Could you move in there now, if you don't mind? I'm expecting some visitors to the shop pretty soon. So they'll be all over this room."

Again, Barb looked up as if startled, blinked at Mimi, then answered. "Certainly, Mimi. That's not a problem at all." With that, Barb gathered her knitting with one hand and snatched her tapestry bag with

343

the other and walked out of the main room into the adjoining workroom. Mimi simply stared after her.

Kelly couldn't hold back. She gestured to catch Mimi's attention. "Now I know what you mean about distracted," she said in a soft voice. "I tried talking to Barb but it was like she didn't even hear me. As if I wasn't even there."

Mimi looked at Kelly, concern written all over her face. "I know. I'm starting to worry about her, and so is Burt."

The front doorbell jingled, and the sound of people talking in the foyer floated into the main room. Mimi's visitors had obviously arrived. "Looks like they're already here, Mimi. I'll get out of their way, too."

"Thanks, Kelly, I appreciate it. There's space up front if you want," Mimi said before walking toward the foyer.

Kelly shoved the laptop back into the briefcase bag, gathered her coffee mug, and evacuated the room as well. Heading through the central yarn room, she noticed four women excitedly touching and examining yarns in the foyer. Mimi was smiling and talking.

Walking into the loom room, Kelly noticed an older woman setting up at the Mother Loom. Straight cut, shoulder-length gray hair, Kelly recognized the woman from previous visits to Lambspun. "Hi, there, you must be Susan," Kelly said, smiling as she paused at the loom. "I was talking with your friend Patty today. She and I have shared some workshops."

"Oh, hey, Kelly," Susan said with a friendly smile. "Yes, Patty started taking classes here about four years ago. Of course, I've been showing up from the time Mimi opened her first little shop in Old Town."

"Really? Wow, I recall her saying that she started years ago with a small shop there." Kelly tried to picture Lambspun's yarns being crammed into a narrow little shop. The image wouldn't come into focus. "I can't picture it, though."

Susan laughed softly. "It wasn't anything like this. Everything was stacked on shelves and such. But Mimi had such a gorgeous variety of yarns that more and more people kept coming. That's how it grew. That, plus her classes." Susan opened her large fabric bag beside her and brought out two spools of yarn that matched the purple and blue fibers of the short expanse of woven fabric on the loom.

Kelly wondered how to broach the subject of Barb, but decided there was no way to dance around it. So she resorted to her usual forthright habits. "You know, Patty and I were sharing our concerns about Barb. She's been under so much stress with her son Tommy and that whole situation. Patty said you'd known Barb since childhood and were also concerned."

Susan's smile disappeared. "Goodness, yes. Barb has not been herself for a few weeks now. She's constantly worrying about Tommy and obsessing about the girl." Susan frowned. "Ever since that girl was murdered and Tommy became a suspect, Barb has just gotten paranoid almost. Of course, I can't blame her. If it was my son, I'd obsess about it, too, I'm sure."

"Patty said you were so worried one time when she missed a get-together that you even went to her house to check on her," Kelly said in a deliberately casual manner. "That was considerate of you. Checking on your friend."

"Well, I was worried. Barb had never missed bridge club before, so I was afraid she might be sick or something. So I drove over to her house, only to find all the lights on but no one there. Barb's car was also gone from the garage. That is very unlike Barb. She adores schedules and keeps on track for all meetings and such."

"It does sound unusual," Kelly agreed,

hoping Susan would continue.

"The next day, when I saw Barb in the shop I asked if she was all right, wondering if she'd had to go to the doctor. She'd never missed bridge before. Barb looked surprised that I'd asked and said she'd decided to go to a late-night movie. Then she walked away to make a phone call." Susan's frown reappeared. That's so unlike Barb, and that's when I started to worry about her."

Kelly's little buzzer became louder as Susan related the story. *What was up with Barb?*

"A late-night movie, huh? I admit, that does sound unusual for Barb. Now I understand why you and Patty have been worried."

Kelly looked toward the adjoining yarn room, thoughts starting to buzz inside her head, making no sense whatsoever. She needed some time to think. Checking her watch, Kelly was surprised by the time. It was late afternoon already. She had to be in Arthur Housemann's office in an hour and a half.

"Thanks for explaining all that to me, Susan. Now I know it hasn't been my imagination. I'm going to have to run back to my cottage now and print off some financial statements. I've got a client meeting in an hour or so." She backed away from the Mother Loom toward the doorway into the foyer.

"You're a busy girl, Kelly. Take care. We'll talk again another time," Susan said, returning to the heddles and the beautiful purple and blue weaving she'd started.

"By the way, that is gorgeous, Susan. Really gorgeous. Great job," Kelly called over her shoulder as she sped away.

NINETEEN

Monday morning

Kelly swiftly walked across the driveway toward the patio garden of Pete's Café. From the time she'd returned from her run and jumped in the shower, her morning had been packed with phone calls with both her clients, solving minor issues before they became problems. Kelly hadn't had a moment to draw a deep breath let alone relax until now.

And now she wanted to give attention to the thoughts that had been simmering in the back of her mind since Saturday afternoon. Kelly headed for the smaller table in the back corner of the patio garden. Perfect. Breakfast was tapering off anyway. She'd have some quiet time at last.

Bright summer flowers were blooming in their sunny and shady spots around the garden. Annuals — scarlet red geraniums and multicolored impatiens — as well as dependable perennials — purple and yellow irises — adorned the flower beds.

But what really made the patio garden so enticing was the greenery — bushes and vines and sprawling ground covers. Tiny blossoms peeked through these leaves, nothing showy or dramatic, simply shades of blue or pink. Vinca vines spread among the flowers. And of course, the tall cottonwood trees that provided most of the shade. The smaller crabapple trees also brought shade, their bright pink spring blossoms long gone. But each year they eagerly announced, "Spring is here," after every winter.

"Julie, could you bring me a large iced coffee, please? Might as well start the summer day off right," she said as she spotted the busy waitress.

"Sure thing," Julie said and continued her path toward her customers' table.

Kelly settled in at the back table and pulled out another ribbon scarf. She decided to make one for herself so she could wear it when she went to the kids' games. The ones she had were looking a little worn. They'd gotten a lot of use. This was also a perfect time for sorting through her jumbled thoughts. She needed to "knit on it," as Mimi always advised. Problems came into focus in those quiet times.

She started the familiar rhythmic motions of knitting. Meanwhile, the thoughts that had been zooming around Kelly's mind, darting into each other, not making sense, began to slowly order themselves.

Could it be? Was it possible that . . . that Barb killed Laura Brewster? The unthinkable thought shimmered for a second in Kelly's mind. There was no doubt Barb harbored a ton of resentment toward the young woman. Laura Brewster had filed a complaint with the police, accusing Tommy of sexual assault in his doctor's office. *Tommy.* Barb's beloved son.

Kelly slid another stitch from the left knitting needle and onto the right. Barb certainly gave new meaning to the phrase "overprotective mother." She remembered Barb's reaction last week when Burt told her that Tommy had willingly submitted a DNA sample to police. Barb was angry that Tommy hadn't consulted her beforehand.

That little buzzer nudged Kelly inside. Was Barb's reaction based on her knowledge that the sample might show some DNA markers with similarities? Perhaps Barb's long-cultivated protective mother persona wasn't the real reason Barb expressed aggravation and anger when Burt told her.

Perhaps . . . it was a protective instinct for herself.

More thoughts popped up, begging for Kelly's attention. Barb wasn't at her house the night of Laura's murder, and her excuse made no sense to an old friend. Another thought, then another zoomed in. Kelly finished another row of stitches, then another, wondering if she was really onto something or if she was jumping to conclusions. As Patty had said, Barb had been through a lot of stress.

Kelly looked up and spotted Burt walking through the patio garden. He hadn't noticed her in the back corner because he hadn't waved a hello. So Kelly waved and called his name. She could bounce these ideas off Burt and immediately know if she was on the right or wrong track.

"Hey, Burt. Do you have a few minutes?" she called. Burt turned and sent her his familiar smile, so Kelly beckoned him over.

"Hi, there, Kelly. Looks like you've found the perfect spot to work in peace and quiet." Burt pulled out a wrought iron patio chair across the table from Kelly. "I'm still with the hot morning coffee." He took a drink from the large mug.

"I've already switched to cold," Kelly said, lifting her mug. "Do you have a few minutes to talk? I've got some things I'd like to run past you, and I'd appreciate your input."

"Sure thing, Kelly. What's up?" Burt placed his mug on the patio table and settled back into the chair. One of his listening positions.

Kelly took a deep breath. "I've been doing a lot of thinking about Laura Brewster's murder —"

"You and Dan and others at the police department," Burt joked.

"Yeah, I'm sure. Well . . . I've been trying to figure out if there was someone else responsible. Someone other than Tommy, that is."

"Are you talking about the violent intruder?"

"Uhhhhh, no. I'm talking about someone else."

Burt's bushy eyebrows shot up as surprise registered. "I'm listening."

Kelly paused, sorting through the ideas, wondering which one to present first. Then, in her usual forthright manner, she simply jumped in. "I'm wondering if Barb killed Laura Brewster."

This time Burt's eyebrows knotted. "Barb? What makes you think that?"

"Well, I learned something the other day that really makes my little buzzer go off.

And you know how I pay attention to that."

"Oh, yeah. So do I. I'm listening."

"We've both commented on Barb's intense feelings toward Laura right after her accusations of Tommy's assault. That was understandable, of course. Protective mother and all that. But I'm sure you've noticed how Barb still harbors this intense, well, I can't find another word but 'hatred.' She's always referring to Laura as 'that evil girl.' "

Burt's skeptical look showed. "That's also understandable. The damage she did to Tommy's reputation survives Laura's death."

"I know. But I always got a cold chill whenever she said that. I wasn't able to explain it. And these thoughts never occurred until the other day. I was talking with Patty, one of the knitters in Barb's advanced class. She mentioned she was worried about Barb and all the stress she's been under. I said we all had noticed how distracted Barb was lately. Then Patty added that Barb had even missed their monthly bridge club meeting, and she'd never missed a meeting in all the years. My buzzer sent a little signal so I asked when that meeting was scheduled. I recognized the day as soon as Patty said it. That was the same night Laura Brewster was killed."

Burt's skeptical look deepened. "I don't have to tell you that is definitely not enough to draw suspicion."

"I know, but then Patty mentioned her friend Susan, a weaver, was so worried she went over to Barb's house that night. It was all lit up but Barb wasn't there, and neither was her car."

Burt sat silently, listening.

Kelly continued. "That aroused my curiosity, naturally. So then I saw Susan setting up at the Mother Loom."

"Yes, Mimi is letting her use it to work on this new table runner Susan is doing. Bamboo yarn."

"Anyway, I spoke with Susan and told her I was worried about Barb and all that. I figured that would get the ball rolling. Well, Susan confirmed everything that Patty said plus she told me that she expressed her concern to Barb the day after the bridge meeting. She said Barb looked surprised. That was her word: 'surprised.' Barb told her that she'd gone to a late-night movie that evening. Then Barb turned and walked away. Needless to say, Susan found that very strange behavior for Barb. And I have to agree."

Burt's eyebrows knotted together. "Yes,

that definitely sounds out of character for Barb. But, again, any theories that Barb missed bridge that night so she could go over to Laura Brewster's apartment and kill her . . . well, I don't have to tell you, Kelly, that's pretty far-fetched."

"What if Barb simply went over to Laura Brewster's apartment to talk with her? Maybe try to convince her to withdraw the charges? I don't know. Maybe the conversation went sour. Maybe Laura refused to listen to Barb. What if Laura called Tommy a bad name or something? Something that would make Barb really, really angry. And maybe Barb simply reacted out of anger. A crime of passion. Choking Laura Brewster to death."

Burt glanced into the garden, not saying a word. Kelly could tell he was thinking over what she said. Kelly decided to mention something else that had piqued her curiosity.

"Maybe that's the reason the DNA results show some markers that match Tommy's. If Barb was the killer, then Tommy's DNA would show a family similarity or connection or whatever scientists call it."

At that, Burt looked back to Kelly. "That DNA sample was puzzling. But that's still not enough to justify accusations."

Kelly pondered what Burt said. He and Mimi had known Barb for years. They were friends. Was that why Burt was not giving credence to Kelly's suspicions? Or was it simply because everything Kelly had told him was easily explained. Nothing really suspicious. Barb really could have gone to a late-night movie. No doubt it would have been the first time in her life, Kelly thought.

The accusing thoughts inside her head, however, were not deterred by Burt's apparent lack of enthusiasm. They still prodded Kelly to find a way to convince Burt to take her suspicions seriously.

Just then Mimi appeared, walking along the flagstone path, several skeins of yarn in her hands. She smiled at them as she approached. "You two have the perfect spot in the shade. This has always been one of my favorite café tables."

"You need some help, Mimi?" Burt said, pushing back the wrought iron chair.

"Thanks. You could bring that bag of fleece on the winding table. I've got a spinning class out here in an hour," Mimi said, nodding toward the tiny cottage on the edge of the patio garden.

Kelly knew she had to say something to capture Burt's interest, but what? Then, a weird thought zoomed from the back of her mind. She voiced it without a moment's hesitation.

"Mimi, would you know if Barb has a CSU jacket? You know, the kind that students and players use. Green and gold."

Mimi let out a little laugh as she paused on her way to the spinning cottage. "A CSU jacket? Goodness, let me think."

Kelly could feel Burt staring at the back of her head, but she kept her attention focused on Mimi. "It might be an old one."

"Hmmmmm, you know, I think she does. She's had it so long I'd forgotten. I think it belonged to her father. Why do you ask?"

Kelly shrugged. "Oh, someone I know was looking to borrow one for a party. Sorry, I didn't mean to slow you down."

"No problem, Kelly," Mimi said, then headed for the cottage.

At that point, Kelly glanced back up at Burt. This time he was looking at her with a half smile. "Pretty slick, Sherlock. That was quick thinking."

Kelly gave a shrug. "It's all the accounting. Numbers keep you on your toes."

"Okay, Kelly. I think the only thing that will settle this is for us to speak with Barb. She's got a class late tomorrow morning. Do you want me to leave her a text message asking her to come in earlier?"

The nagging thoughts finally started to ease off, Kelly noticed. "That sounds like a plan, Burt. I'll be over at the shop as soon as it opens at nine o'clock. Coffee in hand."

"Okay, I'll meet you, and I promise I'll keep an open mind. You've got a helluva track record. You and that damn buzzer," he said with a real smile this time before he walked off.

Kelly had to smile. Thank goodness Burt responded in a positive way. She returned to knitting her red ribbon scarf. She'd done more rows than she thought while ordering her thoughts. This project would be finished quickly, and she'd be wearing her new bright red ribbon scarf while cheering on the kids' teams. *Take me out to the ball game . . .* the words of the old song. *Absolutely.*

The next morning
"You're here early, Kelly," Connie said as Kelly walked into the Lambspun foyer.

"Yeah, I had a real craving for Eduardo's coffee. Couldn't help myself. That specialty coffee I buy still isn't as good as his." Kelly paused beside Connie, who was stacking several small skeins of bamboo yarn on the antique dry sink in the corner of the foyer.

"I have to be careful with Eduardo's coffee. It's so strong it'll keep me awake at night if I have it after twelve noon." Connie gave the pile a little pat when she finished stacking. Cotton candy pink, cantaloupe orange, and lime sherbet green.

Kelly fondled the soft yarn, wondering yet again how something which comes from a tough plant like bamboo can be turned into fiber this soft. Another thought appeared in the corner of her mind. A thought she'd been meaning to ask Connie about.

"How're you doing, Connie?" she asked in a quiet voice, looking into the middle-aged woman's face. A year had passed since that traumatic period when Connie was suspected of killing her husband's lover in Cache La Poudre Canyon.

Connie gazed back at Kelly. "Pretty good, actually. I've been going to that counselor Lisa recommended, and I have to admit she's been a real help. Somehow . . . I never expected that from a counselor."

Kelly gave her an encouraging smile. "That's so good to hear, Connie. Lisa knows the best ones in town because she works with most of the counselors in various groups and organizations."

"Well, the counselor suggested I check out the community college and see if they had any courses I might like. And I signed up for a class in power tools and another in basic home repairs." A smile slowly spread across her face. "I was surprised how much I enjoyed both, so I signed up for another in beginning carpentry. Boy, is that challenging." Connie gave a little laugh.

Kelly blinked in surprise. Who would have thought? "Wow, Connie, I am impressed. Really. Good for you. Those are some challenging activities. I'm not handy at all, so I would probably shoot a nail through my thumb with a power drill."

At that, Connie cackled. "You probably would with a drill, Kelly. You need a hammer for nailing."

"Whatever." Kelly gave a smiling shrug. "I'll leave that stuff in the hands of the talented folks like you."

Burt suddenly appeared in the central yarn room ahead. Barb stood beside him. "Hey, Kelly. Barb and I were going to have a coffee break. Why don't you join us?"

Kelly recognized Burt's subtle way of including her in the conversation, so Kelly played along. "Sure. Connie is making me feel inadequate because I can't tell the difference between a power drill and a hammer, so I feel the need for caffeine." She started toward them.

"I'm as bad with power tools as you are,

Kelly," Burt teased. "Pretty soon, Mimi and I will start calling Connie if we've got a leaky faucet."

Connie simply laughed and gave them all a dismissive wave. "Go have that coffee. I've had my quota of Eduardo's brew for the day."

Kelly followed Burt and Barb through the yarn room and into the hallway leading to the café. Kelly noticed an empty table in the back alcove, small but private. Burt headed right for it.

Jennifer walked up to them as they all settled into chairs. "Good morning, folks. What can I get you?"

"A small hot coffee this time, Jen," Burt answered. "I've had a lot already."

"Nothing for me, thanks," Barb said.

"You can fill my empty mug with Eduardo's gold, if you don't mind," Kelly said, digging out her mug from the large briefcase bag.

"Coming right up," Jennifer said before hurrying off.

"How's this advanced class going, Barb?" Burt asked as he leaned his arms on the table and inclined slightly forward. Kelly recognized his "talking" position, especially when Burt wanted answers.

"They're all doing very well," Barb said,

folding her hands on the table. "Some are more talented than others, but that's always the case in a class."

"That's for sure," Burt agreed with a nod.

"You can put me in that 'less than' category," Kelly joked.

Barb gave her a wry smile. "You're much better than that, Kelly. And you know it." She glanced to Burt, then back to Kelly. "Is that why you asked me to join you for coffee, Burt? I sense you've got something else on your mind."

Burt glanced down at his hands for a second. "Well, you're right, Barb. You've been under a whole lot of stress lately, and several of us are worried about you. Mimi is, for sure."

"And your friends, Patty and Susan. They both told me they were concerned about you," Kelly added in a matter-of-fact voice.

Barb simply listened and nodded. Burt spoke again. "You seem distracted most of the time and stare out the windows a lot. That's not like you, Barb. I've known you for years. You're a take-charge woman and you're always going a mile a minute. So this sudden personality change definitely caught our attention."

Barb continued to listen, not saying a word.

Kelly decided to add the others' comments. "Both Patty and Susan said you even missed your bridge club meeting a couple of weeks ago. They said you'd never missed in all these years."

Barb looked up then and glanced briefly at Kelly, but didn't say anything.

"Susan was so worried she actually went to your house to make sure you weren't sick or something. But you weren't there. That really caused Susan to worry," Burt detailed in his calm voice.

"Susan said you told her you'd gone to a late-night movie," Kelly added, matching Burt's quiet tone.

"Did you really go to the movies, Barb?" Burt asked.

Barb looked right back at Burt, lifting her chin. "Of course. Why wouldn't I?"

"That's really not like you, Barb. I don't recall your ever mentioning a movie." Burt had a half smile.

"Which movie did you see, Barb?" Kelly asked.

Barb looked back at Kelly and paused. "It was that Disney film about the two sisters. Lots of snow and ice."

This time Kelly paused. "That movie left the theaters over two months ago."

Barb stared at Kelly for a long moment,

then a crooked smile formed at the edge of her lips. She glanced down at her hands.

Burt leaned forward over the table. "Where did you really go that night, Barb?" When Barb didn't answer, Burt tried again. "Was it Laura Brewster's apartment?"

At that, Barb glanced up at Burt, then Kelly, then glanced down at her hands again. "I knew this is why you asked me to coffee. I figured Kelly had sniffed it out. But I was hoping, maybe, just maybe . . . you hadn't." She looked up at both of them again. "Yes. I had just gotten off the phone with Tommy. He was so depressed and distraught at how things had changed at the clinic. People were looking at him differently. I could barely listen to him. Later, I went to that evil girl's apartment to try to convince her to withdraw her complaint against Tommy. They were lies, and I knew she did it on purpose. Just like she did to that professor years ago. Lies. All lies."

"What happened when you got there?" Burt asked.

Kelly watched in fascination as Barb's features hardened. "She listened to me without saying a word, just stood there with this smirk on her face. I pleaded with her to withdraw the charges. Then she sneered and said she would never do that. She swore she was telling the truth. Then she taunted me by saying, 'Your son isn't the wonderful young doctor you think he is. I've been in classes with Tommy, and he was always acting so superior. He was the smartest one there. He always got the highest grade. And *he* got the scholarships and the honors and awards. Well, some of us worked just as hard as he did, but there were no awards for us. Tommy got them all. Some of us didn't have it so easy growing up, either. I didn't have a doting mother hovering over me, helping me. I never got any help. *Never.*' "

Barb's voice went cold. "I sensed the malice in her words and could feel it radiating off her, like a foul smell. It was clear that girl had a personal grudge against Tommy and sought to hurt him for the pure malicious pleasure of doing so. She was purposely hateful. That's when I knew she was evil. Pure evil."

After a moment, Burt asked softly, "What did you do then?"

Barb exhaled a short breath. "Something snapped inside. I knew I couldn't allow that evil girl to spread more malicious accusations. What other evil acts was she capable of?" Barb looked out toward the empty hallway. "Suddenly, this overwhelming sense of anger and . . . and something else.

Something powerful swept over me. Laura stood smirking at me, so I grabbed her by the throat and choked the life out of her. She struggled, her eyes bulging out, but I'm very strong and I kept squeezing. Hard, until she went limp in my hands, then I let her drop to the floor."

Kelly stared, captivated by the cold, matter-of-fact description of how Barb killed Laura Brewster.

Barb drew another breath. "As I stared down at her, I slowly realized what I'd done. Strangely, I felt no regret. None. I'd killed an evil presence in our midst. However, I realized I didn't want anyone to suspect me. So I tried to make her death look accidental. Make it appear as if someone was caught ransacking her apartment, encountered a screaming Laura, then panicked and killed her. That's why I opened desk drawers and tossed out papers on the floor. And I deliberately left one page of a bank statement and took the rest. That way it would look like the thief wanted her account number. I left her patio door slightly open and one lamp on. Then I took her purse and slipped out the front door, ducking my head in case there was a camera. I went to my car, emptied her purse, and threw it out the window into the parking lot. I put the purse contents into a plastic bag and tossed it into a Dumpster in a strip mall." Barb leaned back into her chair and stared at the table.

"You did a good job of removing any identifiable traces," Burt said. "Did you wear gloves?"

"No, but I had some driving gloves in my pocket. So I put them on and proceeded to clean everything I might have touched. I used the spray cleaner I found under her bathroom cabinet on the surfaces then used rubbing alcohol on Laura's neck."

"That was clever," Kelly couldn't help commenting. "It must have worked."

Barb gave Kelly a crooked smile. "Well, I knew I had to be thorough because the police would find the slightest trace to investigate. And damned if they didn't find some skin cells under one of Laura's nails. I don't even remember her scratching me, but her arms were flailing around so it must have happened."

"That was puzzling, too. The DNA didn't match Tommy's but there were certain similarities," Burt added.

"But it was enough to continue suspicion. That's when I knew this was going to unravel. And all it took was one tiny bit of skin cells." She shook her head. No sign of remorse. Just disappointment that her elaborate subterfuge hadn't worked.

"What did you do then? Go home?" Kelly asked, curious. "It must have been in the middle of the night."

"Three in the morning when I got home. I threw away my driving gloves, took a hot shower, had a stiff drink of whiskey, and went to bed. Slept like a rock."

"No regret?" Burt asked, looking surprised.

"None," Barb retorted. "I removed an evil presence from the world. No guilt whatsoever."

Burt stared at his folded hands for a long minute. "Well, Barb. It pains me to say this, considering our friendship, but I'm going to have to report all this to the police. You could come down to the department with me, but you need to speak to your family lawyer first."

Barb released a little sigh. "I understand, Burt. I'll call him now. Hopefully he can meet me down at the department so we can get all this taken care of."

Kelly marveled at Barb's no-nonsense manner in describing how she would turn herself in to authorities. Clearly, this confession had allowed Big Barb to return to herself. Almost as if she'd been anxious to do so.

"You amaze me, Barb. You're as matter-of-fact about all of this as you are about everything else." Kelly wagged her head.

Finally a real smile appeared on Barb's face. "That's because in my heart I had a feeling I wasn't going to get away with murder. I've watched you sniff around police investigations for years, Kelly. I knew if they missed something, you would find it. And you did. When Susan told me you were asking questions, I knew you were onto me." She grinned. "It's hard to outsmart you, Kelly."

Kelly had nothing to say in reply as Barb took out her cell phone and proceeded to call her lawyer. Kelly met Burt's gaze and they both exchanged a look of amazement. Big Barb was truly amazing. Killer or not.

TWENTY

Wednesday morning

"Keep those squirrels on their toes, Carl," Kelly advised her dog before closing the cottage front door. She heard Carl barking outside in the backyard, clearly taking Kelly's advice to heart.

Walking across the gravel driveway, Kelly could tell it would be another hot day. Clearly, monsoon season was over. It had only teased them this year. There was some rain at night, but none of the soaking rains that they needed. August now, and it was still hot. The typical cooldown wouldn't come until later in the month.

Back East they called the end of July and beginning of August the dog days. Kelly never knew what that phrase meant. Did it mean it would be so hot they'd be panting like dogs? Or lying in the shade taking naps all day? Or, would it be so hot only dogs could stand it? Whatever, it was a picturesque way of describing summer weather.

As she entered the café's patio garden, Kelly noticed Burt and Mimi sitting at a table in the dappled sun and shade of the early morning. Burt was leaning over the table talking to Mimi. Mimi sat, looking downcast. *Uh-oh.* Kelly recognized Mimi's depressed look. No doubt she was taking the news about Barb very hard indeed.

Kelly slowly approached their table. Burt was the first to glance up and see her. Kelly gave him an encouraging smile.

"Good morning, you two," she said in a deliberately cheerful voice. "I thought I might find you outside enjoying the early-morning temperatures."

"Good morning, Kelly," Burt said with his familiar smile. "Why don't you sit with us for a spell. Mimi could use another friendly face."

"I kind of figured." Kelly settled into a chair between them and set her briefcase bag on the ground beside her. She glanced at Mimi, who had finally lifted her gaze off the table. Kelly gave her an encouraging smile. "How're you doing, Mimi?"

Mimi looked at Kelly with a sad expression. "Not very well, Kelly. I feel like there's been a death in the family."

Burt reached over and patted Mimi's hand in Mother Mimi fashion. Kelly decided to give some verbal pats. They had the same effect. Reassurance.

"In a way, there has been," Kelly said in a quiet voice. "It's a death of an old relationship with someone you thought you knew everything about. And now that's changed. The Barb we knew is gone, I'm afraid."

Mimi shook her head sadly. "I know, I know. I guess I'm grieving. It's still hard to realize someone close to you has actually killed someone. Strangled them to death with their bare hands." Mimi shuddered. "It's just incomprehensible to think of that."

Burt kept his hand over Mimi's. "Well, it helps to know that Barb really wasn't herself at the time she killed Laura Brewster. Not her real self. It was a crime of passion. A rage came over her, she said."

"Yes, she said she felt this anger sweep through her," Kelly ventured. "She also said 'something' came over her. I remember that. I've heard other people say that. Who knows? Maybe some kind of murderer's madness takes over their minds and their good sense."

Mimi stared at Kelly. "Maybe it does," she said softly. "And Barb was trying to protect Tommy, like she always has."

"She's a fiercely protective mother, that's for sure," Burt agreed.

Kelly turned to Burt, hoping to veer off the grim turn of conversation. "You stayed over at the police department with Barb practically all of yesterday, didn't you?"

"Yes, I wanted to be there in case she was brought up before a judge. And she was."

"Did her family attorney agree to represent her?"

"Oh, yes. He consulted with Barb before she gave her confession to detectives. He also was able to explain to her the various steps in the criminal procedures. Barb agreed to cooperate fully with the police. Thank God." Burt closed his eyes, clearly giving thanks. "She even submitted a DNA sample. So when that comes back positive, she'll officially be charged with murder."

"Oh, Lord," Mimi said with a sigh, looking out into the garden.

"I imagine Barb will be talking to Tommy today," Kelly mused out loud. "That's not going to be an easy conversation."

"Poor Tommy," Mimi said, staring up at the gray sky darkening overhead. "He must wonder what's wrong with his family. His grandmother killed someone two years ago and was sentenced to prison. And now his mother has killed someone, and *she* will most certainly be sentenced to prison."

Kelly pondered that for a minute. Mimi was right. It had to be a strange coincidence indeed that two murderers came out of one family. A mother and a daughter. Very strange, indeed.

"What are the chances Barb would be assigned to the same prison where Madge is serving her sentence?" Kelly asked.

Burt shook his head. "I'd say the chances are slim to nonexistent. I don't think the state would want to create a risky situation for either of them. There could be problems."

Kelly could sense the subtext behind Burt's words but decided she really didn't want to know the details. Better left unsaid. "I guess Tommy will be visiting two prisons from now on," she said. "I wonder how he's going to handle it?"

"We'll have to wait and see," Burt remarked. "Some family members will retreat entirely and not visit the prisons at all. They'll simply make regular phone calls."

"I can understand that," Mimi said. "I wouldn't want to be anywhere near a prison." She made a face and shuddered.

Kelly had another thought. "Well, I will try to visit Barb once she's been assigned to a facility."

"You're right, Kelly. It can take a while for the system to assign someone to a penitentiary. And I figure it will take some time to find a place for Barb. There are not as many penitentiaries for women in the system."

"Well, I'm going to think of that as a small rainbow on a stormy horizon," Kelly declared. "At least we'll be able to visit with Barb for a couple of years before she gets shipped off to the Big House or whatever it is." She gave them both a crooked smile.

"That's a good way to think about it, Kelly. And it gets us out of the deep dark mood Mimi and I were in when we first sat down at this table."

"You're both right," Mimi said with a nod. "And let's all send a little prayer that murder and people who want to kill other people stay far, far away from Lambspun from now on." Mimi raised both hands in an impassioned gesture.

"Amen," Burt said with a grin.

"So, there you have it. Big Barb will soon be incarcerated since she's confessed to murdering Laura Brewster. However, I imagine her lawyer will be able to get her out on bond for now. She's certainly not a flight risk. Then there will be a proceeding where Barb will enter her plea of guilty to the charges of murder and be sentenced. That's when she'll go to prison. Judging from how long it takes the justice system to assign some people to a penitentiary, Barb could remain in the Larimer County Correctional Facility for a couple of years." Kelly took a deep drink of iced coffee while Lisa, Megan, and Jennifer sat quietly around Lambspun's knitting table.

No one spoke for a minute. They were all concentrating on knitting whatever pieces they were working on. Finally Kelly spoke again. "I may have missed several legal steps in between, Megan, so fill in whatever I missed."

"I'm not an expert on all those legalities and hoops to jump through," Megan said with a solemn expression. "But I think you've covered the most important ones." Her needles moved at their normal quick pace, more shamrock green rows of stitches forming.

"That is so sad," Lisa observed. "Barb was a skilled nurse and an excellent teacher. Now all her talents and skills will be lost to our community and especially our knitting community here at Lambspun." Lisa didn't look up from the light yellow top she was finishing.

Kelly had nothing to add to Lisa's comment. They would all miss Big Barb. Bossy Barb. And a tremendously talented knitter.

Jennifer looked up from the deep purple yarn forming into a summer top on her needles. "Actually, Barb may have simply transferred her talents and skills from our community to another community where they may be sorely needed."

"You mean prison?" Megan asked, clearly surprised.

Jennifer nodded. "Yes. I'll bet it won't be long before Barb starts teaching knitting to the women inmates. And, who knows? Maybe those women are in greater need of someone paying attention to them than any of the knitting classes Barb's taught here at Lambspun."

Kelly thought about what Jennifer said. It made sense. "You know, you're right, Jen. We all remember how people react when they learn how to knit. They all remark how calming it is. And how they feel better afterward. Well, think about it. Those women inmates are definitely a population of women under a lot of stress. Learning how to knit could be really good for them. Healthwise, I mean."

Lisa looked up. "You know, you make a

good point. Both of you. A prison population is definitely under a lot of stress. We
can't even begin to imagine what it's like."

Jennifer smiled. "That's exactly what I
mean. As much as we'll all miss Big Barb,
we were lucky to have her around for so
long. Now, fate has intervened and Barb
will be going to a place where she is sorely
needed. And her skills will be put to much
better use there. Don't forget. Barb was a
nurse by profession. As traumatic a change
as it will be, I have a feeling that the
experienced nurse inside Barb will recognize
that no matter where she will be assigned,
there will be a great many needy people for
her to help. And her skills will be put to
good use."

Kelly smiled at her dear friend. "Well said,
Jen. Even attorney Marty couldn't have said
that better."

That evening

"Wow. That is one sad story," Steve said,
reaching across Marty and Megan's glass
patio table. He snagged several corn chips
and settled into his chair beside Kelly again.

"Don't breathe on me after you eat those,"
she warned. "They're deadly."

Steve grinned. "I promise."

"Yeah, it depressed me when Kelly told us

this afternoon. Then I told Marty as soon as he got home, and *he* got depressed." Megan sipped from her bottle of iced tea as she leaned back in the patio chair.

"Jen told me today. I sure feel sorry for Tommy," Pete said, turning his bottle of Fat Tire ale on his bare knee. "And Barb, of course."

"Leave it to Kelly to bring us all the bad news that's not fit to print," Greg said with an exaggerated sigh. "For the record, I think Tommy would be better off starting his medical career in another city. Maybe another state. If he stays in Fort Connor, he'll constantly be reminded of what happened." He took a drink from his craft beer.

"You've got a good point," Steve added.

"Yeah, I was so depressed after Megan told me that I couldn't mow the lawn before you guys came," Marty said, smiling as he popped a curled corn chip into his mouth.

"It's fine, Marty," Kelly said with a dismissive wave. "It's grass. Nothing to get excited about." Then she turned to Jennifer and Pete. "Where's Cassie tonight?"

"She's at a birthday party sleepover," Jennifer said. "One of her classmates from school last year. There's a whole bunch of girls going, Cassie said." Jennifer smiled. "Boy, the decibel level is gonna raise the roof over there tonight."

"That's what we need," Greg observed, glancing up at the summer sky, the summer sun still shining brightly. "Raise some decibels. Any suggestions?"

"Yeah, that bad news has got us all down now," Lisa added.

"I'm sorry. I promise not to be the bearer of sad tidings again," Kelly said with an apologetic smile.

Marty set his craft brew on the table beside him. "I know what we need to turn this mood around. Some good news." He slapped his hands on his legs. "And I've got some."

"What? They made you partner?" Steve asked with a smile.

"Don't I wish," Marty said, wagging his head. "No, I'm talking about another kind of good news." He glanced at Megan beside him. "Ready?"

"Ready," Megan said, smiling.

Marty looked around at all of them. "We're going to have a baby." A huge grin spread across his face, which was getting redder.

Kelly stared at Marty then at Megan, her mouth open. She looked at her friends. Their reactions were identical. Shocked. Incredulous.

"What?"

"No way!"

"Yeah, way."

"Really?"

"Oh, my gawd!"

"Fantastic!"

"Congratulations, you guys!"

"When?" Kelly burst out. "When's it coming. I mean . . . when's it due?"

"The OB, uh, obstetrician says I'm about eight weeks along," Megan declared, face flushed. "So, the baby would be due late February or early March."

Greg grinned. "A little ankle biter. I can't believe it."

Lisa beamed at Marty and Megan. "That is such tremendous news!"

"I am *so* happy for you two, I can't stand it," Jennifer said, rising from her chair. "This calls for a hug."

"Oh, yeah," Pete agreed, jumping out of his chair.

"You better believe it," Steve said as he rose.

Kelly popped out of her chair, too, as all the Gang took turns giving both Megan and Marty huge hugs.

"You two are gonna be great parents," Steve said, then gave Megan a big squeeze. Clasping Marty's hand, Steve slapped him on the back. "No offense, Marty, but I sure hope the baby looks like Megan."

"You and me both," Marty said with a quick laugh.

"Now I know why you switched to iced tea," Jennifer said.

"Oh, yeah, gotta watch stuff now," Megan nodded.

Kelly gave Megan a big hug. "Ohhhhh, I still can't believe that you're going to be a mom." She felt her eyes grow moist behind her lashes as she released Megan. "I'm gettin' misty." Kelly wiped both eyes.

Megan gave her arm a squeeze. "Oh, that is so sweet. You don't get misty that often, Kelly. Now you're gonna make me misty." Megan swiped at her eyes.

"Stop that, you two." Jennifer sniffled and waved her hand at them.

"Jen's already started," Pete said with a grin, taking Jennifer's hand.

"It's the hormones," Lisa opined sagely.

"Ohhhhhhhhhhhhhh!" Greg's voice went up two octaves in a theatrical imitation of a famous comedian's hysterical moment. Wrist to forehead, Greg proclaimed in a perfect *La Cage aux Folles* imitation, "It's too much!"

Kelly and all her friends broke out in loud laughter, all trace of tears disappearing.

Lisa reached for her craft brew and offered it to him. "Take a drink. You'll recover. Your hormones are fine."

Greg looked at the bottle and suddenly proclaimed, "This calls for champagne! We need to celebrate!"

"Yes!" Steve said, clapping his hands. "Let's go out. Jazz Bistro is probably booked already. Let's see . . ."

"We can go to Old Town and —"

Just then the screen door to Megan and Marty's family room burst open and Cassie ran out onto the patio. She headed straight for Jennifer and Pete. "Hey, guys! Is it okay if I go with the group to the carnival? It's at that big shopping center lot off East Harmony Road. You know the one at the interstate."

"Yes, I saw it being set up yesterday," Jennifer said, then looked at Pete. "What do you think?"

"Will Jeannie's parents be going with you girls?" Pete asked.

Cassie nodded vigorously. "Yeah, and Susie's parents are going, too."

"How many of you girls all together?" Jennifer asked.

"Eight. So that's two per parent," Cassie replied.

"Smart answer," Greg said, grinning at Cassie.

"Jeannie's parents said we'll stay until ten o'clock, then they'll have to take us back to their house to go to bed. Can I go, *please*!"

Pete smiled. "Sure you can. Let me give you some money." He reached into his back pocket as he rose.

"Oh, Jeannie's parents said we don't need any. It's their treat."

"Well, take some and keep it in your pocket just in case," Pete said. He walked over to Cassie, handed her a folded bill, and gave her a big hug.

Cassie gave him a big hug in return, then went over to Jennifer and gave her a big hug. "Thanks, you guys. See you in the morning." She raced off again.

Kelly looked over at Pete. Talk about parenting. Pete and Jennifer had been doing a fantastic job for over a year. "Good parenting, you two." Kelly lifted her Fat Tire to them in salute.

Megan turned to Marty. "Promise me you'll be as good a dad as Pete."

Marty held up both hands. "I'll do my best, I swear. But, he's a helluva act to follow." He pointed at Pete.

"Ohhhh, I'm getting misty all over again," Jennifer said, waving one hand and swiping at her face with the other.

"Me, too," Lisa said, sniffling.

To her surprise, Kelly felt moisture behind her eyes again. *What was up with all this crying?* "You guys gotta stop. You're making me tear up again," she warned.

"Here we go again." Steve laughed.

"Enough with the waterworks!" Greg decreed, leaping from his chair. "I repeat my earlier suggestion. We need champagne. And more food, of course."

"Hey, I've got a good idea!" Pete said. "Let's go to the carnival and feast on corn dogs and cotton candy and ice cream. We can finish off with champagne when we get back."

Greg's eyes lit up. "*Genius!* Pure genius! Yes! We'll celebrate with carnival food! Let's go!" He started for the screen door.

"Wait! Wait! We've gotta tell Burt and Mimi before they go to bed! They'll be asleep when we get back."

"Oh, yes! We have to tell them! I can't wait to hear Mimi squeal!" Megan laughed.

"Okay, okay," Greg said, pacing on the patio. "Call 'em now. I'm getting hungry again."

Marty reached inside his pocket and handed over his cell phone before Megan could dig hers from her purse. Megan quickly punched in Mimi's number and sat, grinning, while everyone watched.

"Burt? It's Megan. Marty and I have some great news and we wanted to share it before you guys go to bed. Put Mimi on the phone so she can hear, too." Megan held the phone, waiting. "Mimi? Can you both hear? Marty and I are going to have a baby! *Yes!* Really!" Megan looked up at her friends. "She's squealing! I'm putting it on speaker." Megan held up the phone for everyone to hear. A high-pitched voice sounded over the speakerphone, definitely a squeal.

Kelly and all her friends laughed as Mimi's squeal of delight drifted over the phone.

Standing in between concession stands and carnival game booths, Kelly sank her teeth into the sticky, sugary pink froth and took another bite. Cotton candy. Nothing was like it. What felt like a big bite of froth dissolved immediately on her tongue and left an intense desire to take another bite and another. Sugar high.

Steve slipped his arm around her waist as he devoured his batch of cotton candy. "Man, you forget how good this stuff is," he said after he swallowed.

Kelly licked her lips. "Yeah, it's a good thing the carnival doesn't come around every weekend." She gazed up at the Ferris wheel, spinning in its loop. Spotting Megan and Marty rock their seat back and forth, she had to laugh. "You know, it's hard to picture Marty being a father. Megan, yes. I can even picture her organizing nursery school picnics. But Marty? I don't know. He's a great lawyer, for sure. But when he's out of the office, Marty goes totally into goofball mode. Athletic goofball, yes. But, still."

Steve swallowed another bite of the pink confection. "Don't worry. Marty will be up to the challenge. Besides, half of that goofball routine is an act. Marty enjoys making people laugh."

"You're right about that." Kelly savored another sugary mouthful as she watched a woman try to throw a rubber ring over a milk bottle. She spotted Greg and Lisa go by on the Ferris wheel. Greg was holding his hands way up high. Lisa was covering her eyes. Around and around the wheel turned. Laughing people. Children of all ages with their parents. Everyone laughing. Some simply stared at everything, their eyes wide as saucers. She remembered the great view from the top of a Ferris wheel. Wondrous. Looking out over your part of the world.

"They'll both be good parents," Steve said before he took another big bite of froth.

"I wonder how things will change now. Rather, once they have the baby," she said, voicing a thought that had bounced around in her mind. "Will they be able to get together as much? I mean with us. Like now."

"Sure they will," Steve said, not missing a beat. "They'll just get babysitters like everybody else does. You know, like our friends the Carpenters and Bergdorfs." He took another bite.

That made sense, Kelly thought to herself. Just like other couples. She watched the Ferris wheel make another few turns then start to slow down. The ride was over. Time to load up more people who wanted a view from the top.

"C'mon, let's ride the Ferris wheel again," Kelly said suddenly, taking Steve's hand and walking in that direction.

"Third time, huh?" Steve said with a grin as they walked closer to the ticket taker who monitored the Ferris wheel entrance. "The view from the top."

"Can't beat it," Kelly said, finishing off the cotton candy. As she did, she spotted Cassie with some of her school friends laughing and half walking, half running toward the next ride of whirling cups and saucers.

"You know, if Megan and Marty can have a kid half as great as Cassie, they'll be lucky."

"Oh, yeah." Steve nodded, then tossed his empty cotton candy cone into a nearby trash can.

Kelly followed suit, then yanked on Steve's hand. "C'mon. The view from the top awaits." They both laughed as they ran to the Ferris wheel entrance booth.

SILK DELIGHT SHELL

This elegant shell has two simple cables on a reverse stockinette background and a rolled neck.
Sizes: Finished measurements in inches

Bust at underarm (inches): 35 (XS), 39 (S), 44 (M), 49 (L), 54 (XL)

Length (inches): 22 (XS), 22 1/2 (S), 23 (M), 23 1/2 (L), 24 (XL)

*Length is easily adjusted between the bottom edge and the armhole. Changes in length or width change the amount of yarn required.

Materials (Yards):
450   500   660   940   1070
Summit Silk and a sport-weight yarn run together, or any yarn that will give the correct gauge.

Needles:
1 US #8 straight or circular needle
1 US #8 16-inch circular needle

Gauge:
4.5 sts = 1 inch in reverse stockinette stitch

Cable Pattern:
Worked over 12 sts
Row 1 (WS): k.
Row 2: p2, k1, p6, k1, p2.
Row 3, 5, and 7: k2, p2, k4, p2, k2.
Row 4 and 6: p2, k2, p4, k2, p2.
Row 8: p2, sl next 2 sts onto cable needle and hold in front, p2, yo, then k2tog in back, from cable needle, sl next 2 sts to cable needle and hold in back, k2tog in front, yo, p2 from cable needle, p2.
Repeat these 8 rows for cable pattern.

Instructions:

Back:
With smaller needles, CO 79 (84, 89, 94, 99) sts. Work as follows: 18 (19, 21, 23, 25) sts in reverse stockinette st, 12 st cable pattern, 19 (22, 23, 24, 25) reverse stockinette st, 12 sts cable pattern, 18 (19, 20, 21, 23, 25) reverse stockinette sts. Keep first st and last st in garter st throughout back. Work

even in pattern as established until piece measures 14 (14, 14 1/2, 15, 15 1/2) inches from beginning. End on WS row.

Shape Armholes:

Row 1 (RS): k2, p2tog, work in pattern as established to last 4 sts, p2tog, k2.

Row 2 (WS): k2, k2tog, work in pattern as established to last 4 sts, k2tog, k2.

Next row (RS): Repeat row 1. Work 1 row even in pattern as established. Repeat these 2 rows 6 times more, end on WS row. Keeping 2 sts in garter st at each side, work even in pattern as established on 61 (66, 71, 76, 81) sts until armholes measure 7 (7, 7 1/2, 8, 8 1/2) inches from beginning. End on WS row.

Shape Shoulders:

BO 3 (4, 5, 6, 7) sts at beg of the next 2 rows.

Next row (RS): BO 3 (4, 5, 6, 7) sts, work to end decreasing 2 sts at the center of each cable.

Next row (WS): Decrease 1 st at the end of each cable. Slip remaining 43 (44, 45, 46, 47) sts onto a holder for the back collar.

Front:
Work same as back.

Finishing:
Seam pieces lightly. Sew shoulder and side seams.

Collar:
With 16-inch circular needle and RS facing, begin at left shoulder seam, and k43 (44, 45, 46, 47) sts from front holder, then k43 (44, 45, 46, 47) sts from back holder. 86 (88, 90, 92, 94) sts remain. Mark beginning of round and carry marker up. Work even in St st until collar measures 5 inches from beginning. BO all sts loosely. Fold collar down to outside so that reverse St st side shows.

Pattern courtesy of Lambspun of Colorado, Fort Collins, Colorado. Pattern designed for Lambspun by Yvette Silverman.

MIMI'S MUFFINS

1 1/3 cups all-purpose flour
3/4 cup rolled oats
1/3 cup sugar
2 teaspoons baking powder
1/4 teaspoon salt
1/2 teaspoon cinnamon
1 beaten egg
3/4 cup milk
1/4 cup cooking oil

In mixing bowl combine flour, oats, sugar, baking powder, salt, and cinnamon. Mix well and set aside. Grease muffin pans (12 2 1/2″ cups) and set aside. In a smaller bowl combine egg, milk, and oil. Add egg mixture to dry ingredients all at once and stir just until moistened. Spoon batter into prepared muffin cups, filling each cup about 2/3 full. Bake in preheated 400 degree oven for 20 minutes or until golden brown. Cool in muffin pan for 5 minutes on wire rack, then remove from muffin cups onto rack. Serve warm. Makes about 10–12 muffins.

ABOUT THE AUTHOR

Maggie Sefton, the *New York Times* bestselling author of many books including *Yarn Over Murder, Close Knit Killer, Cast On, Cast Off, Unraveled,* and *Skein of the Crime,* was born and raised in northern Virginia, where she received her bachelor's degree in English literature and journalism. Maggie has worked in several careers over the years, from a CPA to a real estate broker in the Rocky Mountain West. However, none of those endeavors could compare with the satisfaction and challenge of creating worlds on paper. She is the mother of four grown daughters, currently scattered around the globe. Author of the nationally bestselling Knitting Mysteries, she resides in the Rocky Mountains of Colorado with two very demanding dogs.

The employees of Thorndike Press hope you have enjoyed this Large Print book. All our Thorndike, Wheeler, and Kennebec Large Print titles are designed for easy reading, and all our books are made to last. Other Thorndike Press Large Print books are available at your library, through selected bookstores, or directly from us.

For information about titles, please call:
  (800) 223-1244

or visit our Web site at:
  http://gale.cengage.com/thorndike

To share your comments, please write:
  Publisher
  Thorndike Press
  10 Water St., Suite 310
  Waterville, ME 04901